A CARNAL CRUISE

FLUFFERS, INC.
BOOK 2

HANK EDWARDS

MITTEN GINGER MEDIA

SUMMARY

Charlie Heggensford, the Idaho farm boy turned L.A. fluffer for hire, is back, and this time, Charlie and the rest of the gang from Fluffers, Inc. are hitting the high seas. Hired to provide fluffing service on a cruise ship filled with gay porn stars, Charlie soon discovers he is no less clumsy on sea than dry land as he continues to over-stimulate his clients. While he works to master the art of his profession, Charlie meets up with a host of new, fetish-sporting men, including a glamorous drag queen with more than one surprise hidden beneath his skirts, a pair of hunky Latin twin brothers who bring new meaning to the term "brotherly love", a hot masseuse with a mysterious past, and the ship's doctor who harbors some surprises of his own.

As the ship steams toward Acapulco, hot, unavailable porn star Rock Harding begins to see ghosts from his past and the shock of his sightings affects his ability to perform. When all other mouths fail to bring Rock up to his task, Charlie is recruited to act as the hunky star's personal fluffer, much to the displeasure of Rock's lover and gay porn director extraordinaire Cedric Wilmington. During the cruise, Charlie discovers not only the healing power of vinegar, the trick to running in heels, and the lengths Cedric would stoop to hang onto Rock, but enough secret revelations to make his head swim!

COCK WATCHER

Charlie Heggensford slowly swallowed the long length of fattening cock. He caressed he shaft with his tongue and paused for a moment with his nose buried in the dark, fragrant bush that surrounded the base. Drawing his head back — slowly, always slowly — Charlie allowed the glistening, pink dick to slide out of his mouth. He kept his lips pressed firmly against the flesh so that he could almost feel the pulse.

The man standing before him groaned and tipped his head back. He set his hips and pumped his dick into Charlie's throat. But Charlie backed off, dropping the penis from between his lips and wrapping a firm fist around it instead. He looked up along the man's well-developed body with a grin and gently stroked.

"Oh, fuck, Charlie," the actor moaned as he looked down at him. "You are one hot fucking fluffer."

"That's why I have a Hummer award on my entertainment center," Charlie replied. "You don't learn this stuff in school, you know."

"Where the hell did you learn to suck cock like that?"

"Idaho."

The actor snorted a laugh and tipped his head back again, closing his eyes as Charlie's fist rode his dick. "You're a piece of work."

"Yeah, I know."

Charlie sensed his subject was ready for more oral stimulation, and he leaned forward to take the cock in his mouth once more. The actor's breath hissed between his teeth and he groaned again. As he sucked, Charlie popped one eye open and glanced at the clock on the wall. He would need to leave soon if he was going to make it to Ken's movie premiere on time, and he certainly didn't want to miss it.

It had been less than a year since he had moved to L.A. from his family's dairy farm in Idaho. He had tried his hand at several jobs when he had first arrived: waiter, valet driver, and bus boy. But Charlie was a clumsy person and always found himself out of a job. Until he walked into the offices of Fluffers, Inc., where the owner, Kinitia Jones, had hired him. She ran a dispatch service providing fluffers for the various adult film studios in L.A., and soon Charlie had been sucking cock all over the city. He was new to the job and eager — sometimes a little too eager — and had quickly gained a reputation for over-stimulating his clients, an act frowned on by the directors as they needed their actors hard and ready, not soft and spent. After several months as a fluffer, Charlie had won The Hummer, an award which recognized achievements in fluffing and was handed out along with the awards honoring actors, directors, and others involved in the gay adult film industry, the Golden Orifices.

Charlie sighed around his mouthful of cock and thought about the friends he had made at Fluffers, Inc. Sharp, beautiful, independent, and mothering in a tough love kind of way Kinitia Jones. Her slightly daffy, loving, joyous assistant from Minnesota, Bernice Tallipepper. And his two closest friends, Billy Ransom, a younger man from Cleveland who had started at the company just before Charlie had himself and could not seem to keep a thought in his head, and older, hot, Ken Carlton, senior member of the team at Fluffers, Inc., and a man who had just been offered a chance to get back into gay porn films as the lead in a rather large budget action porn film titled *Cumuppance*.

Ken had made a name for himself in gay porn films many years prior to working at Fluffers, Inc., but had lost his connections and, supposedly, his desire to be in front of the cameras. However, when a hot new gay porn director had come into the office one day and offered Ken a starring role in what could possibly turn into a film franchise, there was no way Ken could turn it down.

And tonight was the big premiere party for *Cumuppance*. The studio head, Gregory Gianelli, had rented out a large, ornate theater to show the film, and afterwards was hosting a party at his home in the hills. It was going to be a very exclusive affair, and Ken had made sure Charlie, Billy, Kinitia, Bernice, and the other fluffers received invitations. The premiere started at nine on the other side of town, and it was already going on five o'clock. If Charlie could finish up here in the next half an hour, he would have plenty of time to make it to the showing.

"Oh, yeah, get the head," the actor grunted. "Right on the head there."

Charlie slid back and paused with his lips clamped around the thick, mushroom head, slowly pulsing his fist along its length. As he worked the actor's cock, he thought briefly of Rock Harding, gay porn superstar and a man that had worked his way deep into Charlie's heart. He had not seen Rock for almost a month, and it seemed as if every thing Charlie saw or touched brought up memories of him. Each time he checked in on a set, he would survey the area for a glimpse of Rock. But it had been weeks now since he'd seen or heard from Rock, and he wondered what had made the actor lay low.

As he thought about Rock, Charlie's grip on the man before him tightened. He thought back to the times he had fluffed Rock, how the man's dick had slowly expanded in his mouth, and the times he had gotten a little too into his work and made Rock come. That, he had quickly learned, was a major *faux pas* in the world of fluffing. He was supposed to get the men up and keep them hard, not bring them to orgasm. Since those days, Charlie had fluffed Rock several times without making him come, and they had developed a close friendship, much to the annoyance of Rock's lover.

Charlie pushed from his head thoughts of Rock's lover, Cedric Wilmington, evil gay porn director and part owner of the building where Kinitia Jones leased the offices of Fluffers, Inc. He forced himself to focus on his work, and began to suck the full length of the actor's dick. The man groaned and bent his knees, thrusting his hips forward as Charlie dragged his mouth along his prick. Charlie closed his eyes, and suddenly memories of Rock burst into his mind completely unbidden. He could practically taste the salt of his cock and balls, smell the fresh, citrus scent so unique to him, and see the smooth, pink pucker of his asshole as he had turned around and bent over for Charlie to dig in. So much time between them had been spent on work, and Rock had never sucked him, it had always been Charlie kneeling before the muscular, dark haired man, his mouth stuffed full of dick. They had spent time alone together a handful of times, one night falling asleep together atop a desert mesa, but had never really had sex, not in the common use of the word.

The images and sensations brought back on by memories of Rock got Charlie hard in seconds, as usual. His dick strained against his boxer briefs, pre-come soaking through the material of his underwear and into the denim crotch of his jeans. He began sucking the actor before him faster, his right hand tightly gripping the base of the man's dick as his left tugged on his balls.

"Oh, fuck, fluffer," the actor grunted. "I'm fuckin' your hot face and I'm going to shoot off right in your fuckin' mouth."

Consumed by thoughts of Rock, Charlie grunted around his mouthful of cock and sucked harder. Seconds later hot, spicy cum filled his mouth, spurting out over his lips and down along his chin. The sharp smell of the semen pushed into his nostrils and he let the cum dribble out from between his lips as he slowed his sucking. With a heavy sigh and a grunt of his own, Charlie came into the pouch of his boxer briefs which were already slick with pre-come. The smell and taste of semen was enough to send him over the edge every time without so much as a touch of his hand.

It wasn't until he sat back and gazed up at the man that

Charlie realized what he had done. The actor grinned at him and reached down to wipe the cum off his chin.

"Oh, shit," Charlie said with a sinking feeling in his gut.

"Okay, I'm ready for..." The director of the movie walked up, his voice dying out as he caught sight of Charlie's cum=slicked face and his actor's wilting hard-on. "Oh for the love of.... Charlie, what the fuck is wrong with you? Huh? How many times do you have to be told not to make these guys come? I swear, Hummer award or not, you're becoming a real pain in the ass to have on a set, you know that?" The director shook his head and put his hands on his hips. He took a few breaths then turned to shout, "Take a break, every-one. We've had another fluffer issue over here and the next scene will have to wait."

"What? No!" Charlie said, standing up and flinching as his cock pulled away from where it was drying to his briefs. "I have to be out of here soon. Really soon. I'm sorry, I'll.... I'll get him hard again right away, and I promise I won't make him come. Here, I'll start now." Charlie dropped to his knees before the actor and began to suck desperately at the man's softened dick.

The director folded his arms over his chest and narrowed his eyes. "Oh, stop it, Charlie, you look like some kind of ravenous calf trying to feed from an old dried up cow."

The actor shot his director a dirty look. "Uh, Henry, you'd better watch how you say things like that."

"Oh, sorry Adam," Henry replied in a sarcastic voice. "Go get cleaned up, and use someone else to get hard. I'll need a big come shot from you for the end of the movie, so keep it up for an hour at least."

Adam shrugged and walked off, his dick pulling out from

between Charlie's desperate lips and leaving him in mid-suck. Charlie almost fell forward but caught himself in time. Looking up at the director, he sheepishly wiped his mouth and slowly got to his feet.

"I'm sorry, Henry," Charlie said quietly. "I just got..."

"Carried away," Henry finished for him. "Yeah, I know. Just like on the set of my last movie." Henry stepped closer and lowered his voice. "I need to finish this movie tonight, okay? And I'm going to make you stay here with us until we get the very last shot."

"But, Henry," Charlie started to protest.

"No buts, Charlie," Henry said. "You stay here for the full shoot or I'll report you to Kinitia and start using fluffers from Tongue In Cheeks on my sets."

Charlie sighed as Henry turned his back and walked away. Why did this keep happening to him? He risked another glance at the clock and felt his stomach drop. It was a quarter past five. If it was going to be another hour until they started shooting the next scene, Charlie might be able to leave in time to make the premiere by nine. But it was across town, and he would not be able to stop by his apartment and change. He groaned and trudged off to the bathroom to clean up.

An hour later, Charlie knelt before a different actor, a man named Carl, and carefully worked the man's erection, all the while stealing glances at the clock on the wall. The man's cock was enormous, at least ten inches, and thick as a beer can at the base. As he tried to read the clock, the huge dick continually slipped free and bobbed in front of his eyes, blocking his vision. He tried not to think about the sexual possibilities with this man, and kept his mind on the task in hand. He could hear the previous actor, Adam, being serviced by one of the crew over on the set.

"Okay, we're ready!" Henry called out. "Adam and Carl, I need you both on the set. Jan and Dave you're up next. Get over to the fluffer."

Charlie leaned back and watched Carl walk off toward the set, his cock swinging before him like a fifth limb. The man stopped at the foot of a bed and grinned down at Adam as he rolled a condom along the length of his tree trunk of a dick. Adam looked over his partner's equipment with a mix of excitement and nerves as he prepared himself for receiving the deep impact of Carl's massive cock.

"Action!" Henry said and Carl lifted Adam's legs into the air. He adjusted his position then slid his immense cock into the tight asshole before him. Adam grimaced and lay back, groaning as Carl worked himself deep inside.

Carl began fucking his partner with abandon, and Charlie checked the clock again. He would definitely miss the opening credits. He turned back to find two more actors lined up in front of him, both completely soft and shriveled in the chilly evening air of the warehouse. Charlie took a breath, stretched his jaw muscles, and moved in to begin his work.

He left the warehouse at eight-fifteen and ran to the bus stop, pounding up the sidewalk just as the bus pulled away. He did not have enough cash for a cab, and had to wait ten agonizing minutes before another bus came by, bouncing impatiently on the balls of his feet and frightening even the homeless people who roosted in the covered bus stop. He tried not to think about how he looked: crotch stiff with semen and hair that had been mussed by half a dozen hands as he had knelt before the actors. None of that mattered. What did matter was that he had to make it to Ken's movie premiere on time and give his support. He did not want to miss an event this important to someone Charlie had come to consider a very good friend.

The next bus finally arrived and he jumped through the doors as soon as they opened, causing the driver to flinch. Charlie found an empty seat and sat down, fidgeting and keeping time with his hands on the seat back before him as he tried to mentally urge the bus to move faster. At his wit's end and unable to take the slow, groaning transmission and low, relaxed mutterings of the other passengers, he disembarked five stops before he had intended and sprinted along the sidewalk to the theater where he skidded to a stop in front of the glass doors.

With a few deep breaths to compose himself, Charlie pulled the door open and stepped inside. The murmur of the crowd in the lobby washed over him and then began to fade out as all faces turned to stare. Several hundred men and women in formal evening wear surrounded him, and every single one of them stared with expressions of distaste.

"Sir?" a low voice said from Charlie's side.

Charlie looked into the pinched face of an older, balding man with a thick mustache. "Yes?"

"May I help you in some way?"

"Is this the theater for the premiere?" Charlie asked, keeping his voice low. The people in the crowd had begun to speak quietly once again, probably about him.

"Well, yes, we are hosting a premiere tonight, but it is a formal affair." The man let his gaze travel along Charlie's outfit. "And you don't seem to be dressed all that, well, formally. Sir."

"I didn't know it was going to be this formal," Charlie replied, turning to look around the lobby. "I don't see Ken or Kinitia."

"I'm sorry, sir, but I'm going to have to ask to see your invitation."

Charlie's heart leaped. Invitation? Shit! He had left it at his apartment! "Um, I, uh, don't have it on me. But if you would just get Ken Carlton or Kinitia Jones, they can vouch for me."

"I'm sorry, sir, but there is no one here by that name. I'm going to have to insist that you leave." The man took Charlie by the arm and escorted him through the door and to the sidewalk. "Please go before I call the police."

Charlie stepped out from beneath the marquee of the theater and looked up. The word PREMIERE hung above him and below that was listed "ARTHOUSE DEBACLE" A NEW FILM BY EDWARD MARGOLIS.

"Huh?" Charlie said to himself. "Who the fuck is that?" He turned around and looked along the street. Two blocks farther down he could see another theater marquee and rolled his eyes. He had gone into the wrong theater. Tamping down his embarrassment, Charlie jogged down the street and read the marquee twice before entering the building: PREMIERING TONIGHT! A NEW STYLE OF ADULT ENTERTAINMENT! "CUMUPPANCE."

The lobby was deserted except for some well-built models gossiping at the concession stand. They wore tuxedoes and fanned themselves with movie programs. As

Charlie walked in, their heads turned as a group, surveyed his condition, and dismissed him in the space of a minute.

Charlie crossed the lobby and slipped through the door into the dark theater. Projected on the screen before him, so much bigger than life, was Ken's amazing cock. Charlie had become very familiar with Ken's cock over the months, and he would have recognized it anywhere. Eight inches long in person, Ken's dick stretched several feet long on screen and was ready for action as he began working over another actor.

Moving slowly, Charlie eased down the aisle, squinting as he scanned the crowd in the darkness, searching for Kinitia, Billy, Bernice, or Ken. He made it halfway down the aisle between the center and left sections of seats before he heard his name hissed from across the theater. "Charlie! Psst!"

He turned and squinted over the people in the center section who had turned to stare at him. From the right section of seats across the theater, a pale arm waved. "Over here!"

Charlie grinned as the light from the screen reflected off a pair of large, plastic framed glasses. It was Bernice Tallipepper, Kinitia's assistant. She possessed a quick smile and optimistic, down home personality that either won people over or pissed them off. Haling from Minnesota, she had moved out west after her husband of twenty-seven years divorced her for another woman one third his age. Her four children were grown up and married, living scattered throughout the United States, so she had followed a life-long dream and moved west to California. And much like Charlie had himself, she had found her way to Kinitia's door as a receptionist with a temp agency until just a few months ago when Kinitia had hired her full time.

Charlie excused himself through a row of people, apologizing as he squashed toes and scuffed leather, then plopped down between Bernice and Billy Ransom, another of Kinitia's fluffers.

"Where have you been?" Billy asked. He sniffed a few times then reached down into Charlie's crotch to feel the stiff, sticky stain on his jeans. "Jesus, Charlie, not again!"

"Oh shut up," Charlie mumbled. "I'll tell you about it later." He settled into his seat, accepted some popcorn from Bernice, and watched the movie unfold.

Up on the screen, Ken had apparently been taken prisoner, and was enduring a thorough cavity search by a pair of stocky henchmen. The pair stripped him down then inserted a metal speculum into his anus and cranked it open, spreading his sphincter wide. Using their fingers and a lubed up billy club, the two men poked and prodded Ken's gaping hole. Soon one of the henchmen shook his head and said in a horribly over the top Russian accent, "Nah. Ve must geet in deeper dan dees."

The henchman unzipped his coverall and dropped it to the floor, exposing a long, very thick, pumped and ready to go cock. A leather cock ring was fastened around the base, keeping the man stiff as he slid a condom onto his massive pole and then moved around behind Ken. While the other henchman held Ken's head pressed into his crotch, the nude henchman rammed himself full tilt into Ken's hole.

"Ouch," Charlie whispered as on the screen Ken grimaced and let out a shout muffled by the cock in his throat. "That had to hurt."

Billy leaned over and said quietly, "Nah, I was the fluffer

on this set. They had the guy fuck him a little bit first and then had him drive it home. It just looks bad."

Charlie nodded and turned back to the screen. The henchman in front shrugged out of his own coveralls and managed to keep his dick in Ken's mouth the entire time. Ken took both men like a pro, grunting and grinding his hips in a circular motion as the big-dicked henchman pummeled his asshole. Before too long the henchman at the rear pulled his huge cock out of Ken's hole and ripped the condom off. He stroked himself to a splattering climax that covered Ken's middle and lower back, then reached down to slide his fingers into Ken's loose and lubricated asshole. The henchman in front pulled back and shot his load onto Ken's face, spraying him with cum as Ken closed his eyes and mouth and rode the fingers in his asshole. A moment later, he straightened up and launched his own wad onto the belly and crotch of the man in front of him as the man behind continued to finger fuck him.

The henchmen smiled at each other then Ken turned and delivered a couple of high kicks and punches to the men, knocking them out. Charlie and Billy looked at each other with wide eyes.

"That looked really impressive," Charlie said. "I knew Ken was flexible, but not that flexible!"

Billy blinked and said, "I never saw that move while I was on the set."

They turned back to the film and watched as Ken ran through gray corridors, nude and sporting a full erection that bobbed before him. He was searching for stolen microfilm, and to get it he was going to fuck everyone he met. Charlie settled deeper into his chair and stretched out to give his crotch more room to expand as he watched the rest of the film.

After the movie, the crowd gathered in the lobby. The mood was light and everyone was talking about how much they had liked the film. Ken mingled with the well wishers and accepted congratulations on his acting abilities and physical endowments. Charlie, Billy, Kinitia and Bernice stood off to one side of the concession stand and talked about the movie. They had all enjoyed it, Bernice especially since it had been her first time seeing a gay porn movie.

"I'd always wondered how it all worked between, you know, two men," Bernice said. "And now I've seen just about all of it, huh?"

"I'd say you were just getting started, honey," Kinitia replied with a raised eyebrow. "What would your family say if they knew where you worked?"

Bernice giggled and waved Kinitia off. "Oh, I just tell them I'm an assistant at a delivery service. They don't care enough to ask anything more than that. Oh, look, here comes Ken. Ken! Yoo hoo! Kenny!"

Ken sauntered up, his shirt unbuttoned down the middle of his hairy chest and his pants tight enough to reveal that he dressed to the left. He was porn-star-cool as he flashed them a smile and hugged each one tight. Grabbing Charlie last of all, Ken placed a hand over his stiff crotch and asked quietly, "More problems on the set?"

"All right," Charlie replied and backed away. "Hey, nice fight scenes."

Ken grinned. "Thanks. Pretty good for an old timer, huh?"

"So, Ken, great come shots," Bernice said and gave him a thumbs up. "Nice distance."

Ken blushed and looked down at his shoes. "Uh, thanks Bernice. I appreciate you all coming out tonight to see it."

"What, are you crazy?" Billy said. "Of course we would."

"Well, it's just really nice that you all support me in this second attempt at becoming an actor. It means a lot."

"Well, I'd say it's more than just an attempt, but you're welcome," Charlie said and hugged Ken again. "After all, you taught me everything I know."

Cupping his hand over Charlie's crotch again, Ken replied, "And it looks like you need some more training."

"May I have your attention please?" a man standing on a chair called out over the noise of the crowd. The people quieted down and turned to face him. "Thank you all for coming tonight to our premiere. I am Gregory Gianelli, the head of Bruised Knees studios, and I would like to personally invite all of you back to my house for a gathering to celebrate this new era of gay adult film. On your invitations you will find a map to the house, but if you do not have one, any of my trusty assistants in tuxedoes can supply one for you. I hope to see each of you there. Thank you again for supporting *Cumuppance*."

The crowd applauded and then began to file out of the theater.

"I've got the Beetle if anyone wants to ride along with me," Ken offered.

"That's good because I didn't drive tonight," Kinitia said. "Looks like we're all going to be riding with you."

They followed the crowd outside and squeezed into Ken's red Beetle. Bernice got in the front seat and Kinitia and

Charlie sat in back with Billy stretched out over their laps like a Vegas showgirl during rehearsal. The drive was mercifully short, and soon Ken was making his way up the drive to Gregory Gianelli's brightly lit, sprawling house overlooking the lights of the city.

"Wow," Charlie said as he stepped out of the car and took in the house and grounds.

"Yeah, no kidding," Ken replied. "Makes Cedric Wilmington's house look like a fuckin' log cabin, doesn't it?"

Charlie rolled his eyes at the mention of Cedric. "God, did you have to bring up that old bitch?"

"Sorry. But I thought you saw him already."

"What do you mean?"

"You don't know? I was sitting with the cast and crew behind the row you cut through to get to those guys." Ken nodded to where Bernice and Billy were helping Kinitia from the backseat of the car. "You stepped on him and Rock as you went past them."

"Oh fuck," Charlie moaned. "You're kidding."

"Sorry bud. I heard Cedric say something about his new Gucci's right after you stomped by like Godzilla." Ken saw the stricken look on Charlie's face and could not help laughing as he slapped him on the back. "Hey, relax. What can he do to you that he hasn't already tried to do before, right?"

Charlie took a deep breath and followed his friends up to the house. "I'm afraid to find out."

2

OLD TIME'S SAKE

It took almost a full hour without seeing Cedric or Rock before Charlie could finally relax. He had a couple of mimosas and wandered around the large house, peering into rooms and admiring the artwork. There were over three hundred people at the party and Charlie breezed through with a grin, stopping to talk to those he knew and smiling at those he did not but wouldn't mind getting to know.

In one of the upstairs bathrooms, Charlie stood before the toilet relishing the peace and solitude of having a room to himself, even if it was only for a few minutes, when the door popped open. He jumped and quickly tucked himself back into his soiled pants. Fluffer though he was, Charlie was intensely pee shy. After zipping up, he turned to find Brent Harrington, his one time neighbor and sometime lover, standing with his back against the door. His goateed face was creased with a rakish grin that lent a sparkle to his brown eyes.

"Brent?" Charlie gave him a hug and grunted as Brent

wrapped his big, hairy arms around him and squeezed back. "Where have you been for the last few weeks?"

Brent grinned at him. "Working. Got a job on a movie up in Vancouver."

"As in Canada?"

"One and the same. I worked on the movie for a week, fell in love with the place and decided to stay for a while." Brent leaned against the sink and folded his arms. "How about you? What's new in the world of Farm Boy Charlie?"

Charlie shrugged. "Not much, really. Ken's movie was premiered tonight. Did you see it?"

Brent shook his head. "No. I just heard about the party and wandered in on my own. I was hoping to find you here."

"I'm glad you did." Charlie grinned at him. "So what's next for you? Are you back to stay?"

Brent made a face and darted his gaze away, and Charlie felt his throat constrict. He wasn't in love with Brent, not by a long shot, but the man had proved to be a good friend when Charlie had needed someone several months before. Plus he was really hot in bed.

"You're leaving, aren't you?" Charlie asked.

"Just to Vancouver," Brent replied. "It's not that far. You could come visit."

"A whole other country." Charlie forced a smile. "But I'd like to come visit. Are you going to do movies up there or something?"

Brent blushed around his goatee. "Something else, actually. And it's a lot different than what I've been doing."

"Oh? What is it?"

"I bought a pet store."

Charlie laughed. "A pet store? Are you serious?"

Brent laughed along with him. "Very serious. I love animals, and I don't have the attention span or background to be a veterinarian, so I'm doing the next best thing."

Charlie smiled. "I think it's great. I can't wait to see the shop."

"I would love for you to come up and visit."

"I will. I promise."

A frantic pounding on the door interrupted them and a shrill voice asked, "Are you done blowing him yet? For God's sake, there are about forty bedrooms in this place and only six bathrooms! Come on already!"

Brent pulled open the door and waved for Charlie to precede him. As Charlie stepped over the threshold he stopped and gasped. Cedric Wilmington, evil director and man of sour mind and flabby body, stood before him. Cedric wore khaki clam diggers, a leopard print silk shirt, and open toed leather Gucci construction boots, slightly scuffed, with white silk stockings bunched down around his pale, hairless ankles. A bright pink pith helmet completed the safari ensemble.

"Well, well, well," Cedric said through thin, pursed lips. "If it isn't the most notorious fluffer in all the land."

Charlie took a breath and drew strength from the reassuring hand Brent placed on his shoulder. "Cedric. How are you?"

"Practically floating in my own urine, thanks to you and your fat old trick," Cedric snapped.

"Uh, I'm sorry, 'old'?" Brent said with a grin.

"Oh, just get out of my way." Cedric brushed past them into the bathroom before turning back. "Oh, and thanks for ruining my pedicure tonight. Are you wearing clown shoes?"

Cedric dropped his eyes to the stain on Charlie's crotch and smirked. "Well, I see you're still having trouble keeping control of yourself on the job. Better watch that, Farm Boy, or you might find yourself out on the street. Remember that I own a portion of Kinitia's office building and I could raise the rent in a heartbeat."

Before Charlie could reply, Cedric slammed the door in his face and engaged the lock. Charlie considered waiting for the old crow in the hall and having it out with him once and for all, but Brent convinced him to take a walk in the garden instead. Outside, the night air was scented with eucalyptus and jasmine. A meandering brick path made its way through lush, dimly lit landscaping. A few other couples had had the same idea and they passed more than one blowjob in progress as they walked slowly along the path.

After passing a third couple in the midst of oral sex, Brent looked over at Charlie and asked, "What do think? Once more for old time's sake?"

Charlie nodded eagerly, then took Brent's hand and led him off the path and over to a large, decorative boulder. Smaller rocks situated around the boulder turned out to be speakers that piped classical music into the garden.

"Jeez," Charlie said. "Be careful where you step. You might be crushing a speaker disguised as a rock."

"I think Mr. Gianelli can afford more speakers in case I misstep."

Charlie tried to get Brent to sit on the boulder, but the big bear of a man moved Charlie to the rock instead.

"You've been fluffing me for a while now," Brent said with a grin as he knelt before Charlie. "Now let me fluff you."

Charlie smiled and ran his fingers through Brent's dark,

wavy hair. Brent carefully unzipped Charlie's jeans and pulled the elastic of his boxer briefs down beneath his balls. Taking Charlie's cock in his hand, Brent stroked the hardening member, then leaned down to swallow the length of him in one gulp as "Ride of the Valkyeries" began to play softly from the speakers around them. Charlie moaned and closed his eyes, enjoying the feel of Brent's mouth moving slowly along his cock. The gentle scratch of the goatee on the sensitive tip each time Brent pursed his lips and focused all his suction on the head of his dick sent a zap through him. The rhythm and feel of Brent's mouth brought back memories of their nights — and days! — together, and Charlie recalled so many times waking up in Brent's arms. He had missed his bear protector the last few weeks, and he would miss him in the days to come. But right now, Brent was performing a fuck of a good blowjob on him and Charlie meant to enjoy every single suck.

"Oh," Charlie breathed quietly. "That feels really good."

Quiet voices as guests strolled by along the path, but neither of them paid any attention. Brent was concentrating on giving Charlie a blowjob to remember, and Charlie was too involved being blown like never before to care about anyone else in the vicinity. Around them, Wagner faded out to be replaced by the "1812 Overture."

Brent gulped down Charlie's throbbing pole, lodging the head against the back of his throat and struggling against his gag reflex. His left hand wrapped tight around the base of Charlie's cock, and he stroked himself with his right. He moved his head back and sucked harder and faster, moving his left hand higher up Charlie's cock to stroke in time with the movements of his mouth.

"Oh, fuck, Brent," Charlie gasped. "That feels so damn good. Oh, yeah. Just like that, right on the tip. Oh, suck that cock, baby. Yeah."

Brent increased his speed even more and soon Charlie's balls pulled up as he prepared to shoot his load. He braced his hands on the boulder and his legs stiffened as he started to breathe harder.

"Oh, Brent, I'm coming," Charlie groaned. "Oh, God, I'm going to come."

Perfectly timed with the firing of the cannons in the overture, Brent backed his mouth off Charlie's cock and stroked for all he was worth, his grip tightening as the first jet of cum spurted onto his face. It drizzled into his goatee and he moaned. Each blast of semen struck him in the face, spattering across his cheeks, forehead, nose and goatee. Charlie grunted his way through his orgasm until he'd finished, and he took deep breaths to slow his heart rate. Brent rubbed the sensitive head of Charlie's softening cock through the cum that covered his face as he jerked himself off.

"Oh, fuck, I'm coming," Brent moaned moments later. He stood up and Charlie knelt to allow Brent to shoot his load onto his upturned face. Brent's stout cock launched ropy strands of cum across Charlie's cheeks, nose and lips. A puddle of it even landed in Charlie's hair just over his left ear. When he was finished, Brent rubbed the tip of his own cock through the cum then leaned down and kissed him. Their tongues swapped salty licks of semen before Brent straightened up and helped Charlie to his feet.

"So, how'd I do?" Brent asked with a cum-sticky grin.

Charlie nodded and said with a smirk, "You did okay."

"Okay?" Brent asked indignantly. "Just okay?"

"Hey, if I have to hear it, so do you: as a fluffer, you can't make them come. You just have to get them hard and keep them hard." Charlie shrugged. "It's a tough job."

Brent laughed and put his arm around Charlie's shoulders to lead him back to the path. They continued along in companionable silence until they came upon a cupid fountain. They cleaned up in the cold, clear water and dried their faces on each other's shirts. A few yards farther the path opened out on the pool deck in back of the house. Groups of people stood talking around the brightly lit water with drinks in their hands. Charlie could see Kinitia and Bernice speaking with Gregory Gianelli off in a corner near some patio furniture.

"Hey, look there," Brent said and pointed across the pool deck where Cedric stood on the fringes of a group of men, his slitted eyes locked on Kinitia, Bernice, and Gregory Gianelli.

"He looks like the wicked witch in every Disney cartoon," Charlie grumbled.

"Ah, don't break a sweat over Cedric. His bark is worse than his bite." Brent gave Charlie a one armed hug. "You going to be okay now?"

Charlie turned to look at him. "You're leaving? So soon?"

"I accomplished what I came here for. I wanted to see you one last time and say good bye." Brent kissed him tenderly, almost longingly, his tongue sweeping slowly through Charlie's mouth, and then smiled into his eyes. "I'll miss you, Farm Boy. Is it okay if I call you now and then?"

"I'll be angry if you don't." Charlie squeezed Brent's hand and watched with a lump in his throat as he turned and ambled around the pool.

After Brent had disappeared into the house, Charlie made his way over to Kinitia and Bernice. As he rounded a corner of the pool, he was distracted by a group of incredibly handsome men talking together to his left and ran head-on into a tall, muscular chest. As he bounced off the man, Charlie tried to apologize and step to his right but suddenly found himself falling into the sparkling clear water of Gregory Gianelli's pool. He sank slowly to the bottom of and contemplated staying submerged for several minutes just to avoid the humiliation of having everyone stare at him when he resurfaced. What a day!

A pair of strong hands took the decision away from him, however, as fingers snagged his billowing shirt and pulled him back up to the surface. He gasped for breath, swallowed a mouthful of water, and began to cough. His eyes teared up as he was pulled to the side and the strong hands reached lower to grab the back of his jeans and haul him out of the water. Charlie sprawled on the cement deck and coughed the last bits of water out of his lungs.

A small crowd had gathered and he stared blearily up at the faces surrounding him. He could make out Kinitia and Bernice and, after rubbing the chlorine from his eyes, saw Gregory Gianelli looking at him with a mixture of concern and annoyance.

And then the fresh smell of citrus came to him and he turned his head to smile stupidly up at Rock Harding.

"Hi Rock," Charlie said as nonchalantly as possible. "I didn't know you were at the party."

The guests surrounding him straightened up and chuckled. Kinitia frowned down at him and shook her head as she dismissed him with a wave.

"Do you think he's all right?" Bernice asked as Kinitia led her away.

"Honey," Kinitia said. "One thing you're going to have to learn about Charlie is that he is as clumsy as they come. You have no idea how high our premiums would be if the insurance company knew about him."

Rock helped Charlie sit up and patted his back. "You okay, Charlie?"

Charlie nodded and tried to smooth his hair down. "Yeah. Just embarrassed."

"Can you swim?" Rock wondered.

"You ask me that as if you think there's no water in Idaho," Charlie replied. He assessed Rock's face and decided the man was serious. "They do have water in Idaho, and yes, I know how to swim."

Rock smiled. "Well, I'm glad I was here to fish you out anyway." He helped Charlie stand and looked him over. "It's going to be a while before you dry out. Want to go for a walk through the garden?"

Charlie thought about his recent tryst with Brent off the garden path and shook his head with a small smile. "No, not really. I think I'll just see if I can flag down a cab."

"In this neighborhood?" Rock asked. "Cabs don't patrol this area. Look, I'll give you a ride home."

"But what about Cedric?" Charlie said, turning to look across the pool where Cedric was staring at him with blatant hatred. He quickly turned back to Rock. "He doesn't seem too happy about us talking together."

Rock smiled at Charlie without even glancing at Cedric. "We came in separate cars. Come on, I'll give you a lift."

Charlie found Kinitia, Bernice, Ken, and Gregory

Gianelli talking inside the house. He said farewells all around and turned to Gregory. As he thanked the studio head for inviting him to the premiere and apologized for falling in the pool, Charlie tried not to notice that Gianelli was frowning at the small puddle forming beneath his feet on the cream-colored carpet. He followed Rock out the front door, smiling as brightly as he could considering the circumstances. They approached Rock's Navigator and stood at the passenger side. Rock pulled open the door then glanced thoughtfully back to where Charlie stood dripping on the driveway.

"Hang on a second," Rock said.

A few minutes later, Rock nosed his large SUV out the front gate and into the street. Charlie tried not to move around too much as the tarp from the back of Rock's truck tended to crinkle beneath him.

"So, I haven't seen you around in a while," Charlie said. *Crinkle, crackle, rustle.*

"Yeah, I've been keeping a low profile. After I won the Golden Orifice, I decided to take some time off." Rock grinned at him. "How about you? I saw you kissing Brent Harrington. Are you two still seeing one another?"

Charlie shook his head, the tarp scrunching beneath him and his stomach knotting up from nerves. God, how this man affected him! "No, not anymore. He's moving to Vancouver to run a pet store."

Rock cocked an eyebrow. "A pet store?"

"A pet store." *Crackle, rustle.* "So, I was just saying good-bye." *Crinkle, crunch, pop.*

"I see."

They drove on in silence. As he tried to hold perfectly

still, Charlie struggled desperately to think of a topic of conversation, anything to draw the man out and get him talking. But every topic he considered sounded too desperate or trite. He wanted Rock to see him as fun, laid back, considerate, empathetic, and, of course, incredibly sexy. But sitting on a noisy tarp while pool water ran off his body was not going to earn him any points in the incredibly sexy category.

Before Charlie realized it, Rock had turned onto his block and slowed to a stop in front of his building. Shifting into Park, Rock smiled at him. "Here we are. Home sweet home."

Charlie smiled nervously. "Yeah. This is it. I, uh, appreciate the ride." He stopped, staring at the man before him. Was it his imagination or had Rock gotten even more handsome these past few weeks?

Rock frowned at him. "You okay Charlie?"

"Huh? Oh, yeah. Why?"

"You just got a funny look on your face there," Rock said sincerely. "I thought maybe you had hit your head when you fell in the pool or something."

Charlie took a breath and opened his door. Turning, he smiled with as carefree an attitude as he could muster, all the while mentally willing Rock to kiss him. "No, I'm fine. Thanks for giving me a ride home, Rock."

"My pleasure. Hey, do you still work out at the same gym?"

Charlie nodded. "Five times a week."

"Maybe I'll see you there. I need to get back on a regular work out schedule."

Charlie glanced at the bulging arms beneath Rock's tight white T-shirt and felt his cock twitch within the damp confines of his boxer briefs. "Yeah. Maybe we'll run into each other. Thanks again for the ride."

Charlie jumped down out of the car, and when he straightened up was surprised to find Rock walking around the front. His heart jumped and he felt his knees get a little weak. The man strode with such purpose and intent in his expression, he must have made a monumental decision in the last few seconds of their conversation and discovered he could no longer go on without Charlie beside him. Now he would kiss Charlie goodnight and whisk him away to his plush bedroom for a night of unparalleled sex.

Smiling with wide eyes, a palpitating heart, and a stiffening dick, Charlie received a dazzling smile in response as Rock walked up. The big man reached out toward him, their gazes locked. This was it, Rock was going to pull him in close and give him the kiss of his life. Then Rock's hand moved past Charlie and on into the SUV. He grabbed the wet tarp off the leather seat and dragged it out onto the sidewalk. He closed the passenger door, stepped to the rear of the truck and shook the excess water from the tarp onto the sidewalk, then tossed it in the back. Waving to Charlie, he called out, "Night," and walked back to the driver's door where he climbed in and drove away.

Charlie shook his head. He was hopeless. He entered the building, checked his mailbox, and then climbed the steps to his apartment. Trying not to look at the door behind which Brent used to live, Charlie let himself into his tiny studio apartment and went straight into the bathroom where his reflection explained all. His hair was matted down on the right side of his head and curled up in a weird wave on the left, probably from the glob of Brent's cum that had landed therc earlier. The back had spiked up in three cowlicks and, to top it all off, a small runner of mucus had dried just outside of his right nostril.

With a heavy sigh, Charlie took a hot shower, after which he felt more invigorated. He didn't have to be at the office tomorrow until noon, and he was feeling a little restless after riding home with Rock. Perhaps he needed a night out at the bars on his own, without Billy or Ken along for distraction. He got dressed and headed down to the street where he caught a bus for the industrial part of town. Tonight he would prowl through previously unexplored territory. Tonight he would start over with a fresh outlook and a new attitude. Rock and Brent were the past, and someone unknown and exciting was the future.

3

A BIG SURPRISE

A shrill chirping drilled into Charlie's brain and brought him up from the deep realm of sleep in which he was dreaming of fluffing Brent Harrington as the man sat on a boulder flanked by several smaller rocks all in the shape of Rock Harding's head. Each of the heads hummed a different piece of classical music, and somewhere in the distance a group of people played Marco Polo in a large pool.

The chirping again. What was that? Charlie pried open an eye and saw a telephone sitting on the bedside table. The instrument chirped at him and he reached out to snag it, more in the hopes of shutting it the hell up than actually answering. He held it to his ear and said in a raspy voice that sounded nothing like his own, "'Lo?"

"Uh, who is this?" a grating voice asked much too loudly.

"Oh, man," Charlie groaned as his head throbbed. "Who is *this?*"

"Is that you?" the voice asked again.

"Yeah, it's me," Charlie moaned. "Who the fuck else would be answering my phone?"

"Actually," a deep voice said from behind him, "it's my phone."

Charlie jumped and turned to find an attractive older man lying next to him. He stared blankly at the man for a moment, then asked, "Who are you?"

The man smiled and gestured for the phone. Charlie looked at the receiver, realized it wasn't his phone after all, and handed it to the man.

"Hello?" the man said. "Oh. Yeah, it's me ... That was a friend I met last night. What do you want?"

Charlie rolled over and groaned into the pillow, the phone cord stretching across his bare shoulder. He could remember going to some dark, warehouse-style bar and having several drinks with some nice men he had never met before, but after that everything blurred together. He peeked over his shoulder at the man in bed beside him and was pleasantly surprised. Angular, masculine face with a day old dark blond beard, thinning blond hair, bright blue eyes and white, even teeth. The cleft in the chin must have acted as a magnet for him last night, what with thoughts of Rock Harding running rampant through his head.

Charlie got out of bed, moaned quietly at the swell of pain in his head, and padded naked through the bedroom as the man's voice lowered in what sounded like annoyance with his early morning caller. Charlie located the bathroom down the hall and sighed as he peed. What a relief. He washed his hands, splashed water on his face, and smoothed down his hair as best he could. He never snooped in a person's medicine cabinet, but he was desperate and eased open the mirrored cabinet. He found some aspirin and swallowed four, then walked back into the bedroom just as the man was finishing up his call.

"Yeah, don't worry, I'll be long gone by then," he said with obvious annoyance. "Good fucking bye." He banged the phone down and grunted as he turned his back to it with a muttered, "Fuckin' bitch."

Charlie eased into bed behind the man and pressed up against his muscular body. He carefully kissed the top knobs of the man's spine as he slid his arm around the big chest and cupped a firm, hairy pectoral. "Everything okay?"

"Yeah," the man said. "Sorry about that. Just some old business coming back to haunt me."

Charlie nodded into the nape of the man's neck. "I can relate." He pressed his slowly lengthening cock against the crack of his bed partner's firm ass. "Feeling frisky this morning?"

The man rolled over and gave Charlie a sexy smirk. "I could probably be convinced to spend a few hours satisfying you."

Charlie smiled. "Wow, did I know how to pick 'em last night, or what?"

The man grinned. "Actually, I picked you."

"Oh, really?" Charlie blushed. "Last night is kind of a blur for me. I think I was drinking vodka tonics."

The man nodded and pressed the firm line of his long, thick cock against Charlie's thigh. "At first. Then you switched to shots of Jack Daniels."

Charlie flinched. "Ouch. Did I do anything stupid?"

"Well, besides being asked to leave the bar because you were dancing naked on the pool table? Not really." The man laughed at Charlie's stricken expression. "Relax, I'm joking. And by the way, my name is Phrank."

"Frank! Ah, yes, I remember it now," Charlie said and leaned forward to kiss him.

"And it's spelled with a P-H."

Charlie pulled back and looked at him in confusion. "Huh?"

"My name."

"P-H-R-A-N-K? Like that?"

"Yep."

"But you say it like it's spelled with an F?"

"Yep."

Charlie thought about it for a moment, then shrugged. "Okay."

Phrank laughed. "Thanks for your approval." He rose to his knees, looming over him as the sheet fell away from his body and Charlie drank in the sight of his body, immediately becoming fully aroused despite his dull headache. Phrank's body was thick and firm, covered with a moderate layer of dark blond hair that contrasted with the light blond hair on his head and offset his blue eyes. Beneath his flat, taut stomach and sprouting out from a dark tangle of pubic hair, was a long, thick, uncut cock. Beneath Phrank's amazing dick hung a set of smooth, supple balls that made Charlie's mouth water.

"Oh my God," Charlie whispered. "You're gorgeous."

"Thanks," Phrank replied with a bright smile. "And so are you. Now, let's get down to business, shall we?"

Walking on his knees up to Charlie's face, Phrank offered up his pink, low hanging balls and Charlie slurped them into his mouth, caressing them with his tongue.

Reaching up, he ran his hand along the length of Phrank's body, pinching each nipple and ruffling the dark fur. Moving his hand lower, he wrapped his fingers around the solid length of Phrank's cock and slowly stroked.

"Oh, yeah," Phrank sighed. "That's nice." He leaned away, arching his back.

As he leaned back, Phrank's balls settled deeper into Charlie's mouth. Charlie slid his tongue along their smooth surface and tasted the salt of the man's sleep sweat. He gulped them further into his throat and let his tongue run out to caress Phrank's smooth perineum. While he bathed Phrank's balls with saliva, Charlie kept up a steady rhythm on Phrank's cock with his fist.

"Goddamn, Charlie," Phrank moaned. "That's really hot."

Moving from Phrank's balls to his cock, Charlie opened his mouth wide and slowly sucked. The rumpled foreskin covering the slick, bulbed head slid back and forth with Charlie's mouth and tongue. He reached up and pulled the foreskin back to expose the fat pink head and focused his oral attentions directly on the sensitive cap. With his other hand, Charlie gathered the skin just above Phrank's balls and tugged it tight, rubbing the perineum with a finger.

"Fuck, oh, fuck," Phrank gasped. He leaned forward over Charlie, grasping the iron headboard and watching as Charlie sucked at the tip of his cock. "That feels so good."

Releasing the foreskin, Charlie nabbed it with his teeth and pulled it up over the head. He slid his tongue beneath the skin and massaged the reddening tip of the cock as he wrapped his hand around the base and squeezed.

Phrank pulled his cock out of Charlie's mouth and turned his back. He pushed the sheet off Charlie's body and leaned down to take his leaking cock in his mouth. Phrank positioned his asshole right over Charlie's face and groaned as Charlie spread his tight, hairy cheeks apart and lapped at the hot, sweat-slicked anus between.

"Oh, yeah," Charlie groaned up into Phrank's hole. "Suck my cock."

After sucking Charlie's dick for a time, Phrank pulled Charlie's legs up and moved down to lick the smooth pink pucker he had exposed. He rubbed at the tender opening with a thick thumb, working spit into the hole, then pressed down on either side of it to pop the muscle open and worked his tongue deeper inside.

Charlie groaned as Phrank slid his tongue into him and reached up to grab his own ankles and pull his legs back further. He closed his eyes and opened his mouth, planting it over Phrank's asshole and sucking at the wet, hair shrouded skin beneath. He slowly licked along the length of Phrank's crack and nuzzled his nose into the damp darkness of his asshole as he ran his tongue over the surface of Phrank's balls.

"Oh, fuck, Charlie," Phrank said. "That's it. Eat my ass."

"God, Phrank, I'm going to have to get a dick up my ass pretty soon if you keep doing that," Charlie moaned back.

"My pleasure," Phrank replied and bent once more to his work.

After several more minutes of rimming, Phrank moved off Charlie and pulled a condom out of his nightstand. He eased it over his fat prick and lathered a liberal amount of lube along it. Pulling Charlie to the edge of the bed, Phrank slid a lubed finger into him and watched his expression.

"Feel okay?" he asked.

"Yeah," Charlie replied.

Phrank pushed two more fingers into him then grabbed Charlie's ankles and raised his legs to rest on his shoulders. Guiding his hard dick with his right hand, Phrank inched his way inside Charlie's ass.

"Oh my God," Charlie gasped. "That is one monster of a fuckin' dick."

"Nine inches of hot cock, baby," Phrank replied with a smile. "And it's as deep inside you as possible."

"Oh, God," Charlie said. "It's a good thing. I don't think I could take it any further."

Phrank slid out of Charlie's ass and gradually entered him again. He repeated the slow process several times then began to pump his hips faster until he was all out pounding his cock deep into him. Charlie tried to tighten and release his muscles around Phrank, but it took too much thought, so he stopped trying and just rode the waves of pleasure.

At one point, Phrank paused with his dick buried inside him. Charlie opened his eyes and found Phrank looking down at him. When Phrank caught Charlie's gaze, he grinned and wriggled his hips, moving his cock in a circular motion inside Charlie's ass. Charlie groaned and grabbed fistfuls of the sheet beneath him. Phrank chuckled and began fucking him once again, his hips moving amazingly fast.

With Phrank pistoning into him, Charlie felt himself getting close and gasped, "I'm going to come."

"Do it, baby," Phrank said and picked up his pace even more. "Shoot that fucking load. Show it to me."

Charlie looked down and watched his cock jerk as it spurted long, thick loads of cum onto his belly without a touch of his hands. Phrank spread the puddles of cum over

Charlie's torso, his hair-flecked fingers caressing each abdominal muscle and nipple.

"Oh God, that is so hot," Phrank whispered. He closed his eyes as he pumped his cock into Charlie's body then suddenly pulled out and peeled off the condom. Leaning forward between Charlie's legs, he stroked himself to a gushing climax that coated Charlie's chest and belly.

After he was spent, Phrank leaned forward and kissed Charlie on the lips, running his tongue slowly into his mouth and dripping sweat onto his face. He pulled back and grinned. "Have you had a good morning?"

Charlie stroked Phrank's cheek and smiled up at him. "Oh yeah."

They showered together, both too tired to come again but eager to explore each other's body. After a breakfast of toast and coffee, Charlie kissed Phrank good bye and set off to find a bus stop. It was ten o'clock and he would need to be at the office at noon for his assignment.

Ten minutes before noon, Charlie stepped into the familiar outer office of Fluffers, Inc. and smiled at Bernice where she sat behind the front desk.

"Well, there's our very own Olympic swimmer!" Bernice said with a wink. "And how are you, young man? Did you finally dry out from your dip the pool last night?"

Charlie grinned. "Yeah. And I'm much better than last night, thank you."

Bernice raised her eyebrows. "Really? Well, well, well Anything to do with the man who took you home from the party? That Rock Harding is just so handsome. And he seems to be such a nice boy." Bernice sighed and looked off into the distance over Charlie's shoulder. "Nice boys don't come along all that often, Charlie."

"Well," Charlie said. "That one didn't come at all last night. At least not with me."

"Oh," Bernice replied. "I'm sorry. It just looked like he was so comfortable with you and he seemed so concerned when you took that tumble into the pool. I just assumed, you know."

"Yeah, you and me both, Bernice."

"Hey, there you are," Ken Carlton said, walking up from the waiting area. "Have a good night?"

Charlie smirked and shrugged as Kinitia appeared in the doorway of her office down the hall. "Oh, good, Charlie's here. Ken, get Billy from the waiting room and come into my office everyone. You too, Bernice. I've got some big news."

Charlie and Bernice exchanged a puzzled look but followed Kinitia into the office where Billy Ransom and Ken soon joined them. After closing the door behind him, Ken leaned against it and they all directed their attention to where Kinitia sat perched on the edge of her desk.

"I've just gotten off the phone with Gregory Gianelli," Kinitia started.

"He's not asking you to pay to have his pool cleaned, is he?" Billy said and reached out to playfully punch Charlie in the arm.

"Not quite." Kinitia took a breath and smiled at them. "I have just been informed that a large bid I had turned in to Bruised Knees productions has been accepted."

"Bid? For what?" Charlie asked.

"To provide six fluffers and two administrators for their

next three movies which are being filmed simultaneously." Kinitia paused for effect. "On a cruise ship!"

Everyone gaped at her.

"A cruise ship?" Ken asked with a smile. "They're filming a gay porn movie on a cruise ship?"

"Not just one movie," Kinitia corrected him. "Three. And they have rented out the entire ship. Apparently there's a cruise line called Carnal Cruises which rent out cruise ships to porn studios and sponsor gay sex cruises."

"Oh my God," Charlie said with a grin. "So we're all going?"

"Me too?" Bernice said as she clapped her hands.

"You too, Bernice. You and I will share a cabin and we'll break up the fluffers accordingly. Now, it's an all male cast, so we'll need you three plus three other fluffers."

"How about the new kid, Trevor?" Billy asked. "He's been doing pretty well."

"I'll bet," Ken said with a smirk and caught Billy blushing. "We can get the others with no problem, I'm sure. Wow, a cruise ship full of porn stars. Imagine the possibilities. Hey, how long will we be gone?"

"Two weeks," Kinitia said. "And we'll be cruising along the coast of Mexico, down to Acapulco and back up to Los Angeles."

"This is great!" Charlie exclaimed and jumped up to hug her. "Thanks so much."

"You're welcome, Farm Boy. Just remember to hold back and not make them come, okay? This is an important job for us. If we can prove we're the best fluffers in the business, our future will be set."

"Didn't you say the same thing about Charlie winning the Hummer?" Billy asked.

Kinitia gave him a dirty look. She then explained that she would messenger their tickets to them once she received them. They were to be at the docks in two days with enough clothes to last two weeks. Then she sent them all off to their respective jobs.

Charlie couldn't help smiling as he waited for the bus to take him to his assigned job. What an amazing life he was living in L.A. First, he had been humiliated at a party, pretty much snubbed by Rock afterwards, but then got the screwing of his life that morning, and was now about to embark on a cruise for two weeks. How could anything possibly go wrong?

4

———————

BON TOYAGE

Two days later, Charlie squeezed out of the backseat of Ken's VW and gazed around the parking lot. It was a sea of cars riding waves of heat that rose off the asphalt. The cruise line terminal looked like a tiny island several miles away. He wiped his brow, hauled his bag out of the trunk, and then fell in line behind Billy and Ken to trudge through the parked cars.

Inside the terminal, they met up with Kinitia and Bernice. Billy looked around and asked, "Where are Trevor, Casey, and Jon?"

Kinitia rolled her eyes. "I need to find a restroom."

"They called from their cell phone," Bernice replied as Kinitia walked away. "They're having a little car trouble."

"What kind of car trouble?" Charlie asked.

"They were caught jacking a car," Bernice said bluntly. "They won't be joining us."

Charlie and Billy blinked at each other, then Billy

barked a startled laugh as Charlie turned to Bernice. "What did you say? *Jacking* a car?"

Bernice gave them a stricken look. "Oh, did I use the wrong word?"

"No," Billy reassured her. "It's the right word. I'm just surprised. They're carjackers?"

"So it would seem," Bernice said. "From what we've been able to find out, they worked for a gang that strips down cars and sells the parts." She noticed Ken's wide-eyed look. "What is it, Ken?"

Ken laughed and shook his head. "The term *jacking* just sounded so natural coming from you, that's all."

Bernice smiled and raised her ample chin a little higher. "I catch on quick, Kenneth. Best that you remember that."

"Oh, I won't soon forget it," Ken said with a smile.

Kinitia returned. "Since we're down half our team, I'm afraid you three are going to have to do double duty."

"You and Bernice could help us out," Billy said with a grin, and turned away before he could catch the wrath of Kinitia's glare.

"Oh, wouldn't that just burn my ex-husband's shorts?" Bernice tittered as they made their way out of the terminal. "For twenty-seven years he tried to get me to go down on him and I always refused. It would serve him right for me to go down on some strange hunk I hardly know. Ha!"

Charlie shook his head and smiled. This was already turning out to be quite a trip, and they had not even boarded the ship. As he made his way out the door, Charlie looked up and stopped. Towering before them was a massive cruise liner, gleaming white in the hot afternoon sun. It waited alongside the pier and sported several layers of decks and balconies. Each window winked and sparkled in the bright sunlight and Charlie felt his breath stop. It was gorgeous.

"Wow," he sighed. "It's amazing."

Kinitia stopped beside him and looked up at the marvel of nautical opulence before them. "Yeah, it is, isn't it?" All five surveyed the ship in silence for a moment, then Kinitia said, "You do know that's not our ship, right?"

"Huh?" Charlie looked at her, blinking out of his daze. "Oh. It isn't?"

"Nope." She turned her head and leaned back to see around the massive hull of the ship looming above them. "That is."

They turned as a group and leaned back to follow her gaze. Sitting in the shadow of the large ocean liner was a much more petite version. When seen side by side with the ship in front of them, this cruise liner seemed like a child's bathtub toy. It was every bit as clean and sleek, only smaller. Much smaller. Instead of towering above the pier, it merely hovered. The gangway, a much smaller and less ornate affair than the other liner's, wobbled just a bit beneath the feet of the chiseled men who were making their way on board.

"Well," Bernice piped up. "It looks very...clean."

Charlie and Ken exchanged an amused look before all of them picked up their bags and started forward. They threaded their way through the bright floral print crowd of people waiting to board the larger cruise liner and fell into line with the tank-topped, Lycra-sporting muscle men heading to their ship. As they made their way up the boarding ramp, Charlie noted the name of the vessel: *Dominatrix.*

Once on board, they were directed to a handsome Latin

steward who smiled as they approached. "Hello, and welcome on board the Dominatrix. May I see your tickets, please?"

They fumbled their tickets from various bags and presented them, each ticket bent, folded, and haggard looking. He accepted them, smiled at their condition, and leafed through each. "Ah, the fluffer crew. I am Jorge, and I will be your personal steward during the cruise." He graced them all with a megawatt smile and reached out to take the bags from Kinitia and Bernice. "Please allow me to show you to your rooms."

They followed Jorge to a narrow stairway leading down into the depths of the ship. He descended the small metal steps nimbly, obviously comfortable with the ship's layout. Bernice, however, had to turn sideways to get her hips to fit through the narrow opening. Charlie bounced off the bulkhead several times, his bags becoming caught on the doorframe before he finally managed to wedge himself past the doorway and down the steps.

Jorge chatted breezily as he maneuvered the luggage and himself around corners and down hallways. Charlie tried to keep the twists and turns straight, but finally gave up after they had descended a third stairway.

"It may seem like you've been sent to the dungeon," Jorge explained. "But these rooms are actually very nice. The windows are just ten feet above the water, and sometimes you can see dolphins swimming with the ship."

"Oh, I love dolphins!" Bernice said with a bright smile. She had her large, vinyl purse hanging in the crook of her arm and a pair of gigantic black sunglasses in hand as she made her way through the hall directly behind Jorge.

The stocky steward stopped abruptly and turned, expertly maneuvering his broad shoulders in the narrow hallway. His smile was luminous as he opened a door on his right. "This is the state room for the ladies."

"Oh, that's us Kinitia," Bernice said and squeezed through the door. She stood in the middle of the small room and turned in a circle. "Oh, my. It's so nice in here!"

Kinitia slid into the room along with her and looked around. Two twin beds, a small desk, two dressers, and a tiny bathroom with a folding door. She looked out at Charlie and Ken and arched an eyebrow. "Well, it ain't the Ritz, but it's nice enough."

Jorge ignored her comment as he placed the luggage on the beds, then led the three fluffers to the next room. "Since there are only three of you, each can have his own state room. I understand that your other three team members will not be able to join us?"

"Yeah, sucks to be them, but damn good for us!" Ken said with a grin.

Billy smirked at him. "Are you kidding? Those three are loving jail. They're getting screwed six ways to Sunday right about now."

"Sounds like a pretty hot time," Jorge commented and smiled at Charlie as he opened a door. "Who gets this one?"

"I'll take it," Ken said and stepped inside.

Billy chose the next room and Charlie followed Jorge around a corner to his door. "And last, but definitely not least," Jorge said as he opened the door with a flourish. "This will be your room."

Charlie walked into the room and looked around. A carbon copy of the three previous rooms, slightly smaller than his apartment. And it was all his for two weeks. The window looked out over the dock where he could see a crowd of people waving to the larger cruise ship beside them. He turned back to Jorge and smiled. "This is great. I love it."

Jorge nodded and backed to the door. "I'll let you get settled. If there's anything you need, anything at all, just pick up the phone. I'm the steward in this section of the ship and I'll be happy to assist." He winked and closed the door behind him.

Charlie had a chance to unpacked a few things before Billy knocked on his door and invited him up to the deck. He joined them all in the hallway and they only got lost three times before they found their way to the top deck. They stood at the railing and waved to the people on the docks. A jostling at his elbow made him turn to find a tall, handsome black man standing beside him. The man had a shaved head, and beneath his yellow tank top Charlie could see toned, well-defined muscles. As Charlie dragged his eyes back up to the new arrival's face, he blushed when he found the man looking down at him with a smile.

"Hi there," the man rumbled with a smooth, deep voice.

"Hi," Charlie replied.

The man extended a hand. "I'm Theo."

"Charlie." He felt his fingers squeezed by the warm, solid hand, and a spark of longing coursed through his veins.

"Are you an actor?" Theo asked.

Charlie shook his head. "We're fluffers." He gestured over his shoulder and Theo looked at the rest of the team, then back at him.

"The women too?" Theo wondered.

"Oh, no," Charlie said with an embarrassed laugh. "No. Kinitia is our boss, and Bernice is her assistant."

"I see." Theo nodded, then both men jumped as the whistle from the neighboring ship blew. "Well, I should get below and unpack. It was nice to meet you, Charlie."

"Nice to meet you," Charlie replied. "I'll see you around, huh?"

Theo flashed a bright smile. "Oh, you can count on that."

Charlie watched him walk off, his gaze falling to the black bicycle shorts hugging Theo's firm, round ass cheeks, and he let out his breath. It was definitely going to be an interesting cruise.

The larger cruise liner held over a thousand people on her decks, and a few hundred had gathered on the docks to wish them *bon voyage*. The Dominatrix, on the other hand, carried just over a hundred people on board, and about a dozen witnessed her departure. The passengers on board the Dominatrix were determined to be just as loud and far more flamboyant than the ocean liner with its tourists sporting blue hair dye, support hose, and dark socks with sandals. As the ship's rotors ground into action they whooped and shrieked and blew their disco whistles. The larger ship gave another farewell blast from its horn, causing everyone around Charlie to jump. The Dominatrix let out a tiny, less robust blat from her horn as she backed away from the dock, earning many arched eyebrows and catty remarks from her passengers.

Charlie, Billy, and Ken explored the many levels on the ship, smiling at the tanned and muscular actors they passed in the halls. They found several men engaged in a variety of sex acts on the deck or in the hallways, taking advantage of having the ship to themselves. After passing a third blowjob, Billy could take no more and knelt down in front of the receiver as well, getting to work on the man's shaved, dangling balls. Charlie and Ken watched for a few moments, Charlie's dick hardening as Billy really got into it.

Turning away and adjusting themselves, Ken and Charlie headed out on deck to lean over the railing and watch the water spray along the side of the ship. After a few minutes, they turned and leaned their backs against the railing to watch the men stroll past. "Yeah," Charlie agreed. "It's going to be quite an eventful two weeks."

After a few more minutes, Ken announced he was going to check out the sunning decks and sauntered off. On his own, Charlie turned back and watched the land drop away, breathing in the salt-tinged air with a dreamy smile. The wind tousled his hair and the sun was warm on his shoulders. Life was good.

"Oh my fucking God," a scratchy voice hissed from just over his shoulder.

Charlie turned and felt his good mood deflate. Standing before him was Cedric Wilmington, the director who had tried to end Charlie's career and force Kinitia out of business. His hands were fisted on his hips and one leg cocked as he stared at Charlie. A multi-colored silk kerchief was tied over his head to block the wind, and large, dark glasses covered half his face.

"Hello, Cedric," Charlie grumbled. "What the hell are you doing here, besides ruining my peaceful mood?"

"Me? What the hell are *you* doing here?" Cedric demanded and strode up to stand beside him. "What purpose could you have on this ship?"

"We were hired to provide service for the actors," Charlie replied. "And you?"

"Oh my God," Cedric gasped. "He hired *Kinitia's* fluffers for this trip? Oh, that son of a bitch. Wait until I get my hands on him."

"Cedric, why don't you just relax and deal with it, huh?" Charlie suggested. "We're going to be stuck on this ship for two weeks together, so let's just make the best of it, all right?" He turned away, shaking his head.

"Well, we'll see who stays here for two weeks and who is removed by helicopter in a few hours!" Cedric snapped his head around and caught sight of a steward strolling past. "Steward!" With an indignant huff, he stomped off in pursuit of the man.

Charlie closed his eyes and struggled to find the peaceful feelings he had been nurturing before Cedric had appeared, but it was no use. The man had as much of an impact on him as Rock, only in reverse. At the thought of Rock Harding, Charlie's eyes popped open and he looked around, scanning the deck for any sign of the actor. It would stand to reason that wherever Cedric went, Rock was sure to follow, but if he were on board, he was nowhere in sight.

As he swept his gaze over the deck, Charlie's gaze landed on two men of startling beauty. They were Latino, similar enough in facial structure to be brothers, and incredibly handsome. Both had high foreheads, thick, dark hair, simmering brown eyes and full, sculpted lips. They stood at the railing a few yards away with their backs to the sea and their eyes taking in each man that passed. Intrigued, he walked along the railing until he stood beside them. Both men smiled at him, displaying perfectly aligned and dazzling white teeth.

"Hi," Charlie said. "I take it you're actors."

"Yes," the closest man said. "We're brothers. Twins."

Charlie's eyebrows went up. "Really?"

"Yes," the other brother replied. "This is my brother Alpha, and I am Omega."

Charlie shook hands with each of them, their palms warm and dry and the muscles in their arms working with the movement. "It's nice to meet you both. Are you new to the business? I don't think I've seen you around before."

"We are new to the area," Alpha said. "We have just moved here from another place. And you? Are you an actor?"

"Oh, no. I'm a fluffer." Charlie felt himself blush and looked down at the deck.

"Well then, I hope we get the opportunity to make use of your services," Alpha said. "It was nice to meet you. Excuse us, we need to get ready for dinner." After Alpha nodded to his brother, the two men moved off along the deck.

Charlie watched them go, noticing that Alpha was a few inches taller and broader in the shoulders than Omega. He thought about TimXXX, his own older brother back in Idaho, and mentally ran through a sexual scenario involving the two of them. While Tim was handsome and had a good body, Charlie found the idea unattractive. There had been too many battles over toys and the rights to the family car to even think about Tim in a sexual manner. Well, to each his own.

He found his way back to his cabin to change for dinner and nearly knocked Jorge down as he rounded the final corner. Gripping the steward by the shoulders, he smiled and turned his back to the wall. "Sorry, Jorge. Please, go on."

Jorge nodded and, with his eyes locked on Charlie's, turned to face him and inched slowly past. He angled his hips so his bulging crotch brushed against Charlie's. Stopping directly across from him, Jorge grinned and said, "Not a problem, Charlie. Anything I can do for you?"

Charlie smiled back. "I do need to get changed for dinner."

With a nod, Jorge followed Charlie to his room. Locking the door behind him, Jorge stepped up and began to unbutton Charlie's shirt. "First, we need to remove this."

Charlie leaned down and caught Jorge's mouth in a kiss. The steward's tongue was hot as it pushed between his lips. A small groan worked its way from Jorge's throat as he finished with the last button on Charlie's shirt and ran his strong hands through the hair on his chest. They kissed for a few minutes, kneading and groping each other, then Charlie pulled Jorge's shirt tail from his shorts and peeled the garment from his body.

Jorge's upper body was an anatomy textbook of musculature. He was short in stature, but very strong. Crouching down, Charlie nipped at Jorge's brown nipples, bringing each one up into a hard bud of pleasure. He ran his tongue down the middle of the steward's smooth chest and knelt before him with his mouth pressed over the flat, oblong navel surrounded by a thin tuft of dark chair.

"Oh, Charlie," Jorge sighed. "That feels very good."

Charlie breathed in the scent of baby oil as he ran his tongue through the hair around Jorge's navel. He kissed the thin line of hair that disappeared beneath the waistband of

Jorge's white shorts, then unfastened the clasp and slowly lowered the zipper.

"Mmm, that's nice," Jorge said quietly.

Slipping his fingers into the elastic of the steward's briefs, Charlie slid them down his legs and deftly caught the thick, dark skinned cock between his lips. The muscles in Jorge's legs tightened as Charlie leisurely sucked his length. It hardened even further in his mouth, and Charlie estimated it to be about the same length as his own, with a bit more girth to it.

"Get up here," Jorge said through clenched teeth, and he lifted Charlie by his armpits.

Parting his full lips, Jorge kissed him hungrily, their tongues rolling together. Jorge made short work of Charlie's clothes, removed the last of his own, and soon they were sprawled nude across one of the beds. Jorge lay on top of Charlie, his hard cock pressing against Charlie's erection as they kissed and stroked one another.

The steward moved down Charlie's body, his tongue leaving a wide, wet track. Grasping Charlie's dick in his strong hand, Jorge ran his tongue along the entire shaft and then completely swallowed him. Charlie groaned and closed his eyes, pressing his hands onto the back of Jorge's head as the man began to steadily suck him. He felt the steward's body shifting on the bed and opened his eyes to find Jorge's groin positioned directly over his face. Charlie opened his mouth and Jorge lowered his dick into Charlie's throat.

As they sucked, both men spread each other's ass cheeks and used fingers to probe the warm, sensitive holes revealed. Charlie ran his tongue over Jorge's hairy balls and along his perineum to the sweaty, hairy asshole where he began to greedily suck and lick. Jorge's mouth traveled south as well, and soon both men were rimming with abandon.

With strong hands, Jorge gripped each of Charlie's pale ass cheeks and spread him open. Jorge rolled his thick tongue into a tight, hot spike that he pushed deep into Charlie's ass, bringing muffled grunts of pleasure. Sitting up, Jorge plugged Charlie's hole with two thick fingers, sinking them deep inside as he ground his pelvis down over Charlie's mouth.

"Oh, that feels really good, Charlie," Jorge said. "Yeah, get that tongue up inside me. Oh yeah." He bucked his hips and reached down to repeatedly slap his fat slab of dick against Charlie's chest. He grabbed Charlie's hard-on and slowly stroked it. "I want to sit on this big cock of yours, Charlie. Would you like that?"

Charlie nodded up into the crack of Jorge's ass and pumped his hips, fucking the steward's fist. Jorge and spit into his hand, easing the friction as Charlie's dick slid through his fingers. Lifting himself off Charlie's face, Jorge stood beside the bed stroking himself as his eyes traveled the length of Charlie's body. "You're pretty hot to be just a fluffer," Jorge said. "You sure you're not an actor?"

"Not really interested in that right now," Charlie replied. "Maybe later."

Nodding, Jorge looked Charlie in the eye and asked, "Condoms?"

"Over in the dresser. Top drawer."

Pulling open the drawer, Jorge smiled and pulled out a large, double headed dildo. He raised his eyebrows and looked back at Charlie. "Expecting some company?"

Charlie shrugged, a little embarrassed, and said, "I like to be prepared."

Jorge examined the latex toy with a discerning eye. It was about twenty inches long and two inches in diameter. Each end sported a smooth head and a long, thin vein twisted along the shaft between. He looked back at Charlie. "Ever use this with someone else?" Charlie shook his head. "Want to try it?"

"Oh yeah," Charlie said and scooted up on the bed to give Jorge room to lie down.

With the dildo in one hand and a bottle of lube in the other, Jorge positioned himself on his back on the bed facing Charlie. They each raised their legs and lifted their hips, exposing their assholes and sliding closer together. Their legs intertwined and Jorge drizzled lube along the crack of each of their asses. As Jorge eased slick fingers into Charlie's ass, Charlie repeated the gesture on Jorge.

As Jorge spread a generous amount of lube on both ends of the dildo, Charlie licked his lips and spread more lube around and inside each of them.

"Okay, I'll start, then you can join in," Jorge said.

Charlie sat up and took the slick dildo from the steward. He pressed one end against Jorge's twitching hole and applied a slow, steady pressure. The dildo slid into him, bringing a gasp of pleasure followed by a moan. Charlie eased it out a bit, then slipped it in even deeper.

"Oh, fuck," Jorge said. "That feels so good."

With slow movements, Charlie worked the dildo in and out of Jorge's ass until half the toy was inside him. Deciding he was ready, Charlie lay on his back and positioned the free end of the dildo against his own asshole. He scooted forward and felt the toy slowly penetrate him as the other half remained inside Jorge. Charlie's muscles constricted around the dildo as it slid deeper, and he had to pause and relax to be able to take more. He grabbed Jorge's thighs and pulled the man closer, then dropped his head back and moaned as the upper part of their buttocks met and the dildo sank fully into them both.

"Oh, Charlie," Jorge sighed. "That feels so good." He wriggled his hips, moving the dildo inside both of them, and stroked himself. "You like having that big cock up your ass?"

"Oh yeah," Charlie replied, and stroked himself as well. "I like feeling your balls bouncing against mine too."

They took turns rocking back along their spines, effectively pulling the dildo out of each other then sliding it back in. As they became accustomed to the motion, their rhythm increased until they were fucking one another with the shared dildo.

"I'm coming," Jorge grunted. "Oh fuck, I'm going to shoot." Charlie lifted his head and watched as Jorge raised his cock. The cum spurted into the air and dripped down the length of Jorge's cock like a semen fountain.

"That is so fuckin' hot, Jorge," Charlie moaned. "I'm going to come, too. Oh yeah. Uh!" Charlie raised his own cock so that Jorge could watch him come. His muscles constricted around the dildo lodged inside him as his semen burst up over his belly and thigh. When he had finished, Charlie dropped his head onto the bed with an exhausted sigh and they eased themselves off the dildo.

Afterwards, they showered together in the cramped stall, soaping and kissing and washing the dildo as well. After they dried off, Jorge dressed in his uniform as Charlie pulled out some fresh shirts.

"It's not a formal dinner tonight, right?" Charlie asked.

"No, that won't be until the end of the week," Jorge replied. "Tonight you may dress casual." He tucked in his shirt and gave Charlie a lingering kiss goodbye before slipping out the door.

As he dressed, Charlie gazed out the window at the sun-dappled water that seemed to stretch on forever. He was relaxed once again, thanks to Jorge and that marvelous dildo. Hopefully Cedric would keep his distance through dinner and the remainder of the cruise. He wondered briefly whether Rock was onboard, then Ken knocked at his door and called for him to hurry up. Charlie pushed aside thoughts of Rock Harding and finished getting dressed, then followed his friends through the narrow hallways to the dining room.

5
____

THE EARLY BIRD

They were seated at dinner awaiting their main course when Charlie spotted Rock Harding across the room. Rock sat in profile to him, and Charlie was just able to catch a glimpse of his face between diners as they leaned back and forth during conversation. Rock's dark hair was cut shorter than usual, and spiked with gel. As he talked with his dining companions, Rock's brown eyes sparkled and he smiled often, teeth flashing white in his tan face. Even from this distance, Charlie could see the cleft in Rock's chin. His stomach fluttered as he realized he and Rock would be at sea together on a small cruise ship for ten days.

"Charlie," Kinitia said in his ear, making him jump. "Please tell me you're not staring at Rock Harding."

"What?" Charlie asked, his voice going up an octave and a blush pinking his cheeks. "No! Rock's here? On the ship? Nearby? Where?" He leaned right and left, searching the room, looking everyplace but at Rock's table. "I don't see him."

Kinitia gave him a skeptical look. "Uh huh. You just keep away from that man. I've got enough trouble with Cedric Wilmington owning part of one of our competitors, not to mention a portion of our office building. He doesn't need any more ammunition against us. Got it?"

Charlie sighed and hung his head. "Yes ma'am."

Dinner progressed smoothly, Charlie didn't spill anything or upset a single waiter's tray. They ate, the dishes were cleared, they ate some more, the dishes were cleared again, and they ate yet again. By the end of the meal, they were all stuffed and happily drowsy.

All of them, that was, except Bernice. The large meal energized her, and she wanted to hit the ship's nightclubs and dance. "Come on!" she cajoled them, standing up and moving her hips in a terrifying bump and grind routine. "Let's get out there and find the nightlife! Let's go, people! We're on a cruise ship here, filled with hot men. Let's party! Woo hoo!"

The rest of them rose groggily to their feet and followed Bernice out of the dining room, more as a way to remove her from sight of the other passengers than to placate her need to dance. After cruising through a few of the bars, the Fluffers, Inc. team settled around a round table in the show bar to watch extravagant drag performances. There were several impressive female impersonators on board who performed each night and then wandered through the crowds and talked to the handsome men. They all had interesting stage names such as Anna Lingus and her "sister" Connie Lingus, the two of whom performed Abbott and Costello type humor and lip synced to songs from the 1940s. Or Helen of Oy, a Jewish man done up like a Jewish American Princess who sang original, comical songs and did some stand up in between. And then a beautiful black drag queen came on stage in a gown of sequins and feathers. Her name was Chantilly Lace and she lip synced to several dance songs while she performed a series of complicated dance moves with a troupe of six backup dancers. Charlie was impressed by the entire group, but especially by Chantilly Lace.

After the show the performers walked around the tables, accepting tips, compliments and, in some cases, room keys. Chantilly Lace caught sight of the Fluffers, Inc. team and sashayed through the maze of tables to stand behind Charlie and Bernice.

"Hello, fluffers," Chantilly said with a bright smile. "And how are all you cocksuckers tonight?"

They laughed and complimented Chantilly on her performance, handing her tips and introducing themselves. Bernice, wide-eyed with wonder at the sight before her, gave Chantilly an impulsive hug and everyone laughed.

"Oh, babies," Chantilly gushed. "You are quickly becoming Chantilly's favorite people on this trip." She turned her gaze to Charlie and pinched his cheek. "Especially you, you corn fed hunk of beef."

Charlie blushed and nodded his thanks.

"You look even better than you did at the railing during our *bon voyage*," Chantilly said. Charlie blinked up at her in confusion, then his eyes widened in understanding and surprise. Chantilly was Theo, the man who had introduced himself at the railing.

"It's you!" Charlie said.

"None other, baby." Chantilly smiled and squeezed his shoulder.

"Ms. Lace," Bernice piped up. "I just want to say that I think you're the most talented female impersonator I've seen in a long time."

"Oh, aren't you sweet." Chantilly leaned down and hugged Bernice, giving her cheek an air kiss. Chantilly then excused herself to continue to work the room and they watched her walk off. Charlie still could not get it into his head that the sexy, feminine form crossing the room was the same man he had spoken with on deck. A lot of work had gone into his make over.

Following the drag show, they moved on to an electronic and industrial themed bar and bounced and thrashed as a group across the strobe lit dance floor. Several extended dance mixes later, Charlie and Billy stepped up to the bar between two golden brown hunks of actors and ordered a round of drinks for everybody. They each received a bright smile from the bartender and, on their way back to the table, Charlie bumped into Rock Harding.

"Charlie!" Rock said with genuine delight. "I didn't know you were going to be on the cruise."

"Me neither," Charlie replied as he felt his pulse rate triple. "Kinitia didn't know for sure until two days ago. How are you?"

Rock nodded and smiled. "I'm okay." He reached out and squeezed Charlie's shoulder. "It's really, really good to see you. I'm glad you're on board. I wasn't looking forward to spending two weeks at sea with a bunch of shallow porn actors and snotty directors."

Charlie felt his heart leap. "Yeah? Well, that's nice to hear."

"Excuse me!" Kinitia shouted from the table. "I need my drink!"

Charlie turned and gave her a stern look. "Just a moment, please. I'm being polite to a client."

"Well, I don't want to keep you," Rock said.

"Would you like to join us?" Charlie asked and immediately wished he could take the words back. "Unless you're here with someone else."

"No, I'm not here with anyone; I was just sort of wandering through the bars. I'd like to join you, thanks." Rock followed him to the table where Kinitia, Ken, and Billy stared at Charlie in shock. Bernice was sipping the drink Billy had brought back for her and blinked with surprise up at the new arrival.

"Rock," Charlie said after handing Kinitia her drink. "I think you know almost everyone: Kinitia Jones, Billy Ransom, and Ken Carlton. And this is Bernice Tallipepper, our assistant."

"Oh, my," Bernice gushed with a blush and a school girl grin. "Oh, look at you. Oh, well, I must say, it's very nice to finally meet you Mr. Harding. I've heard a lot about you, Mr. Harding, but all those words do not do you justice."

"Please, call me Rock."

Bernice giggled and blushed and Charlie rolled his eyes. He sat between Rock and Billy and avoided looking at Kinitia. It wasn't as if he had planned on running into Rock.

Two hours later, the six of them were well into their third pitcher of margaritas and laughing at just about anything. They had all danced to several songs, Charlie being careful to keep a safe distance between Rock and himself, and so far Cedric had yet to rear his ugly head. The evening was progressing quite well, he thought, until Rock suddenly sat bolt upright in his chair and widened his eyes. He stared across the room, then leaned left and then right as he peered through the flashing lights toward an area beyond the crowded dance floor.

"Rock?" Charlie asked in concern. "Are you okay?" He followed Rock's line of sight and saw the dancers on the floor but nothing alarming. Turning back, he was about to ask Rock what he had seen, but found himself facing an empty chair. When he looked around, Charlie caught sight of Rock wading quickly through the dancers toward the far exit.

"What's wrong with him?" Billy wondered.

"I don't know," Charlie replied. He hesitated then decided that Rock might need help with whatever was happening and slid off his chair.

"Charlie!" Kinitia called, but he ignored her and headed across the dance floor after Rock.

He found Rock standing at the deck railing and looking out over the moonlit ocean. The man's brow was furrowed and his mouth pressed tight in a thin line of tension. Charlie approached him cautiously and asked in a quiet voice, "Rock? Are you okay?"

Rock was quiet for a moment then turned and gave a stilted laugh that sounded hollow and cold. "Yeah, I'm fine. I just ... I just thought I saw someone I knew from ... Well, from a long time ago, that's all."

"In the bar?"

"Yeah. He came out to the deck here, or so I thought. But I guess it was just the lights or something, you know? Besides, it couldn't really be him because..." Rock stopped and glanced quickly at Charlie before looking back at the water. "Well, it just couldn't be him."

"Oh." Charlie stood beside him in awkward silence for a moment. "Is there anything I can do for you?"

"No." Rock shook his head, his mind obviously miles away from their conversation. "But thanks. I think I'll just go on back to my cabin now. Good night, Charlie." He gave Charlie's shoulder a gentle squeeze, smiled a little sadly, and walked off.

Charlie watched him go, his mind racing to figure out just what the hell had happened. Thus distracted, Charlie did not realize anyone was behind him until he turned around and practically bounced off Cedric. The director glared at him, his mouth an angry red slash in his pale, flabby face.

"You stay the fuck away from Rock, fluffer bitch," Cedric snarled. "Do you hear me?"

"Oh, buzz off, Cedric," Charlie said with a sigh, his attitude fueled by the alcohol he had consumed. "I wasn't trying to seduce your man. I just wanted to make sure he was okay."

"Of course he is," Cedric snapped. "Why wouldn't he be?"

"I don't know," Charlie replied. "You're the one who lives with him, you tell me."

Before Cedric could fire off a response, Kinitia, Billy, Ken, and Bernice appeared in the bar doorway. Cedric glared at them and said, "Oh, of course, your back-up singers are here, too. I should have known. You'd better keep this fluffer of yours on a tighter leash, Kinitia. He's really starting to try my patience, and that might reflect in the lease for your office space."

Sipping her margarita through a straw, Bernice stepped out from behind Kinitia for a better look at Cedric and everyone stopped and stared. Bernice's eyes widened as well and she walked up to stand beside the director as he looked at her in horror. They wore the same peach colored rayon pantsuit, scoop necked blouse, light blazer, and palazzo pants. While Bernice wore a simple white mule, Cedric sported a peach Italian sling-back style man's shoe.

Coming up for air from her margarita, Bernice looked Cedric up and down, then cocked her head as she inspected his shoes. "Are sling-backs in style again?"

"Oh!" Cedric said with a huff and stormed off, his peach blazer flowing out behind.

"Hey!" Bernice shouted after him. "Did you get yours at Wal Mart too?"

The group looked at each other for a moment then burst out laughing. Putting their arms around one another, they stumbled off to the casino. After changing in twenty dollars each for cups of quarters, they wandered through the crowd of tanned, toned men and tried their luck on different slot machines.

The lights and bells of the slot machines combined with the night's alcohol to mess with Charlie's equilibrium. In the middle of an aisle of slot machines, Charlie turned too quickly and lost his grip on his cup of quarters. The coins bounced across the carpeted aisle and he cursed before he got on his hands and knees to pick them up. His progress across the carpet brought him to a craps table where he stretched between sets of muscular legs to snag the two remaining quarters lying underneath. He didn't make enough money to just let two quarters go.

Looking up, he found himself staring into a shaved and sweaty asshole. The man before him was on his hands and knees over another man lying stretched out on the carpet beneath the craps table. They were sucking each other's cocks with drunken abandon, their grunts and sighs masked by the sounds of the casino around them. The tanned cheeks directly in front of Charlie were tight and round, evidence of hours on a Stairmaster. The thighs were strong and the muscles bunched as the man pumped up and down, his cock driving deep into his partner's throat.

Charlie stared at the scene before him in drunken fascination as the man on his back reached up and slipped a finger into the asshole right in front of Charlie's face. The man on top groaned and reached back with one hand to pull one ass cheek open and more clearly display to Charlie the penetrating finger. He watched with glassy-eyed fascination as the men sucked and finger-fucked each other, his cock growing harder with every second.

Aroused and intrigued, Charlie quietly moved forward and reached out toward the sweat-shiny asshole before him. He watched as the sphincter opened and closed on the lower man's finger and felt his cock jerk with longing. His finger slid easily into the hole alongside the other man's and the sensation caused Charlie to let out a muffled grunt that caught the attention of both men.

"What the fuck?" The man on top twisted his head around, an angry look on his face. "Hey! This is a private party, fuckhead. Get your finger out of my asshole and back off. Now!"

Charlie was startled by the man's outburst, but managed to pull his finger free from the tight, hot hole. He tried to stand up and leave, forgetting he had moved further under the craps table. His head struck the underside of the table and stars burst across his vision as he fell flat on his stomach. People around the table shouted in disapproval, and the two men beneath the table scrambled to grab their clothes as the craps players crouched down to peer underneath. Charlie lay on the carpet in a daze, watching through bleary eyes as the two men crawled out between the legs of their fellow actors and took off through the casino to many catcalls and whistles.

The ship's doctor was summoned, and he led Charlie through the winding hallways back to his office. He had him sit in a chair and lean forward, standing in front of him as he examined the back of his skull beneath a strong light.

"No broken skin, but you're going to have a bump here," the doctor said. His voice was smooth and deep, a pleasant baritone that washed over Charlie in relaxing waves. "I'll give you some pain reliever and you should put ice on it."

"Okay," Charlie said. He looked up, his eyes inches away from the doctor's crotch, and stared at the bulge in the man's khaki shorts. "You've got quite a bedside manner."

"That's interesting," the doctor said. "Seeing as how you're sitting in a chair."

Charlie sat up then closed his eyes to ride out a head rush. "Whoa."

"You okay?" the doctor asked.

Charlie opened his eyes and looked up at him. The man was handsome with blond hair, high cheekbones, and blue eyes. His crew member shirt was open two buttons at the neck revealing a smooth patch of tanned skin. "Wow," Charlie breathed. "I am now."

The doctor grinned and asked, "Well, now that the professional portion of our meeting is done with, would you like to come by my cabin for a drink?"

Charlie nodded. "Yeah, sure. That would be great."

The doctor's cabin turned out to be through a door in his office. The room was large and neat with a tall armoire and a bathroom only slightly larger than the one in Charlie's cabin. He swallowed two pain relievers and accepted a vodka tonic from the doctor, whose name was Dr. Garth Tanner. After making small talk for a short time, Garth massaged Charlie's shoulders then leaned down and kissed him gently on the mouth.

"Care to have some fun?" Garth whispered in Charlie's ear.

"I love having fun," Charlie whispered back.

"Good." Garth crossed to his armoire and removed a black garment bag. He held it out to Charlie with a gleam in his eye. "Go in the bathroom and put this on."

Charlie took the garment bag and gave him a small smile. "What's in the bag?"

"Just go put it on."

Charlie shrugged and entered the bathroom, closing the door behind him. Hanging the bag on the shower rod, he unzipped it and pulled out what looked to be a long gray dress. He looked through the bag some more and found a pair of blocky-heeled black shoes.

"Are you sure you want me to wear this?" Charlie called through the door.

"Oh, I'm sure!" Garth called back. "Just get naked and put it on. And don't forget the hat and shoes."

Hat? Charlie reached back into the bag and produced a

pillbox hat with a bright flower sticking up from the band. He shook his head but the margaritas, the vodka, the pain reliever, and, most likely, the bump on his head, convinced him to follow instructions. He stripped out of his clothes and left them in a pile in the bathroom. Taking the gray dress from the hanger, he unbuttoned the long row of tiny black buttons and stepped into the garment. The sleeves were a bit too short and the shoulders a little narrow, but he squeezed into it. He struggled to fasten the buttons, then gazed at himself in the mirror. He looked like Mary Poppins on male hormones. Well, nothing left to do but go see what the good doctor's kink was all about.

The stateroom was dimly lit when he opened the door, and he leaned out to peer into the gloom. The lights were low and what sounded like music from a baby's hanging mobile played from a small CD player. Charlie shuffled clumsily out into the room with his feet stuffed into the small, clumpy black shoes. The hat sat at a brazen angle on his head, held in place by two bobby pins he had discovered in the brim.

"Hello?" he said quietly. "Are you there?"

"Is that you, Nanny Charlie?" a tiny voice inquired from the darkness near the bed.

"Um, yeah, it is," Charlie said with a shrug. "And you are...?"

"Baby Garth," the tiny voice replied. "I've been a bad baby Garth."

Charlie grinned. Maybe this would be fun after all. "You have, have you?"

"Oh, yes, Nanny Charlie. A very bad baby Garth."

"Really?" Charlie shuffled to the bed. "You've been that

naughty?" He looked down at the bed and his eyes widened. Garth was dressed in a large diaper with a baby bonnet tied around his head. In his mouth he held an oversized pacifier which he sucked strenuously. Charlie blinked and said quietly, "Oh, my."

Garth removed the pacifier and blinked up at him. "Are you going to spank me, Nanny Charlie?"

"Uh," Charlie stammered, not knowing who he felt more embarrassed for: himself or the doctor. "I don't know. Is that what I usually do?"

Garth nodded with enthusiasm and pointed to the open armoire. "You always use that."

Charlie turned and saw a large wooden paddle hanging on the inside of the door. He shuffled over and removed it from the hook. Hefting it in his hand, he made his way back to the bed. "Okay then. You've been naughty, so here comes the paddle."

"Wait!" Garth said in his normal speaking voice, and then gasped. He reverted back to his high-pitched baby voice and explained, "You have to remove my diaper and spank my bare bottom."

"I do, huh?" Charlie asked, wanting nothing more than to be back in his room with some ice on his aching head. "Okay then, let me get this diaper off you, you bad, bad baby, and then you're going to get it."

Garth looked down to where Charlie fumbled with the Velcro straps of his oversized diaper, gripping the pacifier between his teeth, his eyes wide with excitement. After several attempts to hold onto the paddle and remove Garth's diaper, Charlie finally wedged the paddle under his arm and tore the diaper from the doctor's body. Garth gave an excited little squeak at the sound of the Velcro giving way, and he writhed on the bed, naked but for the bonnet.

Charlie smiled at his accomplishment, then stopped and stared at the sight before him. Garth's dick, in all its erect glory, was maybe four inches in length and as thick as two of his fingers put together. He gazed at the small organ in surprise, caught completely off guard. He was so accustomed to the large length and girth of the porn actors he fluffed, he had not expected to see such a tiny penis. And nestled in the pubic bush beneath the tiny cock, like the eggs of a petite bird, rested a pair of small, shaved balls.

"Spank me, Nanny Charlie," Garth gasped and raised his hairy legs in the air to expose his pale, hairy ass. "Spank me hard."

Charlie nodded to himself and reached out to grab Garth's ankles. He pulled the doctor's legs back a little further and gently brought the paddle down on the man's buttocks.

"Oh, Nanny Charlie," Garth said. "I've been really naughty. Spank me harder."

Charlie let the paddle fall a little harder, wincing at the impact between wood and flesh.

"Oh, harder. I've been really, really naughty."

Gritting his teeth, Charlie let loose on Garth's ass and beat him repeatedly with mighty, arcing swings. The paddle slapped repeatedly against the doctor's buttocks and sent vibrations up Charlie's arm.

"Oh, Nanny!" Garth groaned. "Spank that ass! Oh, God, I'm going to come! I'm coming!"

Charlie leaned over and watched as a thick, massive load of spunk spurted out of the tiny cock to land with an audible plop on Garth's chest. The small balls pumped out shot after shot of cum as Charlie continued to paddle the doctor's ass.

Amazingly, despite the massive quantities of alcohol and the lump on his head, Charlie found he had an erection. It jutted up beneath the gray dress and left a spreading pre-come stain on the fabric. He slowed the paddling to a stop and eased Garth's legs back onto the mattress. The doctor lay on his back, cum dripping down his sides as he caught his breath and gazed up at Charlie with tears in his eyes.

"That was amazing."

Charlie smiled and shrugged. "Just doing my job. You were a naughty baby, right?"

Garth grinned and nodded, then got up on one elbow and reached out to grab Charlie's cock through the dress. "Looks like all that spanking woke up little Charlie."

Charlie watched as Garth opened a few of the buttons around his crotch and reached in to pull out his dick. Garth knew how to use his mouth and tongue on a man's dick, that was clear very quickly. He slowly swallowed Charlie's length, then just as slowly pulled his mouth back. Steadily, he increased the speed of his sucking and tightened his grip on the base of Charlie's cock. Before too long, Charlie felt his prostate tighten and knew he was going to come.

"Oh, Garth," Charlie breathed. "I'm getting close." He curled his toes inside the black, blocky shoes and closed his eyes. "Oh yeah. I'm coming. Oh, God!"

Garth sucked every drop of cum fresh from Charlie's cock, nursing him dry like a baby at his mother's breast. As he sucked him off, Garth gazed up at him with wide, unblinking eyes, watching the expression on Charlie's face until he was spent.

Backing off Charlie's softening cock, Garth gave it one last, gentle kiss, and then got up to brush his teeth and gargle. He came back into the room, his cock small and shriveled like a cold worm, and kissed Charlie deeply on the mouth.

"Lay down with me for a little while," Garth said quietly as he stretched out on the bed. Charlie still wore the bonnet, and he fought to keep from laughing. "Keep the dress and hat on."

With a shrug Charlie kicked off the shoes, sighing with relief as he flexed his toes, and then climbed into bed to spoon the doctor from behind. They lay in silence for a few minutes, and then Charlie heard the man's breathing grow deeper, and cautiously got up on one elbow to peer over a shoulder at Garth's face. He was sound asleep, his head resting on Charlie's arm and a thumb lodged securely in his mouth. He looked for all the world like a baby in his mid-thirties.

Trapped by the doctor's bonnet-covered head, Charlie lay back down and closed his eyes, falling asleep himself a few minutes later.

6

SEAWORTHY

A day later, Charlie stood outside the exercise room, his arms crossed over his chest and a perplexed look on his face. Kinitia had decided to post the fluffer schedule in the one place she knew her team would visit every day: the exercise room. And on this first day of shooting, Charlie's name was missing from the schedule.

Ken clapped a hand on Charlie's shoulder and leaned around his friend to squint at the handwritten list. "Uh oh," Ken said into Charlie's ear. "Looks like you've been shut out, Farm Boy."

Charlie shrugged Ken's hand from his shoulder and stomped away to find Kinitia. There was no answer when he knocked at the stateroom she shared with Bernice, so he began to search her out. After asking several crewmembers if they had seen her with no luck, he ascended a narrow stairway to the top sunning deck labeled as the "Nude Deck."

As he came out of the stairwell, Charlie looked around. Several men lounged in chaises, their swim trunks lying crumpled on the deck beside them as they soaked up the sun. Off at the far end of the deck, set a short distance apart from everyone else, he could make out two people sprawled across lounge chairs: Bernice and a black man. Charlie began walking toward them, his mouth set in a determined line. It wasn't until he was a few feet away and Bernice raised her hand to her eyes and gave him a smile that he realized she was topless.

"Charlie! Hi!" Bernice called and waved. The skin on her upper arm shook and her breasts mirrored the motion. She had large, pale breasts that had definitely been worn down by gravity and the breast feeding of four children.

"Uh . . ." Charlie groaned. "Hi." He averted his eyes, looking instead at Bernice's partner in sun and recognizing him from the deck of the ship and the drag show. "Oh, hi Theo!"

"Hi honey." The man shifted position and reached down to casually lift his large cock and arrange it over his big, black balls. "Aren't you a little overdressed for this deck?"

Charlie grinned and blushed, trying not to look too obvious as he checked out Theo's body. "Yeah, but I'm looking for Kinitia." He turned back to Bernice and made an effort to focus only on her face. "Have you seen her recently?"

Bernice shook her head, her hand still shading her eyes and the skin on her arm flapping in time. "Not for a while. Everything okay?"

"Well, that's what I want to know," Charlie said. "She hasn't scheduled me for any jobs, and I'm a little worried, you know?"

"Oh, honey," Theo purred. "I'll give you something to fluff, if that's what you're looking for."

Charlie smiled shyly at the man and considered the proposal. Theo had a well-developed, smooth chest, wiry, muscular arms and legs, and a shaved, gleaming skull. He was very handsome with high, angular cheekbones and warm eyes. "That would be pure pleasure, I'm sure, but I'm referring to work."

"Oh, listen to you," Theo said coyly and waved him away. "Get away from Chantilly before her body tells on her dirty mind."

"Oh, Theo!" Bernice tittered. "You're so bad!"

Charlie smiled and looked back at Bernice. "Do you know why I haven't been scheduled?"

"I think Rod Mandrake has asked for you exclusively, and he just hasn't started filming yet," Bernice explained. "At least that's what I thought was going on."

"Oh," Charlie replied. "Well, I guess that makes sense." He felt better now that there was some explanation for his lack of assignments. "I was starting to feel like Sandra Bullock in *Speed* 2, you know?"

Theo smiled up at him. "Just standing around on a cruise ship with nothing to do but look pretty?"

Charlie smiled back and nodded. "You got it."

"Honey, I have got 'it,' plus a whole lot more."

"Yes, I see that." Charlie turned back to Bernice. "Okay, I'm going to go. Thanks for the info, Bernice."

"Oh, Charlie," Bernice called after him. "Don't go! Stay up here with us! Get naked and tan your pale Idaho hide!"

Charlie waved goodbye as he descended the steps. He occupied himself by working out, then walking around the deck and observing the water from all four points on the ship: bow, stern, starboard, and aft. It looked the same no matter where he stood, and he sighed heavily. As he leaned on the railing, Charlie felt a presence behind him and turned to find Alpha and Omega standing a few feet away. The twins were smiling at him, their eyes hooded and filled with sexual longing.

"Hello," Alpha said. "We've heard you're a good fluffer."

Charlie grinned. "I've heard that, too."

"Care to demonstrate?" Omega said.

A short time later, Charlie found himself in the stateroom the twins shared. The two muscular Latino men kissed his mouth and neck, their soft, sensuous lips making him moan as they moved over his body. He felt two pairs of strong hands caressing his body and slowly pulling off his clothes. Whenever he opened his eyes, Charlie found himself looking deep into the dark eyes of one of the brothers. At this close range it was difficult to tell them apart.

When Charlie was nude, Omega slid around to press against him from behind, kissing the back of his neck and down along his spine. Alpha fondled Charlie's dick as he continued to kiss his mouth and throat. Omega knelt behind him and spread Charlie's cheeks, licking the crack of his ass then drilling his tongue into Charlie's hole. Alpha moved his kisses lower along Charlie's neck and chest to his flat stomach, slowly dropping to his knees before him. As Alpha moved his mouth closer to Charlie's groin, Charlie tipped his head back and let himself luxuriate in the oral attention of the brothers.

"Oh, God," Charlie gasped. "That's so hot. You two are really fuckin' hot."

Alpha smiled into Charlie's pubic hair and opened his mouth wide to take his dick down his throat. Charlie moaned and pressed his hands against the back of Alpha's head. Bending at the waist, he slid his hands down the bronze skin over Alpha's spine as the man sucked his cock and Omega poked his tongue deeper into Charlie's hole.

As if on an unspoken cue, the twins backed away from Charlie as one and moved him to a bed. He sat on the edge of the mattress and found himself facing two long, thick, uncut cocks. Alpha was just slightly longer than his brother, and a glistening drop of pre-come had collected at the slit. Charlie touched the tip of his tongue to it and slowly moved back. The drop stretched between Alpha's cock and Charlie's tongue, and when the strand broke, Charlie leaned in again to suck the man's cock.

Gripping the base of Alpha's cock in his right hand, Charlie took hold of Omega with his left and stroked him. He worked his mouth along Alpha for a while before shifting position to suck Omega's dick. While he orally serviced the men, he could hear them kissing and touching each other. They were both incredibly sexy men, and Charlie was very aroused by the time the men pulled away and crawled onto the bed with him.

"We have a position we would like to show you," Omega said with a smile. "We call it Seaworthy."

"Oh really?" Charlie replied. "Please, show away."

Alpha coaxed Charlie up onto his hands and knees and presented his cock to Charlie's face. As Charlie sucked on Alpha, Omega got in position between Charlie's legs and rolled a condom along his cock. He slid two lubed up fingers slowly into Charlie's asshole. As Omega's fingers slid into him, Charlie groaned around the slab of meat in his throat and sucked harder on Alpha.

Omega worked some more lube into Charlie, then pulled his fingers out and replaced them with his condom-covered cock. He slid in a short way, then pulled back, then pressed in again. Soon, he was fully seated inside Charlie.

"Oh, fuck," Charlie gasped, dropping Alpha's cock for a moment and lowering his head. But Alpha would have none of it, and put a finger beneath Charlie's chin, raising his head so he could resume sucking. Charlie swallowed the entire length of Alpha's hot dick as Omega pumped into him, and he realized with a smile that he was plugged up at both ends. He was, indeed, seaworthy.

Omega drove into him with long, steady strokes, his hands gripping Charlie's hips tight enough to leave marks. Charlie could feel sweat dropping on his buttocks from Omega's forehead and the very thought of having two brothers filling him up from each end made him even more excited. No wonder these two were up and coming porn stars.

The pace of Omega's fucking increased until he was practically ramming his dick into Charlie's ass, and Alpha's hips pumped hard as well, driving his own cock into Charlie's mouth. Charlie relaxed his throat and took the full brunt of Alpha's face fucking as he heard Omega gasp behind him.

"I'm coming," Omega grunted. "Oh, shooting that load up your hot fucking ass. Uh, uh!" Omega packed Charlie's ass with his cock as he emptied his balls into the condom deep. Omega leaned forward over Charlie and kissed his sweaty back as he eased out of him.

Alpha pulled his cock free and, to Charlie's delight, the

twins changed positions. Omega presented his semi-hard dick for Charlie to suck as Alpha slipped on a condom and embedded himself within Charlie's asshole.

"Oh, fuck!" Charlie choked around Omega's cock. Alpha's dick was only a bit longer, but it was enough to really hit just the right spot. "Oh, God! Fuck that ass, Alpha. Get that cock up in there."

"Oh, yeah," Omega said through gritted teeth. "Fuck his ass. And you, suck my cock. Suck the cock that was just fucking your ass. Suck it."

Charlie closed his eyes as Alpha furiously rode his ass and Omega pounded his own cock deep into his throat. After several minutes of motion and sensation, Charlie rose up to press his back against Alpha's body and fired off long, thick streams of cum that landed on Omega's belly, crotch, and the sheet. He slowly jerked himself to completion, and then Alpha pushed him down flat on his stomach on the bed and moved up over him. Raising himself into a pushup pose with his strong arms and muscular legs, Alpha drove his dick straight down into Charlie's ass.

Omega stuffed his own cock down Charlie's throat with his hands on either side of the fluffer's head. The twins had, for the most part, taken control of Charlie's body and were now fucking him with abandon from the front and the rear. Omega pulled his dick from between Charlie's swollen lips and let loose a hot, pungent splash of semen that splattered across Charlie's face and shoulders.

"Oh, I'm coming," Alpha gasped and nailed Charlie's ass with one last, deep stroke, burying his cock inside him as he filled the condom.

Afterwards, they lay across the bed, limbs entwined,

and caught their breath. Alpha finally stood and pulled the other two up from the bed and into the tiny bathroom where they cleaned up. After that, Charlie bid them goodbye and made his wobbly way back to his cabin. Halfway to his room, he passed Dr. Garth Tanner and noticed the man walked with an odd gait, still a bit sore from a spanking he must have received the night before, delivered by someone else he had lured into his room. In pain though he was, Garth nevertheless smiled brightly at Charlie and said quietly, "Good afternoon, Nanny Charlie."

Charlie smiled drowsily at the man. "Hey, baby Garth."

Back in his cabin, Charlie took a shower and put on his swim trunks. He wasn't about to go out on the nude sunning deck and hang out with Bernice, but he did want to relax in the sun for awhile. Maybe he would run into Kinitia and he could ask her about his schedule.

On the deck, Charlie spread his towel over a chaise and angled it toward the sun. He could hear Cedric Wilmington's shrill voice as the man directed a scene somewhere in the area, but the sea air made pinpointing the location impossible. Probably for the best, Charlie thought, and lay down with a sigh.

Just as he had gotten comfortable, a shadow fell over his face and he looked up. A man stood before him, but with the sun at his back all Charlie could see was a silhouette.

"Can I help you?" he asked.

"I don't believe you're here," the man said and sat on a neighboring chaise.

Charlie blinked the sunspots out of his eyes and found he was looking at the man whose phone he had answered the morning after the premiere party. He had a common name, oddly spelled. "Phrank?"

Phrank smiled. "You remember."

"Hey, I don't easily forget someone like you." Charlie sat up. "What are you doing on the ship? Are you an actor?"

"Nah," Phrank said with a shrug. "Just a hanger on. What about you?"

"I'm a fluffer."

"Wow, great job. You must have amazing jaw muscles." Phrank wiped some sweat from his chest with a towel. "Well, I've been out here all day and am about baked through. I wanted to stop over and say hello, though. Maybe we can meet sometime for a drink."

"I'd like that," Charlie replied. "I'll see you later."

Phrank walked off and Charlie leaned around the back of the chaise to watch him go. The man wore a white Speedo and the material clung to the firm, round globes of his ass which jiggled as he walked away. His back muscles were slick with sweat and tanning oil and Charlie felt his cock twitch in his trunks. Phrank was definitely worth another go.

Before he could properly settle back, Rock Harding appeared beside him, nude and out of breath, his cock hanging long and thick between his legs. Rock glanced at Charlie, then turned in a circle and looked around. His breathing was heavy as though he had run from somewhere, and Charlie sat up, slightly alarmed.

"Rock? Is everything okay?"

Rock looked down at him and had just opened his mouth to reply when Cedric's shrieking cut him off.

"Rock!"

Charlie and Rock jumped in unison and looked up to

find the director leaning over an upper railing, the wind blowing his blond, thinning hair back from his face. "What are you doing? You're up next! Get away from that goddamn fluffer bitch and concentrate on your work! *Now!*"

Rock took a breath and looked back down at Charlie. "Sorry. I thought I saw someone I used to know." Clenching his jaw, Rock walked away and Charlie watched him go as well, definitely appreciating the sight of Rock's bare ass. God how he longed to have his way with that man's ass. The things he wanted to do to Rock Harding, and vice versa.

Charlie took a breath, shook the tension from his arms, and lay back on the chaise. He listened to the sound of the water and the sea birds calling. The sun felt warm on his skin and the sex he had had with the twins had made him drowsy. Before he knew it, he had slipped into a deep sleep.

Almost an hour later, Charlie was awakened by Kinitia and Bernice. They stood before him with wide eyes as he blinked up at them in a sun-soaked stupor.

"What?" he slurred. "What's wrong?"

"Oh my," Bernice said. "You fell asleep."

Charlie nodded. "It's okay, Bernice. I'm not on the schedule."

"No, Farm Boy," Kinitia said as she looked him over. "You fell asleep in the sun."

"Huh?" Charlie rose up and looked down along his body. He had indeed fallen asleep in the sun, and what was worse his hand had been resting on his chest the entire time. His face, stomach, arms, and legs were sunburned, while his chest sported a white imprint of his arm and hand like some crazy tattoo.

"Oh no," he whimpered and looked up at the women above him. "I'm burned. I'm burned bad."

"Oh, sweetie," Bernice said softly and with as much optimism as possible. "Not right here." She reached out and touched the pale, hand-shaped outline on his chest.

They helped him up and he winced at the tight feeling already beginning in his legs and face. "It's going to be bad."

"Don't worry, Charlie," Bernice said with a wink. "I've got just the remedy for a bad sunburn!"

Sometime later, Charlie stood in his small bathroom, naked and miserable as he dabbed a washcloth over his glowing red skin. At each touch of the cloth he hissed in his breath and let it out slowly. He had taken a quick shower and had been dismayed to find his skin glowing hot pink when he stepped out. And then Bernice had shown up with her home remedy: a bottle of white vinegar. She had instructed him to apply it full strength to his burn and let it soak in, that it would take out the sting and ease the heat. Charlie had been dubious, but he had tried it and been pleasantly surprised at how well it worked.

He managed to dress without too many tears, and when Ken and Billy knocked on his door, he even found the energy to smile in greeting.

Both men wrinkled up their noses and squinted at him.

"Whoa," Ken said and took a step back.

"Jesus," Billy agreed. "What did you do? Over douche yourself?"

"It's vinegar for my sunburn," Charlie said. "It's an old Minnesota cure."

"For what? Too many friends? Whew!" Ken waved his

hand in front of his face. "You're going to walk behind us on the way to dinner."

Charlie hung his head but took a stabilizing breath and closed the door behind him. He wasn't going to let something like how he smelled keep him from enjoying this cruise. He squared his shoulders, hissed at the flash of pain, and slowly followed his friends down the hall.

7

THE VINAIGRETTE AND THE PORN STAR

Kinitia entered the dining room several steps ahead of everyone else. Charlie thought she looked stunning in a red sequined, hip-hugging dress with a plunging neckline and open back. The dress made everyone who passed them in the hallway turn to look at her. Her hair was piled high on her head, and it appeared as if she had invested in a make over in the ship's spa. She made her way down the center steps and paused on the landing where more steps to the right and left led down to the main floor of the dining room. Kinitia surveyed the room full of men who all seemed to be looking up at her. She looked to Charlie like a queen peering out over her subjects.

Charlie descended the center steps behind Kinitia. He missed the final step and stumbled forward, bumping into Kinitia's back and sending her stumbling into the railing at the edge of the stairway landing. She let out a rather loud and unladylike grunt as she doubled over the railing, and

Charlie winced. Several men gasped, but most smiled and a few even laughed. Damn his natural clumsiness!

"Sorry, Kinitia," Charlie said. "I lost my balance."

Kinitia gave him a tight smile after she pushed herself upright. She turned for the steps down into the dining room and he moved to join her, but she held him at bay with a freshly manicured hand. Turning her head with her right foot on the first riser, she said quietly, "Let me go down first and then you can follow. I don't want to end up in a pile on the floor. Okay?"

Charlie lowered his gaze and nodded. As he watched Kinitia descend the steps, he managed to hold back a tear. Everything about this cruise was going wrong: his lack of fluffing assignments, his sunburn, the combination of Rock and Cedric, and now Kinitia didn't even want to walk beside him for fear he would end up rolling her down the stairs. He let out a sigh, and before he could start down the steps himself, Bernice linked arms with him.

"Will you escort a lady to dinner, sir?" She wore a flowing white gown that accentuated the tan she had spent all day perfecting. Her glasses reflected the lights in the ceiling and Charlie could see a touch of highlight in her soft curls that had been brought out by the sun.

He grinned down at her. "I would be delighted."

She leaned in and sniffed at his collar. "Oh, I must say, your cologne is exquisite."

They made it down the steps and around the tables without incident. Pulling out Bernice's chair, Charlie waited until she was settled then sat beside her, noticing that Ken had done the same for Kinitia. Billy was off talking to a table full of blond, tan actors he had met during his afternoon fluffer duties.

Several men stopped by the table to talk and each one sniffed warily when they got too close to Charlie. They glanced around with questioning looks on their faces, and one actor asked Charlie, "Did you order extra vinaigrette dressing?" Charlie opted not to respond.

During the meal, Charlie noticed Rock and Cedric sitting a few tables away. Rock looked distracted and edgy, his eyes jumping from face to face around the dining room and, from what Charlie could see, he barely touched his dinner. Charlie frowned then winced as he creased his sunburned lips. How was he going to fluff anyone in this condition? He found himself actually hoping he did not get scheduled for at least a day or two, until his sunburn healed.

Following the four course meal, they were all working on dessert when Gregory Gianelli stood up and tapped his fork against his water goblet. The steady murmur of conversation died away and he smiled as he looked out over the men surrounding him.

"I would like to take this opportunity to welcome you all aboard the Dominatrix. As you know, we are sailing down the coast of Mexico, docking in Acapulco for two nights, and returning to Los Angeles. I chartered this cruise line to inject some passion and excitement into the films my directors have been working on. There were three directors recently signed to my studios that I felt would make good use of this time and be able to produce quality, interesting images for the adult gay film industry. At this time I would like to introduce them to you, starting with Rod Mandrake. Rod, would you stand up please?"

Rod stood up and took a bow as the room gave him a round of applause. Several men at a neighboring table lifted their bare feet into the air and whistled. Everyone laughed, including Charlie who was surprised that so many people knew about Rod's foot fetish.

"Next I would like to welcome Cedric Wilmington who has just signed on with us as a director. The movie he is working on will be his first for us here at Bruised Knees Studios, and we're all very excited to see what he will create. Cedric, if you please?"

Cedric stood up to mild applause during which he smiled brightly and turned to wave to the entire room. He sat down beaming and Charlie noticed with interest that Rock did not acknowledge Cedric nor did he applaud for him.

"And last, but most definitely not least, please welcome one of the newest directors in the gay adult film industry, Simon Marshall. Simon?" Gregory held out his hand and a young, bookish looking man stood up with obvious embarrassment. He was attractive in a college professor kind of way with round silver glasses, close cropped dark hair, and quick, alert eyes. He had a shy smile and deep dimples that immediately endeared him to Charlie and everyone else at his table if their quiet sighs were any indication. Simon waved to the room and quickly sat back down.

"He's a porn director?" Charlie asked, leaning over to whisper to Billy.

"He looks like a history teacher I had in high school," Billy replied. "Too bad my teacher wasn't gay, I may have gotten a better grade."

"Or not," Ken said with a grin. "Depending on how well you performed."

Billy gave Ken a dirty look then turned his attention back to Gregory Gianelli.

"In closing, I would like to thank all of you for joining me on this cruise. I wish you a great amount of fun, sex, and adventure over the course of the trip. Thanks again."

A loud round of applause and many whistles as Gregory Gianelli resumed his seat at the captain's table. He smiled and nodded and raised his hand in response, and then everyone ordered after dinner drinks from their handsome waiters.

"So," Ken said as he leaned back and patted his full stomach. "What are the plans for the evening?"

"Obviously nothing that involves much movement for me," Charlie moaned. "I'm thinking of taking a bath in aloe vera gel and calling it a night."

"Hey, you can't poop out on us like that," Billy said. "I need a dance partner."

Charlie rolled his eyes, but felt his spirits pick up. He may have been having a tough time so far on this cruise, but his friends would always be there for him. With his mood lightened, Charlie followed them to a disco where a trio of drag queens was dancing, including the flirtatious Chantilly Lace. Bernice immediately joined her new friend on the dance floor. Several songs later, she returned to their table, face glowing beneath a sheen of sweat.

"I just love gay men!" she exclaimed and fell laughing into Kinitia's arms.

Kinitia laughed along with her. "I know exactly what you mean, Bernice."

Some time later, Charlie left the disco and strolled along the deck. He paused and leaned on the railing, taking a deep breath of the salt-tinged air. A full moon hung luminous in the clear night sky and he sighed with content. Maybe this cruise wasn't so bad after all. A footstep from behind startled him, and he turned to find the ship's doctor, Garth Tanner, standing nearby. The man was dressed in a dark suit and looked very handsome as he smiled at Charlie.

"I heard you have a bad sunburn," Garth said, coming up beside him. He sniffed and frowned. "Did you spill salad dressing on your suit?"

Charlie sighed and shook his head. "No. It's a Minnesota recipe for relieving sunburn pain: white vinegar."

"Ah." Garth nodded. "I've heard of that."

"Really?" Charlie asked with surprise.

"No." Garth shook his head and smiled. "Hey, I've got a gallon of aloe vera in my cabin that should help. Do you want to stop by?"

"Oh, yes," Charlie said with relief. "I didn't bring any with me. Thank you, thank you."

Back at Garth's cabin, the doctor helped Charlie ease out of his clothes and spread the cool, green gel over his simmering skin. Charlie jumped and shivered as the gel touched him and goose flesh broke out over his arms and legs.

"Oh, man!" Charlie said through clenched teeth. "That's cold!"

"Your skin is hot, so the difference is making you shiver." Garth finished applying the gel and stepped into the bathroom to wash up. He returned a few moments later with two pills in his palm. "Here, take two plain aspirin. They may help the sting."

Charlie swallowed the pills and then looked up as Garth examined his nude body. "What?"

"Well, I know you're sunburned and all, but I was just thinking how much fun I had the other night ... Nanny Charlie." Garth gave him a sexy smile. "Think you can still wear the dress?"

Charlie shrugged. "Why not? Probably the closest I'll get to sex in a couple of days."

"Ah, you should be fine day after tomorrow. Stay out of the sun and keep putting aloe on the burned areas to prevent peeling." Garth opened the armoire and pulled out the garment bag. His eyes were twinkling as he handed it to Charlie. "Here you go."

"Okay, I'll be right out." Charlie entered the bathroom and closed the door. He carefully pulled the dress on over his head, sucking in his breath at the pain in his shoulders and trying not to smear the aloe gel. Once he had the dress buttoned, he slipped into the black, clunky shoes. Finally, after pinning the hat on his head, Charlie stepped out into the dimly lit room and approached the bed.

Garth lay on the sheets in his large, Velcro fastened diaper and baby bonnet. Charlie put his hands on his hips and cocked his head, the hat tipping a bit with the motion.

"Have you been a bad baby, Garth?"

The doctor nodded and Charlie reached into the armoire to grab the paddle. He pulled the diaper free and raised Garth's hairy legs to expose his ass. He tried not to look at Garth's small penis and balls, and concentrated instead on delivering a firm, sound spanking. The paddle whacked faster and faster against Garth's hairy ass, turning his cheeks red and causing Charlie's sunburn to sting.

Garth cried out with each slap of the paddle and soon pumped out another surprisingly heavy load of cum. Charlie slowed the paddling to a stop, his forearm aching from the exercise and his sunburned shoulders tingling as he surveyed his work. The doctor's ass cheeks were a bright, cheery red and Charlie reached down with both hands to spread the firm globes open and expose pink, puckered asshole between.

"Oh," Garth moaned. "My ass is stinging. That feels good when you touch it like that."

"You've got a nice, tight hole here, doc," Charlie said, his voice deep with lust. "I'm getting the urge to just plow my cock right up that chute of yours."

"Oh, do it," Garth said breathlessly. "Fuck that tender red ass of mine."

Charlie got a condom from the wardrobe and opened two buttons of the dress. He pulled out his cock, rolled the condom onto it, and lubed up the doctor's asshole. He slapped the man's cheeks a few times, grinning at his sighs and moans, then eased himself into Garth's hole. Charlie watched as his cock spread the sphincter open, the shaft sinking deep inside. He held Garth's ankles and closed his eyes until he had penetrated the doctor as deep as possible.

"Oh, God!" Garth cried out. His fingers grabbed into the sheet beneath him and his toes curled tight. "Get your dick up inside that hole. Yeah, fuck that spanked ass. Get it in me."

Charlie pumped into him, hips picking up speed until he found his rhythm. He pulled Garth's ankles up to his shoulders and hung them behind his neck then leaned over the bed and fucked the doctor good and deep. The dress billowed around him and he felt sweat break out on his tender, sunburned skin, but he didn't care. The man had such a tight, narrow hole it was amazing.

A few moments later, Charlie could feel his orgasm closing in. He pulled out of Garth's asshole, yanked the condom off, then directed his dick at the doctor's face. Garth opened his mouth and slurped up the majority of Charlie's load, sucking and licking the warm, thick cum as it slowed to an oozing stream.

Afterwards, Charlie wiped up and crawled into the bed, falling soundly asleep beside the still-bonneted doctor. He had not removed the dress or the hat, being too tired and still a little too sore around the shoulders.

The following morning, Charlie awoke to the sound of Garth scurrying around the cabin. He rose up in bed and watched the doctor as he stuffed clothes into a laundry bag and tried to get dressed at the same time.

"What's wrong?" Charlie asked through a yawn.

"Someone paged me," Garth explained as he ran around pulling on socks and shorts. "Must be sea sick or something. And I need to get my laundry down to the cleaning crew this morning. The stuff I'm wearing is the last of everything in my drawers and closet." He trotted up to the bed as he buttoned his shirt. "Thanks for last night. I left a bottle of aloe on the counter in the bathroom. Sorry I have to run." He kissed Charlie quickly and headed out the door with the bulging laundry bag in tow.

Charlie stretched then hissed at the tight feeling of his skin. Maybe it was just wishful thinking, but the sunburn did feel a little better. He got up and shuffled into the bathroom to pee. After he had washed his hands, he turned to pick up his clothes where he'd left them on the floor of the bathroom, but they were gone. He searched the entire cabin but found nothing he had been wearing the night before. Garth must have stuffed Charlie's clothes in the laundry bag along with his own. Even the towels were gone!

"Dammit!" Charlie said. "Now what?"

He wasn't about to parade through the ship's halls in the nude, not with all the porn actors sporting muscular bodies strolling around. And especially not with a pale hand print on his chest. He looked at himself in the mirror, sighed, and then reached up to remove the bobby pins holding his hat in place. He had no other choice.

Walking down the hall to his room, the gray nanny dress swished along the walls and brushed against Charlie's legs. He had left the hat and shoes in Garth's room, hoping against hope he would encounter as few people as possible. As luck would have it, he saw more people in the hall than he had the entire cruise, some of them two or three times. He had a sneaking suspicion that a few of the men had circled around the hallways to get a second look.

Rounding a corner at a brisk pace with his head down, Charlie ran into Rock Harding and fell to the floor with a startled yelp. He looked up along Rock's muscular, hairy legs to the thong barely covering his crotch, then up over his flat, hairy stomach and hard chest to the man's dark, amused eyes.

"Charlie," Rock said with a nod. "Auditioning for the ship's musical?"

Charlie felt himself flush beneath his sunburn. "No." He tried to get up with as little pain as possible, but it was no use. Every time he moved his shoulders the skin stretched tight and sent barbs of pain through his system.

"Let me help you." Rock held out a hand and easily lifted

Charlie to his feet. He looked the dress over and asked, "What's with the outfit?"

"It's a long story." Charlie looked down and shuffled his bare feet.

"I can only imagine. Do you ever have any short stories?" Rock frowned and reached down to run his finger along a sudden, spreading stain on the front of the dress. "What is this?" He sniffed at it cautiously. "It's not cum."

"Oh, shit." Charlie removed the bottle of aloe and found it had come uncapped and started to leak. He snapped the cover back tight and shrugged. "It's aloe. For my sunburn."

"Ouch. It looks pretty bad. Doe it hurt?"

Charlie nodded. "Yeah."

Rock locked his gaze on Charlie's. "Need some help applying the gel?"

Charlie's breath caught in his throat and his heart stumbled over a couple of beats. "Uh ... Yeah, that would be nice."

"Great. Where's your cabin?"

Charlie led Rock to his cabin and opened the door. The room reeked of vinegar and he felt himself blush again as Rock followed him inside.

"Whoa," Rock said, his eyes beginning to water. "What is that smell? Did you over-douche yourself or something?"

"What? No!" Charlie said and waved his hands through the air, trying to fan out the smell. "It's a remedy for sunburn pain that Bernice told me about."

"Oh, wait," Rock said with a smile. "White vinegar, right?"

Charlie looked at him in surprise. "You've heard of it?"

"No. I just recognized the smell." He grinned and Charlie swooned. "Okay, get that dress off and hand me the lotion." Rock stopped and cocked his head. "Jeez, I haven't said something like that since I went to my high school prom."

Charlie let out a braying, nervous laugh as he unfastened the buttons on the dress and let it drop to the floor. He remembered he was naked beneath the dress just as the garment hit the carpet and he almost reached down to cover his penis and balls. But Rock had seen him naked once, the day they had first met. Or at least, he had seen Charlie's cock. It shouldn't matter that he was standing naked in front of Rock, should it? Rock was a gay porn star. He had seen hundreds, maybe over a thousand, men naked.

But had the air ever felt quite as charged between Rock and those actors as it did right then? Charlie's heart didn't pound, it *slammed* in his chest.

Maybe he should get a towel or something to cover up.

"Just a second," Charlie blurted and dashed into the bathroom. He looked around frantically, but the maid had been in and taken all the towels and failed to return with a fresh set. The only towel remaining was a tiny wash cloth lying forgotten in the corner. Charlie held up the wash cloth and assessed its ten square inches of material. Not likely.

"Dammit," he whispered and edged around the bathroom door to find Rock standing in the middle of the room with a patient look on his face, a palm full of aloe in one hand and the bottle in his other.

"Sorry, just a second," Charlie muttered and darted to the dresser. It wasn't until he had pulled open the top drawer that he remembered he had left his clothes out for the laundry service as well and had no clean underwear. The only objects that occupied the drawer were the double headed dildo, a bottle of lube, and two boxes of condoms. The drawer stuck halfway open and the dildo bounced up and out, landing on the floor with a quiet thump. Charlie closed his eyes and prayed for a tidal wave to capsize the boat and divert Rock's attention.

"Wow," Rock said. "Nice one. It's like the dirtiest tandem bicycle ever made. Does it get much use?"

Charlie laughed and turned around. "Sorry for acting so odd. I just... I felt uncomfortable being naked in front of you after all the... you know... all the stuff that's happened with Cedric and everything. Kinitia's constantly telling me not to piss Cedric off by talking to you and stuff." Charlie took a breath and shrugged. "And all my clothes are being washed and I have no towels. So, I guess I'll have to be naked."

Rock smiled and motioned for him to come closer. "Come on, Charlie. I'm a porn actor. I've seen plenty of dicks. One more won't hurt."

Charlie didn't know whether to feel relieved or hurt. Was he not something special to Rock? Shouldn't his nudity mean more to Rock than just another actor he was getting paid to fuck and suck? Was he overreacting or should this bother him?

"Charlie?" Rock asked with a slight frown. "You okay?"

Charlie blinked then nodded and smiled. "I'm fine. Sorry. Must be the sunburn." He took a mental breath, then turned to fully face Rock and walked across the room to stand before him. As he stood straight-backed and stiff-legged before Rock, Charlie fought to keep his mind on subjects that would not arouse him. "Okay, I'm ready."

Rock took a moment to look him over. "Well, you certainly know how to grab a man's attention, Charlie," Rock said in a husky voice. "Looks like you've been working out a lot." He squirted some more gel into his palm and rubbed his hands together to warm it up.

"Yeah, I guess I have." Charlie sucked in his breath as Rock approached him, but then let it out when he began to lightly rub the gel on his skin. "Wow, that feels a lot better than it did last night. I thought I was going to freeze to death."

"He didn't rub his hands to warm it up first," Rock replied, his eyes narrowed as he concentrated on the task at hand. He grinned at the pale mark of Charlie's hand and arm across his chest. "I hate when I leave my hand on my chest while I'm sunbathing."

Charlie snickered and tried to hold still as he concentrated on keeping his cock from growing hard. As Rock slathered him with aloe, he would feel blood rushing south and quickly switch his mind to other topics. His erection would recede, only to return once more as he focused again on the touch of Rock's hands. It became especially difficult when Rock knelt before him to rub aloe on his legs.

"Good thing you were wearing your trunks," Rock said as he stared at Charlie's dick. "I'd hate to see you burn that handsome cock of yours."

"Thanks," Charlie muttered and closed his eyes. He thought about Cedric Wilmington and was relieved to feel his hard-on diminish immediately.

Rock spread the aloe over Charlie's thighs and calves, his head lowered as he worked. When he was done, he leaned forward slightly to stand up once again and his lips barely brushed the head of Charlie's penis. As Rock stood to his full height before him, Charlie stared up at his face and felt his cock spring into full readiness with a mind of its own.

"I was hoping to find you this morning, Charlie," Rock said quietly, wiping the excess gel over his own chest. "I've been wanting to talk with you about something."

"Really?" Charlie said, his eyes wide. "What?"

"Well, I've been doing a lot of thinking and..."

A knock interrupted him and they both turned to glare at the door. There was a pause, and then another round of knocking, more forceful than before.

"Charlie?" Kinitia called through the door. "Are you okay in there?"

Charlie took a breath and stepped back from Rock to gather his wits. He had found in the past that the closer he stood to Rock, the more stupid he became. As he stepped back he bumped a small folding tray table and it fell to the floor with a thump.

"Charlie?" Kinitia called again. "Are you okay?"

"I – I'm fine," Charlie stammered, his voice cracking. "Just a minute." He looked around and noticed a pair of shorts he had overlooked earlier sticking out from beneath his bed. He pulled them on and, with a quick glance at Rock, opened the door.

"I thought I heard you in here and I was worried that you..." Kinitia stopped when she saw Rock standing awkwardly in the middle of the room wearing just a thong bathing suit and holding the bottle of aloe. "...Were doing something stupid." She turned her withering glare to Charlie. "And look, I was correct."

"I'll just leave this with you," Rock handed Charlie the aloe as he headed out the door. "And I'll catch up with you later." He nodded to Kinitia and walked quickly down the hall.

"Charles Heggensford..." Kinitia began and closed the door to block out most of her stern, but well-intentioned, lecture.

8

GOING TO TEMPLE

The Dominatrix docked in a bustling Mexican port the following day. Charlie, Billy, Kinitia, and Bernice signed up for the ship's tour of the city and the ruins of a temple that lay deeper in the jungle. Ken could not attend the tour as he was scheduled to work the set of Simon's movie, a scene of which would be filmed somewhere on shore.

The four explorers stocked up on bottles of water, a few snacks, and gathered at the foot of the gangway at the appropriate time. They were joined by several of the actors, all of whom had managed to get the time off from their shooting schedules. Charlie kept his eyes open for any sign of Rock, but tried not to appear like he was looking for Rock.

"I don't think he's coming," Kinitia whispered.

"What?" Charlie asked a little too innocently, widening his eyes as he turned to her. "Who?"

She gave a quiet huff. "You know who: Rock Harding. I think he's scheduled to work today."

Just then Rock appeared at the top of the gangway. He was dressed in tight black shorts, a tight white tank top, and hiking boots. A flannel shirt was tied around his waist and a small digital camera jutted from a fanny pack stuffed full of water bottles. He bounced down the gangway and smiled at Charlie.

"Hi there," Rock said. "Going on a tour?"

Charlie shrugged. "No. We just thought we'd hang out here for awhile."

Rock blushed and grinned. "Very funny. Okay, I'm Mr. Obvious."

A hunky steward approached the group and introduced himself as Harmon. He made sure everyone was properly attired and ready to do some hiking, grinning at the little walking shoes Bernice had chosen. Leading them through the city streets to a bus, Harmon warned them as they boarded that the ride ahead was going to be rough. Rock and Charlie shared a seat and Billy saved a spot for their tour guide. Harmon gave Billy a wink as he swung his tight ass into the seat.

The bus ride was like nothing any of them had ever experienced before. The vehicle bounced over deep holes and bumped along barely discernible ruts in the jungle. By the time the bus came to a shuddering stop, they were all sore and tired. Harmon helped each of them off the bus then led them along a narrow path overgrown with vines and ferns until, insect-savaged and cursing, they stepped out into a field from the middle of which loomed a tall, ancient Mayan temple. The sides rose up in a rough pyramid shape with many plateaus arranged like staircases.

"Oh my God," Charlie said in awe. "It's amazing."

Harmon smiled beside him. "It is, isn't it? I never get tired of seeing this place." He looked at the entire group. "Okay, everyone, listen up. We can go inside the temple a short distance. For those of you who are more adventurous, we can climb up this side facing us. There are steps leading to the top. We can't go to the very top, but we can go to the first level just beneath the point. There's a platform around the entire temple from which you can see for miles. The stone steps are worn, however, and can be tricky, so please be careful."

With Harmon in the lead, they approached the temple and disappeared inside. The air was damp and cool and only the light filtering past them from the doorway broke the darkness. Charlie shivered, his sunburn multiplying the chill in the air. Rock noticed that Charlie was cold and untied the flannel shirt from around his waist. He held it open and helped Charlie slip it on.

"Thanks," Charlie said quietly. Everyone spoke softly due to the somber atmosphere of the temple. He pulled the extra large shirt tight over his chest and, when Rock had turned away, leaned down to inhale the man's citrus scent. Photos were summarily taken both within and outside the temple.

They all opted to climb to the top of the temple and soon they were mounting the steps. Charlie noticed Billy and Harmon were both missing from the group and assumed they had remained inside to fool around.

The view from the top of the temple was staggering. They could see the city and port off in the distance, the ocean twinkling blue beyond.

"Amazing," Rock said. "Have you ever seen anything quite like this?"

Charlie gazed at the man with open adoration and said, "Oh, some things. Not many, but some."

"Really?" Rock turned to look at him and Charlie quickly blinked the fawning look from his face. "Where?"

"Well, there was the desert that night when we sat up on the mesa a few months ago," Charlie replied. "Remember that?"

Rock smiled and nodded. "Yeah, I do. You're right, that was close. But there's something about being here. The energy of this place, the craftsmanship of the temple; it just feels so ancient and powerful." Rock shrugged. "But, then again, I've been going insane on the ship, so maybe I'm just glad to be back on land."

"What do you mean?" Charlie asked.

Rock took a breath and looked around for the others. The rest of the group had circled the perimeter of the platform and were busy looking at the view deeper into the jungle, so they were alone for the moment. "I've been seeing things on the ship. Well, not really things: a person. Someone who should not be on board the ship."

"A stowaway?" Charlie wondered.

"Worse, actually." Rock sighed and looked back out over the trees. "Someone I thought was dead."

"What?" Charlie said, his voice a little louder than he had intended. He caught Kinitia leaning around the corner of the temple to eye them suspiciously and gave Rock an apologetic look. "Sorry."

"That's all right. I'm kind of stuck here, you know? I don't know if being with Cedric all these years has made me paranoid or delusional or what, but I could have sworn I've seen this guy twice on the ship." Rock shook his head and folded his arms over his chest. "Maybe I am crazy."

"Well, tell me about the guy you're seeing," Charlie said. "Explain it to me."

Rock gave him a sideways look. "It's a pretty long story."

Charlie shrugged. "I've got nowhere else to be."

"Okay, then." Rock took a breath. "Eight years ago I was new to California and the industry. I had yet to make any movies, but I had posed for some magazine layouts and wanted to become an actor. I was young and naive and didn't know anything about the world of gay porn. I met Cedric at a bar one night and he was really nice to me and liked me and invited me home with him."

"And you went?" Charlie asked, his voice bordering on disbelief.

"Cedric was different back then," Rock replied. "He was nicer, more easy going. Now he's just too full of himself and has become bitter and angry. Anyway, we started to hang out together. It was nice because I didn't have a lot of money, and Cedric knew a lot of people in the business and pretty soon I was auditioning for a movie. He really helped me out. Until..."

Charlie nodded. "I knew there as going to be an 'until' in there somewhere."

Rock smiled and glanced at him. "You really don't like Cedric, do you?"

"Do you blame me? He tried to set me up when I first started working for Kinitia." Charlie let out a breath and shook his head. "Okay, this is not about me. It's about you. I'll keep my opinions to myself. Please continue."

Rock nodded. "Thank you." He gathered his thoughts for a moment then resumed. "I met a guy on the set of my first movie. He was really hot. Nice body, handsome face, great dick, and we got along really well. However, he was also doing drugs, which I was not into, but I liked him, and we started going out. I was, however, still living at Cedric's, and he didn't want me to bring this guy back to the house, so I started spending more and more time at this guy's place." Rock paused and Charlie saw him swallow and try to rein in his emotions. "One morning I woke up after a really long, really hot fuck session with him and he was lying beside me. I was pretty hung over, and when I tried to wake him up, I couldn't. He had died."

"Oh my God," Charlie whispered. "How awful."

Rock did not acknowledge him; he was reliving the past as he told the story, his eyes distant as he stared out at the sea. "I freaked. I didn't know what to do. And I had a police record. Nothing big, just breaking and entering and another arrest for hustling, stuff I was doing to try and get by until I made it in movies. Because of my record I didn't want to call the police, so I called Cedric."

"Oh no," Charlie groaned.

"Yeah, well, hindsight is 20/20, right?" Rock shook his head. "He told me to get cleaned up and wipe down every-thing I had touched, then drive over to his place. So I did it. He was gone when I got there and I sat in the dark for hours waiting for him to show up. I was afraid to turn on the lights, afraid to move, afraid of everything. I didn't know what Cedric was doing or if he would be bringing the police back with him or what, you know?" Rock paused and shook his head. "When he finally showed up, he was alone. He told me he had taken care of the body so that no one would ever find it. But he wanted something in return."

"You," Charlie said and shook his head. "That manipulative fuck."

Rock laughed and looked down at his muddy shoes. "That's putting it mildly."

"And you've been with him all these years because of that one morning? You had nothing to do with that guy's death, Rock," Charlie said earnestly. "You didn't kill him. If he was doing drugs like you said, he probably overdosed."

Rock shrugged. "Maybe. But we were pretty wild the night before, what if I had injured him without realizing it?"

"But he was alive when you went to sleep, right?"

"I guess so. I had had a lot to drink, it's all kind of a blur." He shrugged again. "I freaked out. And I've paid for it over the last seven years."

"Well, I for one say it's time to stop paying for it. You need to dump that tired old bitch and live your life. You're handsome, fun, caring. Any man would be lucky to have you." Charlie took a breath and was about to go on when Harmon approached them.

"Looks pretty serious over here," Harmon said. "Everything okay?"

Rock smiled and nodded. "Everything's great, Harmon. We just got carried away by the view, that's all."

"I know what you mean, Rock. How about I take a picture of the two of you?"

Charlie smiled. "That would be great, thanks."

"Yeah, it would." Rock handed the man his camera, and then reached out to put his arm around Charlie's shoulders. Charlie smiled so wide he thought his face would split, and he didn't even care that his sunburned shoulders hurt where Rock touched him.

Harmon snapped a few photos and handed the camera back. He turned to the group and said, "Everybody ready to head back down the steps? Just a mile through the trees and we can get back on the bus. Okay, let's go!"

Kinitia pulled Charlie aside before he could begin the descent and asked, "What the hell are you doing with Rock?"

"We were just talking, Kinitia," Charlie replied. "We're not making plans or declaring our love for each other. We were just talking about someone on board the ship."

"Don't fuck this up, Charlie," Kinitia said and pointed a mud speckled finger in his face. "I mean it. Cedric Wilmington is no one to mess with. I dislike him just as much as you, but I know when to walk away from a barking dog, you know what I mean?"

Charlie snickered. "You've been hanging around Bernice too much on this trip. You're starting to talk like her."

"Hey!" Harmon called to them from the bottom of the steps. "Let's go, you two!"

Kinitia shook her head, but then reached out and put her arm around his shoulders, hugging him to her side. "Charlie, I know you think I'm a real hard ass, but I only want more for you than what you think you deserve. Do you understand? I think you're a very special person with a good heart and I want you to be happy. Don't get mixed up in any fucked up head games, okay?"

Charlie smiled at her and hugged her back. "I promise. Thanks for the vote of confidence. Does this mean I can get scheduled for work tomorrow?"

Kinitia laughed and headed down the steps, saying over

her shoulder, "I've already put you down for an eight hour shift, Farm Boy. You're going to be working the Luau Deck all day tomorrow, so take your sunblock."

Charlie and Rock did not get a chance to speak much on the bus ride back to the ship. But they did ride comfortably together like two old friends, and Charlie enjoyed the feel of Rock's leg pressing up against his own.

The next day, Charlie worked for Rod Mandrake. He was set up in a corner of the deck that had been blocked off from all other passengers and basically sat in a deck chair until he was needed. He passed the time by leafing through magazines and trying to keep out of the sun.

"Okay," Rod said with an edge in his voice. It had been several hours already and he was leading up to a major come shot for the end of this particular scene. "I'm going to need five guys up and ready to go at the same time, got that Charlie?" Rod turned to look over at him and Charlie nodded.

"Got it, Mr. Mandrake." Charlie grinned at the smile Rod shot him and thought back to the time he had gone to Rod's house for dinner. The director had revealed his foot fetish and asked permission to eat his dinner under the table off Charlie's feet. Charlie had agreed and had found the experience strangely exciting. Not to mention the foot fucking he had delivered to the man afterwards.

"All right, here we go," Rod said. "I need Robert and Jon up and ready to go first. Get over to Charlie and have him get you up to start the scene while we set up the lights."

Charlie got out of his chair and knelt on a small cushion by the railing in the shade as the actors walked up. He smiled at each and reached out to fondle them before opening his mouth and sucking first one then the other. As he fluffed the men, Charlie opened his eyes and assessed their bodies. The men were, naturally, in phenomenal shape, every muscle defined. Both men had waxed their chests for the trip and were smooth and tan, glistening with sweat and oil. Charlie sighed into the pubic hair of one of the actors as he slowly took the man's cock down his throat. He really did enjoy his work.

"Okay, let's go you two!" Rod called and the actors thanked Charlie as they turned to get in the scene. Two other men took their places and Charlie set to work on them, feeling their dicks start to harden in his hands and mouth.

A short time later, Rod was up to four men in the scene and Charlie was fluffing the final actor. The man was tall and muscular and sported a thick, dark mustache and a hairy chest. As Charlie sucked the man's cock, he found it filling up more and more of his mouth and throat. The man was a horse! Charlie backed off the dick then took the cock deep down his throat, gagging a little as the head tickled his gag reflex.

As he sucked, Charlie glanced over the railing and caught sight of Rock lying in a chaise. He was sunning himself and Charlie noticed very quickly that he was nude. Shifting position a bit so he could see better, Charlie urged the actor to move with him and continued to suck the man's dick as he spied on Rock lying sprawled out a deck below him.

Rock's body was a gleaming network of muscle and tanned skin. The light coating of dark hair sported sun-bleached tips in some places and drops of sweat and tanning oil glimmered in the strands. Rock moved his leg, the muscles in his thigh bunching as he bent his knee slightly then reached down to adjust his thick cock to a new position. The new placement of his cock allowed Charlie a view of Rock's tanned, supple balls and he felt himself grow hard at the sight. He could remember sucking that low hanging sac on a set by a waterfall. He could perfectly recall the taste of Rock's skin, the flavor of dried spunk after Charlie had accidentally made him come, the citrus scent of his body. Charlie closed his eyes and tried to keep his mind focused on the man before him and not on the one lying below, but he kept turning to look through the railing, his mouth full of cock.

As Charlie watched with a mix of shame and excitement, Rock, with his eyes closed and a small smile on his face, reached down to begin idly stroking his penis. He raised his left arm up over his head and sighed, a sound that touched Charlie's ear like a lover's hot kiss and made his cock twitch painfully inside his shorts. Charlie groaned around the actor's fully engorged cock and started to suck harder.

Rock pulled lazily at his dick until it was fully erect and stretched up over his belly to its full nine inches in length. It was a thing of beauty, tanned and soft with several thick veins running along the shaft and a great, tanned head perched at the top. Charlie could almost taste that sweet cap of skin glistening with oil from Rock's palm. He watched as Rock turned his head slightly and, eyes still closed, ran his tongue along the hollow of his hairy, sweaty armpit. Charlie was hypnotized by the man below him, caught up in the masturbation he was witnessing as he sucked the actor's dick. He reached out and wrapped his fingers around the thick root of it, squeezing it tight.

Rock licked his armpit a few more times and his stroking

picked up speed. His cock stood in full bloom now, ready for action. Lowering his left arm, Rock placed his fingers around the base of his cock and balls, the loose sac surging up and over his hair-flecked fingers as he pressed into the sensitive spot beneath. The rapidity of his strokes increased even more and Charlie could almost feel Rock's hand gripping his own cock where it lay trapped in the confines of his swim trunks.

"Oh, fuck!" the actor grunted and Charlie suddenly got a mouth full of cum that streamed out over his chin and onto the man's feet. "Oh, God!"

Charlie kept his eyes on Rock and, when he saw the man's balls pull up in preparation for his orgasm, felt himself let go. The smell and taste of the actor's semen coupled with the sight of Rock stroking himself spiraled into his crotch where he shot his own wad with several deep groans. Rock arched his back and fired off a number of loads of cum that splattered over his chest and belly, sinking into the hair and liquefying in the heat to drip down the sides of his torso.

"Charlie!" Rod screamed and he jumped. "What the fuck?"

"Jesus," the actor moaned, pulling his dick out of Charlie's mouth. "That kid can really suck cock."

"Yeah?" Rod said to the actor. "Fat fucking lot of good it does me when I need you for the final come shot!" He glared, watching as Charlie meekly wiped the come from his chin. "You are driving me crazy! Why can't you be consistent? One day you're fine and have no problems fluffing men to just the right point, and the next day you're sucking them dry like some kind of fucking semen vampire!"

Rod stopped with his mouth hanging open and shifted

his eyes to look out over the water. "Hmmm, a semen vampire. That's not a bad idea." He tapped his finger to his chin and considered the idea.

"Does that mean I'm forgiven?" Charlie asked quietly.

Rod looked back down at him and his face clouded with anger once more. "No! I'm very angry! Now, get this guy hard again and keep him hard and don't make him come! Got it?"

"Got it," Charlie said.

"Good!" Rod stormed back to the set where he commenced yelling at the other four actors.

The well hung actor stepped up once again and smiled sheepishly down at Charlie. "You really do give a good blow job."

Charlie grinned up at him. "Thanks, I guess. Seems to just be getting me into trouble lately."

"Hey, I won't let you get too carried away this time, okay?" the actor said. "I'll make sure I stop you if I feel I'm getting too turned on."

"Thanks," Charlie said and began to massage the man's softening penis. "I appreciate that."

As he sucked the man back into tumescence, Charlie risked a glance over the railing and found, to his combined dismay and relief, that Rock had left. All that remained was the ship's towel he had used to wipe up, clumped with drying semen.

9

CROUCHING FLUFFER, HIDDEN HARD-ON

Still a day away from docking in Acapulco, Charlie found he was once again not scheduled to work a movie. Two of Rod's actors had injured themselves playing volleyball in the nude and the director decided to shut down filming for a day. During this time, Charlie reflected on his recent fluffing screw ups and wondered if maybe he was supposed to be something other than a fluffer. Cameraman? Crew member? Whatever the hell a gaffer was? He really did need to pay more attention when he was on a set.

He wandered the decks aimlessly, staring out over the ocean and thinking far too much for being on a cruise ship filled with porn stars. He was slipping into a deep funk and did not know how to stop his descent.

Fortunately, he literally bumped into Bernice as he rounded the main deck for the fifteenth or sixteenth time. A splash of her mai tai dribbled onto his bare feet and he jumped back with a quiet, "Oh!"

"Charlie!" Bernice said with tipsy joy. She threw her

arms around his neck and hugged him tight. "Hi! Good to see you! What are you doing?"

Charlie shrugged. "Nothing."

Bernice took a step back and surveyed him. "Nothing at all?"

"Nope. Just walking the deck."

"But, Charlie, there's so much to do on this ship."

"Like what?"

Bernice rolled her eyes as she sipped from her drink. "Um, they're playing volleyball on the top deck." Charlie shook his head. "Uh ... aerobics? No? Okay, how about some shopping?"

"No money."

"Hmm, that is a problem." Bernice thought again then her face brightened. She slurped up the remainder of her drink and set the empty glass on a nearby table. Grabbing Charlie's hand, she led him along the deck and inside to the main concourse then into the spa center and up to the desk.

"May I help you?" a handsome, tan young man asked with a smile.

"Yes," Bernice replied with a smile of her own. "I need a full treatment for myself and my friend here."

"Bernice," Charlie hissed in her ear. "I can't afford this."

"Charlie, honey," Bernice said with an indulgent shake of her head. "That's why God invented credit." She produced a credit card from her bra and handed it to the man behind the desk, who took it between two fingers with barely a flinch.

A few minutes later, Charlie was getting out of his clothes in a changing room. He put on the soft cotton robe hanging on a hook and entered a short hallway with several closed doors leading off it. Bernice appeared wearing her own robe and Charlie could not help noticing the bright pink polish she wore on her toes. Bernice followed his gaze and turned her foot to show off the polish.

"Like it? I got a pedicure and some new sandals for when we hit Acapulco."

"Looks great," Charlie said with a nod. "What color is it?"

"Electric bubble gum."

"Great name."

"Oh, I'll say it is!" a chipper voice piped up, and a tall, tan man with shoulder length blond hair approached down the hall. "Hi, I'm Dirk and I'll be working on..." He consulted a clipboard. "Bernice." Dirk looked between them and flashed Bernice a bright smile. "You must be Bernice." She tittered bashfully in response. "Why don't you come right this way?" Dirk extended a hand and led Bernice down the hall and through a far door.

As she entered the room behind her masseuse, Bernice dropped her robe from her shoulders, effectively mooning Charlie with her large, white buttocks. He flinched, and then shook his head with a smile. Bernice had really opened up in the last few months.

A door behind him opened and Charlie turned, then stopped and smiled. "Well, hi there."

Dressed in white shorts and a white polo shirt with the ship's logo on the breast, Phrank looked up from his clipboard and blinked in surprise. "Oh, hi. I guess I never knew your last name." He looked back at the clipboard and frowned as he sounded the name out. "Heg-gens-ford?"

"That's me." Charlie folded his arms. "I thought you said you were just a hanger on. Why didn't you say you worked on the ship?"

Phrank shrugged, embarrassed, and lowered his voice. "It's a long story. Suffice it to say it's a short term solution."

"Okay," Charlie said, curiosity eating him up.

"So, come on in the room and we can get started." Phrank led him into a pleasantly decorated room lit with scented candles. Ocean surf sounds played from hidden speakers and Charlie immediately felt himself begin to relax.

"Now then," Phrank said as he consulted his clipboard. "Looks like you're in for the full treatment." He looked up with a crooked, sexy smile. "Guess we'll be spending a lot of time together this afternoon."

Charlie felt his cock twitch beneath his robe. The man was incredibly sexy. Even in the low candlelight, his blue eyes were twinkling. "Well, how awful, huh?"

"Why don't you get up here on the table and I'll start your massage."

Charlie shrugged out of the robe and climbed up on the table, thankfully without falling off it. He lay with his face in the padded opening and gazed down at the floor as Phrank covered his ass and legs with a lightweight sheet. Charlie watched Phrank's bare feet move into view at the head of the table, and then sighed as the man began to knead his knotted muscles with large, strong hands. Charlie closed his eyes as blood began to flow back into his sore, tense muscles. A thought occurred to him and he asked, "You are trained to do this, right?"

Phrank stopped the massage and leaned down, his lips brushing the pink surface of Charlie's ear lobe and sending a shiver of longing through him. "Of course, Charlie. Now relax and enjoy, okay?"

Charlie took a breath and let his mind go blank. No

traces of Rock, his questionable career, Cedric, or what Rod might be saying about him to Kinitia clouded his thoughts. He let himself relax beneath Phrank's firm hands.

An hour later, Charlie felt as if he would never be able to walk out of the room. His muscles had turned to liquid beneath Phrank's touch. The man had massaged the back of his entire body, kneading muscles and joints and applying pressure to points on his body that Charlie never knew existed. Phrank spent so much time working on the bottoms of Charlie's feet, it made him wonder if he had a fetish in common with Rod Mandrake. Then it felt so damn good, he realized he didn't care.

"Okay," Phrank said quietly. "Roll over and I'll work on your front."

"Oh, God," Charlie moaned. "I don't know if I have the muscle control to be able to do that." He had to concentrate to get his body to obey, but soon he lay stretched out on his back, the sheet crumpled and forgotten on the floor beside the table.

As Phrank massaged his chest and shoulders, Charlie could practically feel the man gazing down along his body. "Wow, I must have been pretty hung over."

"When?" Charlie said dreamily.

"When we slept together. I just don't remember you having a body like this."

"Thank you, I think."

"It was definitely meant as a compliment." Phrank worked his way down Charlie's torso and over his firm stomach. "Very nice definition."

Charlie did not answer. He had started to get an erection and tried valiantly to fight it off. Would that seem unprofessional to Phrank? The man was massaging his hips and groin, how could Charlie not be expected to get hard?

"Huh, bigger than I remember too," Phrank said quietly. He wrapped both hands around Charlie's full blown erection and squeezed. "Nice dick, Charlie."

"Thanks. Sorry about the boner, I couldn't help it with you massaging me."

"The hell with sorry," Phrank said and placed Charlie's hand on his own bulging crotch. "How about we do this a little more intimately?"

Charlie opened his eyes and smiled. "I like the sound of that."

Phrank locked the door, then pulled off his clothes and approached the table to resume the massage. Charlie looked the man's body over and sighed. Phrank was over six feet tall, thinning blond hair cut close to his scalp, bright blue eyes, defined cheekbones, a square jaw, and a body built for sex. A moderate amount of dark hair covered his body and, just as Charlie remembered it, swinging between his legs hung a long, uncut cock with a low hanging set of balls. Phrank was half hard and quickly rising, prompting Charlie to reach out and grab the dick in his fist.

"Oh, God," Phrank moaned. He paused with his eyes closed a moment, then moved down to stand at Charlie's feet, reluctantly pulling his cock free, and continuing with the massage.

As Phrank reached up and kneaded his thighs, Charlie brought his feet together and clasped the man's fully erect penis between them. He shifted his feet slowly up and down until Phrank had to stop what he was doing and lean on the table with his head down and his eyes closed.

"Charlie," Phrank said with quiet intensity. "You're driving me crazy."

"Good," Charlie replied with a smirk.

At that, Phrank reached down to release a catch and the lower portion of the table collapsed. Charlie gasped as his legs bent at the knee, then laughed when Phrank spread his thighs and moved up to stand between them. The intense look on the man's face silenced Charlie's laughter and he sat up to pull Phrank toward him.

Their tongues met first, and then their lips pressed together in a hot, wet kiss as they hungrily mauled each other. Charlie slid down along the table until he felt his cock press up against Phrank's own erection. He reached down and grabbed both dicks in a two-handed clutch. At the touch of his hand, Phrank moaned into Charlie's mouth.

Moving his mouth along Charlie's jaw, Phrank ran his tongue into his ear, sending shudders racing along Charlie's spine as he slowly stroked their cocks. Phrank moved his tongue down Charlie's throat to his chest and licked and sucked each nipple. He rose up now and then to slide his tongue into Charlie's mouth, then dropped down lower along his body.

Phrank slipped his cock from Charlie's hand and knelt before him. He devoured Charlie's erection in one gulp, sucking fast and hard and pumping his hand along its length. Charlie grunted and reached down to press his hands against the back of Phrank's head as the man took his dick deep into his throat. Phrank paused with his nose embedded in the surrounding bush, tongue and throat working the full length of his meat. When he resumed sucking, he moved more slowly, his full lips clamped tight around the shaft and his tongue lapping greedily at the soft head. Slurping up the drops of pre-come oozing from the slit, Phrank reached under Charlie's balls and pressed a strong thumb to a spot at their base, sending a fireworks display of sensation through Charlie's body.

"Oh, fuck," Charlie gasped and arched his back. "Oh, yeah."

Phrank sucked him a little longer, his hot mouth and wide tongue evoking a marvel of sensations as his hands found pressure points and massaged tightened muscles. When he let the dick drop from his mouth, Phrank ran his tongue along its length and set to work on Charlie's balls. He sucked them into his mouth and held each one on his tongue, then released it and licked its smooth pink surface as Charlie groaned and sighed, his hand slowly pulling on his wet, hard cock just above Phrank's head.

Phrank lifted Charlie's legs and rested them over his shoulders, pulling him farther down the table so his hips hung over the edge. He pushed Charlie's hips up and used strong fingers to spread open his ass cheeks. Phrank leaned in and ran his tongue slowly over Charlie's anus, sending a shiver through him.

"Oh, God," Charlie groaned. "Get your tongue up in there."

Phrank rolled his tongue into a tight spike and poked it between the folds of Charlie's hole. The soft sac of Charlie's balls fell over the bridge of Phrank's nose as he gave him the most intense rim job he'd ever experienced. Phrank sucked, licked, and spit into Charlie's asshole for several minutes as Charlie moaned, sighed, and gasped. When Charlie's hole was sopping wet, Phrank slowly pushed a finger inside. A second finger soon followed, and then a third, all the while he sucked and licked Charlie's balls and taint.

"Oh, fuck," Phrank said in a husky voice. "I like watching my fingers sink into your ass."

"Get them up there," Charlie said.

"You have got a fucking hot ass." Phrank shook his head as he pumped three fingers in and out. "So fucking hot."

"Oh, God," Charlie groaned and tipped his head back. "That feels so good." He lifted his head and met Phrank's gaze. "But I know something that would feel a fuck of a lot better."

Phrank didn't respond. He withdrew his fingers and moved to the pile of clothes he had left by the door. Extracting a lubricated condom from the pocket of his shorts, he tore it open and rolled it on as he crossed back to the table. Hefting Charlie's legs up high, Phrank bent at the knee and positioned his cock at Charlie's hole. With a sure, steady motion he burrowed forward, muscle parting before the thick, rounded head and folding back over the long shaft.

"Oh, Jesus!" Charlie grabbed the edges of the table as his body tensed around Phrank's long, slow penetration. With one steady thrust, Phrank was soon buried deep within him, and Charlie raised his head, looking down along his torso to where the man's muscular, sweat-streaked body was coupled to him. Charlie ran a hand along Phrank's chest, twisting each nipple and feeling the line of every defined muscle.

"Oh, God," Phrank sighed. "Your ass is nice and tight."

"Fuck me," Charlie said with clenched teeth. "Fuck me hard and fast."

Phrank smiled and draped Charlie's legs over his shoulders, then leaned forward to place his hands on the edges of the table. He pulled his hips back until he had almost completely withdrawn from Charlie's ass. He stood poised like that for a breathless moment, the head of his formidable dick barely parting the lips of Charlie's hole and his eyes gazing with heated lust down into Charlie's. Then he dropped his hips and plowed his cock deep into Charlie's ass, burying himself completely once again.

"Oh, fuck!" Charlie exclaimed and raised up to kiss Phrank as the man pumped into him at a quickening pace. Charlie sucked Phrank's tongue into his mouth and turned his head to press his open mouth tight over Phrank's lips. He wanted to be filled up by the man at both ends of his body.

Phrank kissed Charlie once more then leaned back and gripped his ankles tight, lifting them into the air and spreading them wide. In this position, Phrank looked down, watching as the thick body of his cock embedded itself in Charlie's hole.

"So fucking hot to watch my dick pumping into you."

"Fuck my hole," Charlie said between gasps. "Get that ass."

Words evaporated from Charlie's mind as Phrank fucked him even harder and faster. He rode Phrank's dick with his mouth open and his eyes squeezed shut, fingers gripping the edge of the massage table. Phrank drove into him with such force his cock seemed to be butting up against the bottom of his stomach. Charlie felt himself approaching orgasm and raised his head.

"I'm going to come."

"Shoot your fuckin' load, baby," Phrank said and, incredibly, picked up his pace to fuck him even faster. "I want to see it blow all the way up to your face. I want to come on your face, shoot my hot cum on that pretty face of yours."

"Oh yeah," Charlie said and, at the thought of Phrank's semen plastering his face, felt himself topple over into orgasm. "Oh, uh!"

He jerked himself off, his load splashing onto his throat, chest, and belly. He squeezed the last few drops from the head of his cock and laid his head back as Phrank continued to fuck his ass.

"Oh, yeah." Phrank pulled out of him. "Here it comes," he said as he rounded the table, peeling the condom from his bulging cock and aiming it at Charlie's face.

Charlie turned his head and closed his eyes just as the first shot of cum splashed over his forehead. He breathed in the smell of Phrank's semen and felt his cock twitch exhaustedly. Blast after blast of cum covered his face until Phrank finally let out a loud gasp and lowered his mouth to kiss Charlie tenderly on his cum-smeared lips.

"You're a hot fuck, fluffer," Phrank whispered, and licked a puddle of cum from Charlie's face. "I'm glad you came in for a massage today."

"Me too," Charlie said and smiled up at him.

Hours later, after a quick shower followed by a visit to the whirlpool with Bernice, Charlie spent some time in the sauna and endured a slightly painful, but still enjoyable, facial. It was nothing like the facial he had received from Phrank, but it still felt good. When his pampering had come to an end, Charlie thanked Bernice profusely for her generous treat, and then watched her sidle off to the bar for another mai tai. He wandered the decks a bit until he finally sat down and watched two men rimming and sucking a third on the shuffleboard court. That was where Ken found him.

"Thank God I found you," Ken said gasping for breath and leaning over with his hands on his knees.

"What? What's wrong?" Charlie asked with concern.

"We need your help."

Charlie was already on his feet. "Who? Kinitia? Billy?"

Ken shook his head and gave him a small smirk. "Just come with me. And you can thank me later."

Charlie followed Ken to the top deck of the ship where a film crew sat around on deck chairs talking. The men fell silent as they caught sight of Charlie, each turning to look at him. Charlie caught Ken's shirttail and leaned forward to whisper, "What's going on?"

Suddenly Cedric appeared before him and Charlie jumped. The director wore a bright floral print muumuu and folded his arms over his sagging chest. Large, dark glasses shielded his eyes, but Charlie could tell from the tight pale line of his lips that he was not pleased.

"Uh, Ken...?" Charlie said unsurely. "Why did you bring me up here?"

"Oh for God's sake," Cedric huffed and turned to Ken. "You didn't explain it to him?"

"That's not my place, Cedric," Ken replied, and stepped back with a smirk, leaving Charlie and Cedric standing a few feet apart.

"Fine," Cedric turned and looked at Charlie for a moment before he said, "One of my actors needs help getting hard."

Charlie blinked. "Oh. Well, can't Ken do it?"

Cedric rolled his eyes behind his glasses. "We've tried

using Ken. We've tried using Billy. We've tried using the other actors in the scene. Hell, we nearly flagged down a coast guard cutter we saw off the bow but it was too far away. He just can't get it up."

"Well, I'll, uh, I'll see what I can do." Charlie looked around. "Where is he?"

Cedric jerked a thumb over his shoulder. "We put him in the storage closet to try and remove any distractions. I really need this scene, okay? This is the first movie I've done for Gregory Gianelli and I need this guy to deliver in a big way, if you get my drift. And I can't afford a fuck up like what you did on Rod's set yesterday, got it?" Cedric leaned in closer, hands on his hips. "Do not make this man come."

Charlie smiled tightly and nodded. "Got it. Let me see what I can do." He walked around Cedric and headed for the storage closet door. On the way, he passed several actors standing in a group talking and their conversation died out and they turned to watch as he approached the storage closet. Charlie hesitated outside the door, taking a breath and steeling himself for whoever waited behind it, then turned the knob and entered the dimly lit room.

The first thing Charlie noticed was all the deck chairs. There were hundreds of them, folded up and standing in precise rows. The air was thick with the smell of plastic and aluminum. Off in a corner, sitting on a single, upright chair, was Rock Harding. Tension creased his sweaty face, his eyes were squeezed shut, and the muscles in his arms stood out as he gripped the seat of the chair. It appeared as if Rock was concentrating so hard on becoming aroused, he was distracting himself.

Billy Ransom knelt between Rock's tensed legs, his face

also bathed in sweat as he worked his mouth up and down the actor's penis. Billy made wheezing, desperate grunts each time he came up for air, and the sweat from his exertions ran down his face to drip onto the floor. But still, Rock would not harden.

Charlie cleared his throat and both men jumped. Rock blinked at him in a kind of daze as Billy smiled with relief, his swollen lips a testament to how hard he had tried to fluff Rock into readiness. He looked like a collagen experiment gone awry.

"I tried, Charlie," Billy said, his voice husky with exhaustion, "I did. But he won't respond to anyone. I tried my best, like you taught me."

Charlie walked up and placed a comforting hand on Billy's shoulder. "It's okay, Billy. Leave him to me now. Go on outside and get some air."

Billy stood on shaky legs and crossed to the door. He looked back once, watching as Charlie knelt to take his place and Rock turned his glazed eyes down to him, and then he retreated to the cool sea air.

Charlie ran his hands lightly up and down Rock's thighs as he looked into his face. Rock's haunted expression, dark rings beneath his eyes, and glazed eyes gave Charlie great concern. He continued to stroke Rock's thighs, then his calves — his amazing, glorious calves — then his thighs again, slowly moving higher until he gently brushed his fingers along Rock's penis

"You okay, big fella?" Charlie finally asked.

"I keep seeing him, Charlie," Rock whispered. "I've seen him twice more now. I think I'm going crazy." Rock shook his head and closed his eyes. "I can't get it up because I keep thinking about him. What if he's come back to haunt me? To get even?"

Charlie held a finger up to Rock's lips to quiet him. "It's okay, Rock. We'll figure it out, I promise. But first, you have to get this scene shot for Cedric. Do you understand that? He needs to film this one scene and then you'll be done for the day and we can focus on this man and work everything all out, okay? Put him out of your mind for now. Just relax, it's all going to be okay. I'll help you figure it out, you're not alone in this."

The creases in Rock's face eased and he closed his eyes and straightened his back. He took slow, deep breaths and shook the tension from his arms.

Charlie watched Rock relax and slowly stroked his cock. When he felt the time was right, he leaned down and caught the flaccid dick between his lips. He closed his eyes and sighed as he worked his tongue around the pliable shaft and over the tender head. He really did love sucking Rock's dick. He enjoyed the taste, the citrus smell of his body, the feel of his powerful legs on either side of his face. No other man made him feel this way.

Reaching up, Charlie took hold of Rock's balls and gently twisted as he tugged them down. Rock groaned, a good sign, and Charlie increased the pressure of his grip.

"Oh, Charlie," Rock sighed. "That feels good. No one does this quite like you."

Charlie moved his mouth faster along the length of Rock's cock and was relived to feel it begin to fill out. If he could just keep up this momentum, he would be able to get Rock up and ready to film his scene.

After several minutes, Charlie had only managed to get

Rock to half-mast. He sucked and licked and stroked and pulled, but Rock's body seemed to refuse to want to become fully aroused. Finally, after what seemed an eternity, Charlie had an idea. He moved back and said to Rock, "Stand up and turn around."

Rock stood up without question, completely trusting in him, and turned his back to Charlie. Leaning forward, Charlie parted Rock's ass cheeks and ran his tongue up the length of his crack. Rock groaned and bent at the waist, supporting himself on the back of the chair, and Charlie licked and sucked at the soft folds of his anus. Using the fingers of one hand to keep Rock's ass spread apart, Charlie reached up between the man's legs to pull on his dick. He was rewarded with several deep grunts and a steadily hardening cock. With renewed vigor, Charlie dug into Rock's ass, rimming him deep, plunging his tongue into the soft tissue and pulling harder on the man's dick.

Several minutes later, Rock slammed the door to the storage closet open and strode out onto the deck with a massive hard-on and a broad smile on his face. Cedric squealed with delight and everyone else on the deck applauded. As the crew scurried into position, Charlie appeared in the doorway and Ken and Billy rushed over to him.

"How did you do it?" Ken asked in something short of awe. "How did you manage to get him up like that?"

Charlie shrugged with tired, heavy-lidded eyes. "It's a gift, Ken. I don't own it, so I can't explain it."

Billy rolled his eyes and they turned to watch as Rock began to fuck another actor's ass. He slapped the man's ass cheeks and clenched his teeth as he pounded into the hot ass.

His well-known, well-used, and well-hung cock slipped in and out of the actor's hole and Rock closed his eyes and threw his head back. He continued to hammer at the actor's asshole until the man straightened up and fired thick, wet shots of semen up onto his own chest. Rock reached around and grabbed hold of the man's balls, squeezing them as the actor pumped out his load. When the man had finished, Rock pushed him forward once again and continued to fuck him until he brought himself to climax. He pulled out, stripped off the condom with a practiced hand, and blasted his thick, white shots onto the actor's back.

As he watched Rock's come shot, Charlie folded his arms and took a satisfied breath. His doubts from earlier had been erased. This was what he was meant to do, and boy, oh boy, he really did love his job.

10

SOMETHING SHINY

The following morning the Dominatrix docked in Acapulco. The passengers gathered at the deck railings, an excited buzz jumping from one person to the next. The entire ship had rented out a moderately priced hotel to stay in for the next two nights as the directors were going to shoot some land-based scenes and everyone would have a chance to tour the city. On the third day, they would board the ship once again and head back to Los Angeles. Charlie, Bernice, Kinitia, Ken, and Billy crowded up along the railing with everyone else, waving to the people on the docks.

A bump at his left elbow brought Charlie around and he found Theo standing beside him in full drag as Chantilly Lace. She wore a bright orange scarf wrapped around her head and a long, flower print dress. Wicked looking red nails extended her fingers more than an inch as she batted her eyelashes at Charlie and gave him a sly smile.

"Hi, baby," Chantilly said in her golden honey voice. "How's Chantilly's favorite fluffer today?"

Charlie smiled. "Just fine. And how are you, Ms. Lace?"

"Take your fine and multiply it twice, honey. Are you going into town to go shopping?"

"We all are."

"May I join you?" Chantilly inquired.

"We'd be delighted."

The tall drag queen looped one arm through Charlie's and the other through Bernice's and together they descended the gangway to the docks. As they made their way through the crowds of people, they passed Alpha and Omega, the Latin twins, and Charlie received two winks and smiled in return.

"You don't want to be getting mixed up with those two," Chantilly said quietly when they were out of earshot of the twins and Bernice had darted off to look at some jewelry.

"Why not?"

"They're trouble, baby," she said, her face serious. "And I mean bad trouble."

"Really?" Charlie glanced back at the men. "What kind of trouble?"

Chantilly shook her head. "I can't say. But just keep yourself and your friends away from them, got it? They're bad news."

"Oh, Chantilly!" Bernice exclaimed as she ran up to them. "Come see this necklace! I've just got to have it!"

"No, honey, uh uh," Chantilly warned as she allowed Bernice to lead her away. "You are not buying any of this shit. This is all tin and plastic."

Charlie grinned as the tall black man in women's clothes began haggling with a shopkeeper and Bernice hovered nearby, nodding with excitement. He turned to look back through the crowd and wondered about Alpha and Omega. What were they involved in that made Chantilly so nervous?

Later that afternoon, Charlie, Ken, and Billy signed up for scuba diving along the coral reefs. Charlie and Billy had never been scuba diving before and took some quick lessons from an instructor before following Ken down into ten feet of water and swimming around the sharp-edged coral. Colorful fish darted around them and up through their lines of bubbles as they swam slowly through the diluted rays of sunlight.

Twenty minutes later, their rental time was expired and they were out of the water. Charlie was first out of his wet suit and stood at the end of the dock drying off and watching the people walk past. A familiar face caught his eye and he shifted position to see around a large cluster of American tourists. He watched as Omega entered an upscale hotel across the road. The man wore a white T-shirt and dark sunglasses and before he entered the glass revolving door of the hotel, he looked around as if checking to make certain he had not been followed.

"What're you looking at?" Ken asked, coming up behind him and making Charlie jump. "Whoa, you're edgy. Did you spend too much time breathing bottled air?"

"No, nothing like that." Charlie turned back to watch the hotel entrance as Billy joined them.

"Who's Charlie cruising?" Billy squinted in the direction of the hotel. "That bellhop? He is kind of cute, but pretty young for your tastes, Charlie."

"No, not the bellhop. Come on, but be careful not to be seen." Charlie headed across the crowded road.

Charlie led the way across the road and ducked behind a

large potted palm tree. He realized that Billy and Ken had adopted outlandish spy attitudes when Billy broke two broad palm leaves from a small tree and hid behind them as he trotted up to join him, and Ken crawled up on his belly.

"I thought I told you not to be seen," Charlie hissed.

Billy parted the palm fronds long enough to say, "We took extra spy precautions to blend in," then snapped them back together to hide his face. "I'm in disguise."

Charlie snatched the leaves from Billy's hand and tossed them to the ground. He jerked Ken around from where he was standing with his chest pressed against the wall to make as small a target of himself as possible. Pointing his finger in their faces, he said, "This is serious."

"Oh, okay, sorry," Ken and Billy said together, then glanced at one another and started to laugh.

"Oh for God's sake," Charlie threw his hands in the air and turned to the revolving door. "Stay here."

He pushed into the hotel lobby and stopped to look around. The grandeur of the place caught him off guard, as did the air conditioning. It felt like a fall day in Idaho inside the building, and he breathed a sigh of relief. After the hot sun on the open dock it was like stepping into a cool bath. He assessed the layout of the lobby and was surprised to find so many shops and restaurants surrounding the plush furniture and brass lamps. Towering palms reached toward bright, sparkling skylights and blooming tropical flowers overflowed decorative pots.

"Wow," Charlie breathed. "I bet these guys leave more than just a light on for you."

Ken and Billy stepped in behind him and looked around, just as impressed. Charlie turned to find them looking over each of his shoulders and jerked his head to lead them away from the doors. They walked quickly across the lobby to stand outside a shop entrance.

"What are you doing in here?" Ken asked quietly. "This is a little more upscale than we're used to."

"I know, that's what's so weird," Charlie replied, looking around for any sign of Omega. "I can't imagine what he might be doing here."

"Who?" Billy asked impatiently. "What the hell is going on?"

"Omega," Charlie said.

"Omega?" Ken repeated. "One of those Latin twins?"

"Yeah, the shorter one," Charlie replied. "He came in here looking around and acting suspicious. I thought I'd try to find out what he was up to."

"Why the hell should you care?" Billy asked. "Maybe he makes more money than lowly fluffers and he upgraded his room."

"Hey," Ken snapped. "Cut the negativity. Besides, actors don't get paid this much, that's for damn sure."

"Oh yeah," Billy said with a grin. "I keep forgetting you're a fluffer *and* an actor."

"Knock it off, both of you," Charlie said. "Look, this is what I know." He told them about Chantilly's warning.

"So?" Billy said with a shrug. "A drag queen thinks these brothers are bad news. Maybe they shop lift or skipped school when they were growing up. Who cares?"

"No, it's something else," Charlie said. "Chantilly was really serious about her warning. Like, really, really serious."

Suddenly a deep voice from over Charlie's shoulder said, "Gentlemen, may I help you?"

The three of them jumped and let out tiny yelps of surprise. Turning, they found a hotel detective standing behind them with a slightly amused look on his face, the light glinting off his badge. He was tall and dark, handsome in an older, authoritative kind of way.

"Oh, I'm sorry," the detective said. "I did not mean to startle you. I was just curious if you are perhaps guests of our fine establishment?"

They all started speaking at once in high, nervous voices, each of them saying something completely different from the other. The detective listened to their babbling for a moment then raised his hand and the three stopped chattering at once and stared at him with wide eyes.

"Please stop talking and come to my office."

They took a collective breath and followed the tall, broad shouldered man down a quiet, carpeted hallway and into a small, windowless office. The detective closed and locked the door behind him then leaned his large body against it and folded his arms as he smiled at them. "Now," he looked at Charlie. "Tell me what it is you are doing in this fine hotel dressed as you are?"

Charlie looked down at his bare chest, damp trunks, and faded flip-flops and felt his stomach sink. He looked up at the detective and said with a bright smile, "We were looking around to maybe stay here in the future?"

The detective arched an eyebrow. "You're lying. Do you know what happens to thieves in this country?"

"We're not thieves," Ken said and stepped forward. "We came in on the Dominatrix and are all staying at a different hotel. We followed a friend in here to see what he was up to and ask if he might want to join us for lunch."

"I see." The detective looked at them each in turn. "The Dominatrix, eh? Are you actors?"

Billy smiled and jerked his head to Ken. "He is. Charlie and I are just fluffers."

The detective's eyebrows went up. "Really?" He lowered a large, hairy hand and squeezed his bulging crotch. "What if I don't believe you? What if I need a demonstration of your skills?"

The three looked at each other and grinned. The detective moved across the room and stood before the desk as all three knelt before him. Ken reached out and opened the man's pants and pushed them down his legs. He then shucked his boxers down to his ankles, exposing a long, fat, uncut cock. The black pubic hair surrounding the base of the man's dick was soft and tightly curled.

"Wow," Billy said. "Nice piece of meat, detective."

"They don't call us hotel dicks for nothing," the man replied. He reached down and lifted his soft dick to expose a set of large bull balls covered with dark black hair. "See something you like?"

"A couple," Ken said and leaned forward to take the man's left nut into his mouth.

Charlie leaned down and began sucking the detective's right ball as Billy shifted his position to kneel between them and sucked the man's dick. Billy gripped the base of the big dick with one hand and stroked its length with the other, focusing all of his oral attention on the top quarter of the steadily lengthening cock.

"Oh, that's it," the detective breathed. He removed his blazer and unbuttoned his shirt to expose a broad chest covered with black hair. "Lick my balls. Suck on them."

Charlie and Ken ran their tongues along the furry surface of the detective's balls. Every now and then one of them would slip his tongue in the other's mouth for a quick kiss before returning to work on the man's sac. Billy pulled the foreskin back and revealed a wide, heart-shaped head. He touched his tongue to the drops of pre-come that had collected at the tip then opened his mouth and took the exposed head down into his throat.

"Oh, yes," the detective gasped. "Suck it! Take my dick all the way."

Billy worked his mouth along the expanding shaft then pulled the foreskin up over the head of the man's dick. He slid his tongue into the tiny, wrinkled opening and around the interior of the sheath of skin.

Charlie moved down along the detective's taint as Ken took up sucking both heavy balls. Running his tongue through hair, Charlie got to the damp, sensitive pucker of the detective's asshole and slid the tip of his tongue between the folds of muscle.

"Oh, fuck!" the detective gasped. He leaned forward, placing a hand on the back of Billy's head and stuffing his cock deeper into Billy's throat as he gave Charlie more room to maneuver. "Eat my asshole!"

Charlie followed the detective's direction, licking and sucking the man's hole. He spread the hairy cheeks apart and nipped gently at the dark skinned ring of muscle he had unveiled, impaling it with his tongue.

After several minutes, the detective suddenly straightened up and stepped away from them. His dark eyes were clouded with lust as he removed the last of his clothes.

"Strip," he ordered and moved behind his desk. "And straddle each other on the floor."

The three fluffers shed their clothes and Ken got down on his hands and knees. He lowered the upper half of his body to the carpet and nodded to Charlie who moved on top of him and did the same. Billy climbed up on top of Charlie and balanced himself with his legs slightly bent. All three had their butts in the air, eager and waiting.

The detective stepped back around the desk as he rolled a condom along his dick. He was big, Charlie estimated about eight inches, and thick. The detective knelt behind them and rimmed them in turn, licking and sucking first one hole, then another, and then another. As he moved between them, the man slipped probing fingers into the other two assholes. All three groaned as the detective prepped them for his cock, and when he'd finished, he stood up and bent his legs, sliding into Billy.

"Oh, fuck!" Billy said right into Charlie's ear. "Goddamn, how big is that fucker?"

"Give me a minute and you'll find out," the detective said. He pulled out, aimed his cock again and this time drove it all the way home.

"Oh, God!" Billy gasped. "So fucking big."

"Hang on tight," the man replied. He reached out and took hold of Billy's shoulders then began to hump him with wild intensity.

Billy grunted and moaned, and in a surprisingly short space of time, ejaculated onto Charlie's back without touching himself.

"Oh, shit," Billy groaned. "You fucked the come right out of me. Oh, yeah."

The detective slowed and pulled out of Billy. He replaced his condom with a fresh one, then began the whole process once again with Charlie. He drove his cock halfway in on the first push, pulled out, and completely impaled him on the second thrust.

"Oh, fuck!" Charlie echoed Billy's sentiments as the detective pummeled his asshole. He wrapped his hands around Ken's chest and held on, his eyes shut tight as he felt his balls constrict. In minutes, the detective's fucking had pushed him over the edge and he shot his own load onto Ken's back, also without touching himself. The detective got a third condom and knelt behind Ken to repeat the process. Ken rode the man's dick like the professional porn actor he was. His mouth hung open and his hands made fists in the low shag carpet. Charlie and Billy climbed off and stood aside to watch as the detective drilled Ken hard and deep. In a short amount of time, Ken rose up, grabbed his cock, and stroked himself to climax. Billy fell onto his back beneath Ken's big dick and let the load splatter across his face and throat.

With a grunt, the detective came into the condom while buried inside Ken. When he had finished, the detective pushed Ken forward and fell across his back, smearing Charlie's load between them.

"You have proven yourselves," the detective said as he pulled out of Ken's red, raw hole. "Now get out of my hotel."

The three got dressed and walked a little unsteadily down the hall to the lobby. The detective followed along behind to make sure they exited the hotel to the street. Once they were outside they could see him standing behind the glass doors with his arms folded and a stern look on his face.

"He's a great fuck, but he's got a shitty attitude," Billy said.

Charlie and Ken shook their heads before heading back to their own hotel. As they made their way along the street, they spotted Omega walking a block ahead of them, his broad shoulders puffed out beneath the tight T-shirt and his dark glasses giving him a dangerous air. In his left hand he carried an aluminum briefcase that bumped against his muscular leg with each step.

Sunlight glittered along the briefcase, catching Charlie's eye, and he nudged both Ken and Billy and nodded toward it. They picked up their pace, angling through the crowded sidewalk to get a little closer to Omega. They fell into step fifty yards behind, and Charlie's gaze kept dropping to the briefcase as it winked and sparkled in the sun. Omega led them back to their hotel and they watched as he crossed the lobby, got on the elevator, and the doors closed after him.

"Well, that was uneventful," Billy said with a shrug. "Great sex, but overall a let down. I'm going out to the pool."

Charlie stood with his hands on his hips and his gaze focused on the elevator where Omega had dropped out of sight. The lobby of their hotel was not nearly as extravagant as the hotel they'd just left, but it was still comfortable. And it contained a bar that he and Ken decided to visit for an afternoon cocktail.

After the first round of margaritas, Ken looked up and smiled at Kinitia heading toward them. "Hi there, boss lady. How's it going?"

"Charlie," Kinitia said, an edge to her voice. "I need your help."

Charlie blinked up at her. "What's wrong?"

"Your expertise is needed once again." She glanced at Ken. "Sorry. Hi, baby," she said and leaned down to kiss Ken on the cheek. Turning back to Charlie, she asked, "Can you come with me?"

"Sure," Charlie said with a shrug. He slurped up the rest of his frozen margarita and stopped as a piercing pain drilled into his forehead. "*Ah!* Brain freeze! Give me a minute. Oh, God!"

He put his head in his arms and blinked away tears. Slowly, the headache subsided and he stumbled out after Kinitia. She led him outside to the pool area, around the length of the sparkling blue water and along a path built through a tropical garden that reminded him of Gregory Gianelli's backyard. The path opened up on a steaming whirlpool where three actors lounged naked in the bubbling water. They looked up as Charlie and Kinitia approached and nodded in greeting.

"Thank God," one of them said. "We've been waiting here for hours."

"No we haven't," snipped another of the actors. "We've only been in here for twenty minutes."

The first actor shrugged. "Well, I'm coming down from my hit and it's felt like hours. Stop harshing at me."

Charlie followed Kinitia around the whirlpool to a small maintenance shed set off behind some decorative rocks and trees. Through the door he could hear the sounds of conversation and, from the tone of the voices drifting through the thin walls and door, it was a tense one. They paused and it looked like Kinitia was debating whether or not to interrupt the obviously emotional issue.

"I've seen him, dammit!" Rock's voice came through loud

and clear. He sounded distraught and concern clutched at Charlie's heart. "I know it's him! But every time I try to catch him he's gone."

"Goddammit, Rock, that was eight years ago! He's gone, okay? Gone for good!" This was Cedric, the sharp, shrill voice was unmistakable. "I need you here and now, in the present, to get this motherfucking scene over and done with so I can try to piece together something resembling a movie from all the scenes you've been fucking up. If I don't deliver a quality movie to Gregory Gianelli, he's going to drop my ass and I'll end up doing that tired old shit back at Four on the Floor again for half what I can make at Bruised Knees! Now, clear your fucking mind of that fucking dead beat you were fucking eight fucking years ago and let's shoot this fucking scene!"

There was silence and Charlie and Kinitia glanced at one another. Before she could decide to knock, the shed door banged open and Cedric stepped out. He stopped, startled, then glared at them.

"Oh, is eavesdropping on your list of talents as well?" His cold, faded blue eyes zeroed in on Charlie.

"I brought Charlie over like you requested, Cedric," Kinitia replied. "We couldn't really hear anything that was being said."

"Whatever," Cedric snarled. He bowed and waved in an exaggerated manner for Charlie to enter the shed. "Please, oh great and powerful fluffer, enter the king's chamber and proceed with your duties. We all bow at your fucking feet."

"Hey!" Kinitia snapped and took a step toward the director. Cedric flinched and backed up a pace, but Charlie moved between them, facing Kinitia with a calm smile.

"It's okay, Kinitia," he said quietly. "I'm fine. Just go back in the bar with Ken and I'll join you guys as soon as I can."

Kinitia moved her head around Charlie to glare at Cedric, but then shifted her gaze back to Charlie's face. Her look softened and she gave him a tight smile. "Go to it, Farm Boy."

Charlie stepped into the dark, damp shed and closed the door behind him. After his eyes had adjusted, he saw Rock sitting on a barrel in the corner. The man was naked and sweaty, gaze cast down at his hands clasped between his knees. Looking up, he smiled sadly and Charlie saw the glint of tears in the corners of his eyes and his heart ached even more.

"Oh, Rock," he said softly. "It's okay." Stepping up to him, Charlie put his arms around Rock and settled the man's head on his shoulder. Rock's back and shoulders shook as he started to cry softly, and Charlie's eyes filled with tears as well. A few minutes later, Rock sniffled and wiped at his eyes as he pulled away from Charlie, clearly embarrassed.

"Sorry," he muttered thickly. "I'm an asshole."

"No you're not," Charlie replied. "You're just kind of emotionally confused right now." He backed up and stepped on two garden rakes that immediately sprang up and clubbed him across the shoulders. Charlie cried out and lurched forward which allowed the rakes to tumble into a small regiment of gardening tools that all fell to the concrete floor with a loud clatter and a small cloud of dust.

Charlie grimaced and, when the dust had settled, looked over at Rock with a shrug. "Oops."

They both started laughing, and soon Rock was once again wiping tears from his eyes, only this time they were tears of laughter. Charlie had Rock position himself more comfortably on the barrel, then knelt between his legs and gently stroked his soft penis. It started to lengthen, slowly, and Charlie took it between his lips, closing his eyes as he breathed in Rock's citrus scent, the salt of his sweat, and the earthy smell of the shed that brought back memories of the days when he had had sex with Ben Whistler in his family's barn. Funny, he hadn't thought of Ben once until just this moment, and then the thought was gone and he was focused on getting Rock up and ready for someone else to finish him off.

Rock sighed as Charlie worked his mouth along his cock. After twenty minutes of intense sucking and stroking, Rock strutted out of the shed and over to the whirlpool, his cock jutting out before him like the prow of a ship. Around the base of his penis and balls a silver cock ring glittered in the tree-filtered sunlight. Cedric eyed the new adornment then nodded.

"I like the cock ring," he said to Rock. "It looks very masculine."

Rock gave Cedric a quick nod then sat on the edge of the whirlpool. Filming began, and Charlie leaned against a tree to watch, rubbing his aching jaw and drinking from a water bottle he found nearby. He smiled as the cock ring, which was in actuality a simple metal ring he had found in a box of engine parts, winked at him. It did look very masculine and somehow right on Rock's body.

The three other actors moved in to begin orally working over Rock's rigid cock and Charlie flashed back to the oral worship he, Ken, and Billy had performed on the hotel detective. Art imitating life? Two of the men sucked and licked

Rock's balls as the third opened wide and swallowed his dick. Rock's cock and balls were sucked and licked for several minutes, a sight that got Charlie hard all over again.

He watched the scene progress for a few minutes then decided to track down Ken and Kinitia and order another margarita. He had earned it.

11

A PHRANK DISCUSSION

After he had cleaned up in the hotel room he shared with Ken and Billy, Charlie left to meet the others for dinner. The lobby was crowded with all of the Dominatrix passengers trying to arrange dinner and drinks, and Charlie stood off to the side looking around for his friends. The crowd was a marvelous collection of tanned and tattooed flesh and testosterone. Ken and Billy joined him a few minutes later and they found a house phone to call up to Kinitia and Bernice's room.

"Oh, Bernice is still trying to choose her outfit for the evening," Kinitia said with sarcasm. "It's quite a decision, what with a whole ship full of gay men to impress, you know?"

"I just want to look good, is that a crime?" Bernice called out good naturedly in the background.

Several minutes later, after Billy had made plans to meet a number of men in their rooms at some point in the evening, the two women finally stood before them. Kinitia had dressed casually in khaki shorts and a floral print blouse. Bernice had chosen a long, white cotton dress with purple sandals. The three men blinked at Bernice's colorful footwear and then the group headed out to a restaurant.

Following dinner, they decided to go bar hopping. They danced for awhile in one bar, had a couple of drinks, and then moved on to a new location. At a reggae bar, Bernice started a conga line and soon had a majority of the crowd dancing along with her as she wound through the tables and dance floor. Charlie was at the end of the line, dancing and enjoying himself until he stumbled and bumped into a waitress who held a tray of drinks over her head as she made her way through the dancers. The multi-colored refreshments doused the woman and the glasses shattered around her feet, leaving her standing in a puddle of sticky drink mixes with stains on her clothes and grenadine clumping with her hair gel. She glared at Charlie as the entire bar turned to stare. She stomped her foot, splashing her leg with margarita mix, let out a strangled cry of frustration, and stormed off to the kitchen.

They quickly left the reggae bar and wandered from place to place, drinking and laughing and forming a human shield around Charlie to protect the wait staff. At one point in the evening, Charlie spotted Alpha and Omega at a bar and pointed them out to Ken and Billy.

"I wonder what was in that briefcase," Charlie said more to himself than anyone else.

"Who gives a shit!" Billy replied over the music. "Let's dance!"

Winding through the city, the group decided to make the bar in the lobby of their hotel their last stop. When they entered the dark, tiki-themed bar, Charlie saw Rock sitting with a miserable look on his face, surrounded by the cast from his movie. No one spoke to him, conversing around him as he simply sat and stared at the dance floor with his chin in his hand.

"Hey guys!" Billy shouted and ran up to talk to the table of men. Rock looked up and saw Billy, then turned expectantly and smiled when his gaze landed on Charlie.

"Hey there Steel Cock Ring Man," Charlie said, approaching him with a drunken grin. He greeted the other actors who nodded back in reply and smirked as they watched him and Rock.

"Hi yourself," Rock replied. "Having a good night?"

"Besides drenching a waitress with sticky alcoholic beverages? You know it." Charlie ordered a drink and as the waiter walked away, he caught sight of Cedric standing in the door to the bar. The director looked around as if searching for someone, even going so far as to stand on his toes and peer over the heads of the people in front of him, and Charlie turned his back as his mood deflated.

But the alcohol he'd already consumed emboldened him, and he smiled at Rock as they talked. Charlie was waiting for the inevitable arrival of Cedric and his screeching voice, but he never arrived. With a glance over his shoulder, Charlie saw Cedric making his way through the crowd in the opposite direction from where they sat. Maybe he needed to use the bathroom before he came over to ruin everyone's mood.

"What are your plans tomorrow?" Rock asked, pulling Charlie back to their conversation.

"Huh?" Charlie blinked at him. "Oh, I was, uh, going to go parasailing off the beach."

"Really?" Rock said. "That sounds like fun. And a little dangerous... for you."

They laughed, and then Charlie heard himself say, "Would you like to go with me? Bernice said she would go, but I think she really wants to go shopping."

"Yeah, all right. That sounds like fun. What time?"

"Eight o'clock."

"In the morning?" Rock asked in surprise. "You're not back on the farm any more, you know."

Charlie laughed. "I like to get an early start on these things. Eight a.m. in the lobby, Mr. Harding."

Rock nodded and saluted. "Okay, I'll be there."

"Charlie!" Bernice called from the dance floor. "Come on! Come dance with us!"

Charlie waved then held up his index finger to indicate he needed a moment. He excused himself from Rock and shouldered his way through the crowd toward the bathrooms. Just as he was about to enter the men's room, the door banged open and Phrank strode angrily through and ran right into him. Charlie bounced into the wall with a grunt, prompting Phrank to stop and apologize.

"Oh my God, I'm so sorry," Phrank said. "I didn't see you, Charlie. I'm sorry."

"It's okay, just a mild concussion," Charlie said with a grin as he rubbed the back of his head. "Everything okay? You look pretty pissed off."

Phrank rolled his eyes. "Everything's fine. I just need some air. I'll see you around. Sorry again."

He walked off and Charlie cautiously entered the men's room. Other than occupants in both stalls, the room was empty. He relieved himself at a urinal then stopped at the sink to wash his hands and check his hair. As he primped in the mirror, one of the stall toilets flushed and the door opened to release Cedric Wilmington. Charlie rolled his eyes, then recalled how angry Phrank had been upon leaving the bathroom and decided Cedric, the tired old bitch, had probably made a pass at Phrank as he had taken a leak. The director narrowed his eyes when he saw Charlie.

"Eavesdropping again?" Cedric asked icily.

"On your bowel movements?" Charlie said. "Not likely."

Cedric turned up his nose and approached the sink as Charlie tore off paper toweling and stepped back to dry his hands. Behind him, the occupant of the handicapped stall flushed and pushed the door open. The door banged into Charlie's backside and sent him stumbling forward just as Cedric turned. He had his mouth open to fire off a sarcastic comment and his hands were dripping wet.

Charlie closed his eyes as he collided with the director. His hands sank into Cedric's soft belly and his lips connected solidly with Cedric's partially opened mouth. The man's lips were cool and dry, and Charlie had the nauseating sensation of kissing bad beef. He tried to pull away, but the floor was slippery and he lost his footing, the motion pressing him even more firmly against the director. Cedric's arms had been trapped between them, his wet hands pressing weakly into Charlie's chest and leaving damp handprints over his nipples. To top it all off, Cedric had horrid breath. He had eaten authentic Mexican food and washed it down with some kind of sugary drink that had coated his throat. Charlie let out a muffled groan of disgust, and when he thought he felt the tip of the director's tongue press against his lips, nearly screamed.

"Oh," the man in the stall said with a start. "Sorry." He scurried out of the bathroom without looking back.

Charlie managed to get his feet firmly planted and pushed himself back as Cedric was finally able to leverage his arms enough to shove him away. Charlie bumped into the stall, tripped over his own feet, and sat down hard on the toilet. As he struggled to stand, his hand connected with the flush toggle and water roared into the bowl, the force of the spray hard enough to splash up and soak his ass.

"Oh, God!" Cedric moaned. He turned and rinsed his mouth out at the sink as Charlie sagged onto the toilet in defeat. His shirt and shorts were soaked, and his lips felt chapped where they had touched Cedric's mouth.

Cedric stepped forward and pulled the stall door open wide so he could glare at him. "Don't ever mention this to another living soul."

"Not top priority on my list of things to do, trust me," Charlie grumbled. "Use some lip balm or something, huh? And chew some gum. Gross!" Charlie ran his forearm over his lips and spat onto the floor a few times.

"You know you did that on purpose," Cedric snapped. "Just trying to get on my good side and give you a break. Well, fluffer, this is one problem you're not going to be able to fuck your way out of." And with that, Cedric turned and stomped out of the bathroom, leaving Charlie to sit dripping on the toilet with his mouth hanging open in shock.

Cedric actually imagined he had done that *on purpose?* He struggled to his feet and made his way to the sink where he turned his back and peered over his shoulder at his reflection. His shorts were drenched. Charlie turned to face the mirror, shuddering at the memory of Cedric's lips and breath as he turned on the water. The faucet splashed water up onto the crotch of his shorts and he hung his head. It was time to give up and leave.

When Charlie returned to the table, he found that Rock had left. The discovery did not surprise him in the least, and he plopped down in the space where Rock had been sitting. The rest of the actors were out dancing with Billy, and Ken and Kinitia were dancing with Bernice. They motioned for him to join them but he shook his head and waved good night. His wet shorts were starting to chafe, and he needed to be up early anyway for parasailing. As he left the bar and headed for the elevators, he saw Phrank standing at a payphone. The man hung up just as Charlie approached and turned to smile at him nervously.

"Hi there," Phrank said. "Done for the evening already?"

Charlie nodded and stifled a yawn. "Yeah. It's been a long day."

Phrank looked him over, taking in his wet clothes. "Have a little trouble in the bathroom?"

"Touchy water pressure in this country." Charlie smiled stiffly and stretched his back. "I am a little sore, though."

"How about a massage?" Phrank said. "The least I could do after almost knocking you out. I've got a room to myself here at the hotel."

Charlie raised an eyebrow. "Oh yeah? Sounds good. Let me get a change of clothes. What room are you in?"

Phrank opened his mouth and then froze, his eyes widening as he looked over Charlie's shoulder. "Uh, I'm in, um, 224. Let's say thirty minutes?"

Charlie turned to see what Phrank had been distracted by and saw Alpha and Omega walking across the lobby to the elevators. The men were looking straight ahead and had not seen Phrank and Charlie at the pay phones. When Charlie turned back, Phrank had vanished and a nearby stairwell door was just hissing closed. With a shrug, he turned and followed the twins to the elevators, just missing their car.

After taking a quick shower, Charlie changed into comfortable shorts and an oversized T-shirt and made his way to Phrank's room. His knock was answered in seconds, and Phrank ushered him inside quickly before closing and bolting the door behind him. Turning, he smiled a little nervously and said, "Okay, ready for that massage?"

"What's wrong?" Charlie asked. "You're as jumpy as a cat on Red Bull."

"Me? No, I'm not jumpy. I'm just, you know, excited you're here." Phrank lurched forward and hugged him tight.

Charlie let out a grunt of surprise at the impact of Phrank's hug. "Why'd you disappear when you saw Alpha and Omega?"

Phrank leaned back and gave him a confused look. "Who?"

"The twins who were crossing the lobby when you took off." Charlie narrowed his eyes. "Did you have sex with them, too?"

Phrank let out his breath and, dropping his gaze, nodded. "Yeah, I did. And I was just a little embarrassed by it, you know? Two guys at once, and twin brothers to boot, you know. Kind of out there. Like, how big of a slut am I, right? So I took off." Phrank turned away and Charlie fidgeted for a moment, thinking briefly of his own encounter with the twins. Phrank turned back to him, flashed a sexy smile, and shrugged. "Anyway, that's not why you're here, right?" He shrugged. "Come on, get those clothes off and let's get your muscles relaxed."

Charlie slipped out of his clothes and sprawled nude across the fitted sheet of the bed. Phrank stripped as well and crawled up to straddle Charlie's butt, his cock nestled within the crack of Charlie's ass. He poured oil into his palm and kneaded Charlie's muscles.

"Wow, you are tense," Phrank said. "Had a lot going on?"

"You could say that," Charlie replied and moaned beneath Phrank's touch. "That feels really good."

Phrank massaged Charlie's aching muscles for almost an hour, after which he sported a rigid boner and pre-come had leaked from the slit to run down the shaft.

"Oh, wow," Charlie said upon rolling over and catching sight of Phrank's condition. "Great minds think alike."

Phrank looked at Charlie's own erection and smiled. "They certainly do."

He took Charlie's dick in his mouth, sucking on the head and wrapping a tight fist around the shaft. Charlie groaned then shifted position to open his mouth and swallow Phrank's long, uncut cock. The pre-come lathered his tongue and throat and he raised his head from the mattress to deep throat as much of the man as possible.

"Oh, that's nice," Phrank said. He lay on his side and pulled Charlie's body over to lie beside him and they both eagerly sucked each other. Charlie pulled the masseuse's foreskin up over the rounded head of his thick cock and slid his tongue into the wrinkled casing. He caressed the soft head with his tongue and then opened wide to gulp down the entire length once again.

Not long after, Phrank's legs stiffened and he grunted around Charlie's cock where it lay lodged in his throat. "I'm going to come."

Charlie pulled the man's dick from his mouth and jerked him off, sending a spray of thick, hot cum over his face and shoulders. Phrank gasped as he continued to suck Charlie's cock, his hand and mouth picking up the pace until Charlie moaned and shot his own load over Phrank's handsome face and strong, tanned shoulders.

"Oh, God," Charlie sighed. "I really like your massage technique."

Phrank laughed then helped him up and into the bathroom where he started a cool shower. Stepping in, Phrank held the curtain open for Charlie and then tipped his head back to let the water run down his body. Charlie stood transfixed, watching Phrank's body hair darken beneath the flow of water. The stream ran along his softened penis and dripped to the surface of the tub. He was like the most beautiful garden fountain ever created.

After he had lathered up, Phrank stepped aside to allow Charlie to stand beneath the spray. Charlie let the cool water rush over him and sighed. It felt so good to just stand still for a moment. Then he felt an abrasive scrubbing across his back and shoulders and groaned. Turning his head, he peered over his shoulder to find Phrank holding a large loofa sponge bubbling with soapy lather.

"This should help peel away some of the dead skin from your sunburn," Phrank said with a smile. "I'll do your back first then wash your front."

Charlie lowered his head and let the water beat the top of his skull as Phrank washed away the dead skin on his back with the loofa. Surely he had died and gone to Heaven. When the masseuse finished washing his back, including his buttocks and legs, Charlie turned and luxuriated in the feel of the water washing the soap off his back as Phrank worked on his chest and stomach. The loofa stung just a bit over his burned skin, but it was a good pain, and Charlie rode it out, thinking about how much better he was going to look in the morning.

After he had rinsed off, Charlie returned Phrank's bathing favor and used the loofa to scrub the man down. He slowly scoured the man's rippling back and shoulder muscles and felt his cock hardening once again. Phrank was a gorgeous, outgoing, kind man; where the hell had he been keeping himself?

"Have you lived in Los Angeles for very long?" Charlie asked as he lathered the small of the man's back.

Phrank shook his head. "Not really. I used to live there a number of years ago, but then I moved away and recently joined the cruise line and came back on a tour I was working. That's when I met you."

"Have you always been a masseuse?"

"Yeah, I got my license when I lived in L.A. the first time."

"So that's just what you've always done?"

Phrank shrugged. "Pretty much."

"How did you find out about working on the ship?"

Phrank turned and looked at him with a grin. "My, you're full of questions tonight."

Charlie smiled and reached down to rub the loofa over Phrank's firm ass cheeks. "I'm just curious. We've had sex three times now, and I hardly know anything about you."

"Yeah?" Phrank turned to display his rising hard-on. "Will this help you solve the mystery?"

Charlie assessed the thickening cock and nodded. "I think it will do for starters." Kneeling in the tub, he closed his eyes and sucked Phrank's quickly swelling cock. Water splashed down over his face and back, wetting Phrank's body as the man groaned.

"Oh, man." Phrank looked down at him. "That is so hot, watching you suck my cock."

Charlie reached up and pulled back Phrank's foreskin and centered his mouth on the fat, slick head. He sucked long and hard on the top inch and rolled his eyes up to watch Phrank's face as the man bent his knees and clenched his fists.

"Oh, shit, Charlie!" Phrank pulled his cock free and turned around to present his tight, pale ass. "Eat my ass. I want your tongue up inside me."

Charlie moved in and set to work on Phrank's trembling hole. The sphincter twitched around his advancing tongue, sometimes clamping down on it and other times allowing it to pass deeper inside. He pressed his hands against the firm ass cheeks and spread them open wide, encouraging Phrank to bend even lower as he began to stroke his long, uncut dick. Charlie pressed his lips around the swollen pink center of Phrank's body and blew a hot stream of air inside him followed by quick flicks of his tongue. Phrank moved back to press his asshole more firmly against Charlie's face then began to bounce his hips up and down, rubbing his sensitive hole along the five o'clock shadow around Charlie's mouth.

"Oh, fuckin' eat that hot ass," Phrank gasped. He closed his eyes and leaned his forehead against the tile of the shower. "Yeah, let me ride that pretty face of yours. Oh yeah, lick it. Suck it."

Phrank continued to hump Charlie's face with his ass for a few minutes, then abruptly straightened up and shut off the water. Turning, he helped Charlie stand up and kissed him feverishly. Their tongues coiled together and moved from one mouth to the other with a hungry rhythm. Phrank grasped their hard-ons in both fists and pumped along them, tightening his fingers as his excitement grew more intense.

Phrank broke the embrace, leaving Charlie gasping for breath and watching him with lust-filled eyes as the man stepped out of the tub. He helped Charlie out and led him dripping wet to the bed where he pulled Charlie down on top of him and resumed kissing and fondling him.

Charlie returned Phrank's embrace for a few minutes until he thought his head would explode, then moved his mouth down to suck at the hollow of Phrank's throat. Phrank moaned and writhed beneath him, encouraging him to move lower still to the man's armpits where he eagerly licked and sucked at the soap-scented skin. He ran his tongue through the dark blond hair of the man's pits, savoring the taste of Phrank's clean pre-sex sweat then moved over to bite lightly at each nipple.

Rising to his knees, Charlie assessed Phrank's hard, red organ and wrapped a steady hand around its base, using his fingers to peel back the foreskin and expose the oozing purple head. He slid his lips over the slick head and tightened them at the ridge where the cap met the shaft where he sucked with a steadily increasing force.

"Oh, God!" Phrank balled up the fitted sheet in his fists and arched his back, sweat standing out on his body as

Charlie continued to suck the pre-come from his pulsing dick.

As Phrank raised his hips from the bed to try and cram more of his cock into Charlie's mouth, Charlie reached down to probed the man's asshole with a gentle but determined finger. Phrank nodded with his mouth open and lowered his body to the mattress then reached down to spread his cheeks apart and allowed Charlie's finger to penetrate him further.

Sliding his hips back on the bed, Charlie shifted position so he could get to Phrank's cock and asshole. He fully inserted his finger inside the hot, quivering hole and bent it slightly as he twisted it in a circular motion, pressing hard against the lump of Phrank's prostate before finger fucking him. As his finger worked Phrank's hole, Charlie deep throated him.

"Goddammit," Phrank panted and raised his head. "I want you to fuck me, Charlie. I want your cock to bang my ass. Fuck me."

Charlie raised his head and, licking his swollen lips, gave Phrank a smile as he continued to twist his finger inside his ass. "I've been waiting for an invitation." He withdrew his finger and crossed the room to grab a condom and a bottle of lube. After applying both, he had Phrank slide down to the edge of the bed then raised the man's muscular legs and gripped his ankles as he leaned over his hairy, sweaty torso.

Looking into Phrank's crystal blue eyes, Charlie pressed his cock steadily into the yielding resistance of the man's flesh and sank completely into him. Phrank closed his eyes and dropped his head to the mattress, his mouth open in a silent cry of pleasure.

Charlie paused for a moment, relishing the feel of

Phrank's muscles as they gripped and released along his invading prick. He pulled completely out of Phrank's hole and realigned his hips to drive himself back in once again to the hilt. He repeated the action, withdrawing and penetrating completely, pausing after each movement until he could stand it no longer. With his dick embedded in Phrank's ass, he adjusted his stance and grip on the man's ankles then began to fuck him. Starting out slow, Charlie soon built up speed until his hips slapped against Phrank's buttocks as he plowed the man's willing hole.

Sweat ran down his face and over his chest and Charlie still found the energy to move his hips faster. His abs clenched and released in time with his pelvis, each thrust delivering the full length of his cock.

"Oh, fuck that ass," Phrank groaned. He had closed his eyes and wrapped his hands around his long, hard cock. "Yeah, fuck me hard."

Charlie banged Phrank's ass tirelessly and watched the big, loose sac of the masseuse's balls as they bounced in time with his thrusts. He wanted to shoot his load over Phrank's clean-shaven balls and long, arching dick.

The thought of coming on Phrank's balls and cock brought him dangerously close to orgasm and Charlie tried to back the spasm off, but it was too late. He could feel the load rushing up through his body and pulled out of Phrank's ass. Stripping the condom away, he aimed his cock and shot his load across the silky surface of Phrank's balls and the length of the man's dick.

"Oh, shit," Phrank gasped and raised his head to look down at the semen covering his balls and cock. He swiped up what he could see and used it as a lubricant as he jerked himself to orgasm. "That was so fucking hot, Charlie. I love having your cum all over my cock. Oh, I'm coming. Oh, God. Oh, yeah."

Phrank's first shot fired over him to land on the sheet a foot above his head. The next shot hit him square in the face, and the final shots hit his chest and belly. Phrank gasped for breath and slowed his hand, finally squeezing out the last few drops onto his palm and raising it to his mouth where he licked it clean as he smiled at Charlie.

"That was an incredible come shot," Charlie said with a grin. "You could be a porn star."

Phrank smirked, closing his eyes and shrugging. "Maybe I was and got tired of it."

They took another shower then crawled into bed, both of them exhausted. Phrank tossed an arm casually over Charlie's chest as they lay naked beneath the single sheet. The spots of cum from Phrank's load lay drying just in front of Charlie's face, and he breathed in the smell of the man's semen as he slipped into sleep.

12

A ROCK BY ANY OTHER NAME

Charlie awoke with a start the next morning and looked around the strange room in confusion. Where was he? Then he smiled as he remembered meeting up with Phrank outside the bar the night before and the hot sex afterwards. He rolled over, his cock twitching in anticipation, then frowned at the empty half of the bed that greeted him. Rising up on his elbows, he looked around the room until his eyes landed on the clock by the bed. It read 8:10 a.m. and he blinked and yawned sleepily. Why did he feel like he was forgetting something?

He got up and staggered into the bathroom to pee, then moments later bolted back out to the room, his heart pounding. He had told Rock he would meet him in the lobby at eight to go parasailing! As he rushed to the phone, Charlie smashed his little toe against the foot of the bed and collapsed in pain. White hot stars of agony blasted through his foot as he grabbed his toe and rolled groaning on the floor. He risked a glance at his toe and cringed at the swollen, red appendage and the beginnings of a purple bruise. Shocking how the smallest part of a person's body could generate so much pain.

He crawled to the phone and dialed the front desk.

"Hi," Charlie croaked after a desk clerk picked up. "I'm looking for a man by the name of Rock Harding. He's tall, dark, and handsome with brown eyes and hair and may be sitting down in the lobby waiting for someone."

"Just a moment please," the young girl said. Charlie could almost picture her scanning the lobby, her eyes narrowed as she assessed the men lingering before her. He wondered idly if what he considered handsome would also be her definition of handsome, and was relieved when a moment later Rock's deep voice came over the line.

"Hello?"

"Hi, it's Charlie."

"Where are you?"

"Getting ready."

"But I called up to your room and Ken told me you didn't come back last night." Rock paused, and when he continued Charlie could hear the smile in his voice. "Did you get lucky and forget about me?"

"Well, yeah." Charlie's eyes popped open as he realized what he had said. "No! I mean, no, I didn't forget about you. I spent the night with someone and overslept, that's all." He felt funny admitting his latest sexual encounter to Rock and hoped it didn't have an affect on their friendship. Which was strange since the man was a porn star and fucked a number of different men each week. But Charlie really cared for Rock and wanted the man to respect him, crazy as that might sound.

"Oh, okay." Rock chuckled quietly. "I'm just teasing you, Charlie. Get ready and come down here. I'll be in the restaurant. Do you want me to order you breakfast?"

Charlie sighed and gave Rock an order of scrambled eggs and toast. He limped into the bathroom and showered quickly then dressed in his clothes from the previous night. After using the edge of a washcloth with a bit of toothpaste on his teeth and tongue, he opened the small complimentary first aid kit and used two band aids to secure his black and blue toe as well as possible. With that done, he limped out the door and down the hall.

The elevator was empty and he took several deep breaths to calm himself on the ride down. As he tried to control his breathing, he noticed small particles floating around him and frowned. What the hell were those? He looked up, saw more hovering above, and panicked. Were they spores? Were they dangerous? He ducked and moved erratically around the elevator car to avoid touching them. As he danced around the small space, he caught sight of himself in the mirrored back wall and came to a sudden halt, his mouth dropping open. His sunburn had begun to peel along his chest, shoulders, and face. The floating particles were flakes of his skin!

Horror filled him as the doors opened on the lobby, and he crossed as quickly as possible to the restaurant, leaving a trail of dead skin wafting behind. Looking around frantically, he spotted Rock in a booth and was about to run over when he stopped. Rock's head was lowered, a plate of eggs before him as he read a folded newspaper placed to the side of his breakfast. Wearing a bright blue tank top, white linen shorts, and sandals, with tousled, gel free hair, he looked like a handsome newlywed groom waiting for his bride.

Charlie's heart jumped at the sight, and he stood in the door to the restaurant for a moment to watch unobserved, forgetting about his peeling sunburn and possibly broken toe. All he could think about was the fact that he was about to spend the morning with Rock Harding and have his undivided attention. Charlie smiled as his heart doubled its beats and his cock began to harden.

A waitress approached Rock's table to drop off a plate of eggs with toast, obviously Charlie's breakfast, and Rock looked up to smile at her. After she had walked off, he glanced toward the door and Charlie felt himself blush when their eyes met. Rock smiled and cocked an eyebrow as he glanced down at his naked wrist as though checking the time.

Charlie laughed and shook his head. He crossed the restaurant and slid into the booth, his blush growing deeper at Rock's assessing gaze. Finally, he could stand it no longer, and he asked, "What? What are you looking at?"

"You're leaving a trail of something behind you," Rock said with a quizzical look. "What is that?"

Charlie sighed. "It's from my sunburn. I'm peeling. I forgot to put on my aloe last night and my skin is peeling." He speared a forkful of eggs with dismay and averted his eyes in embarrassment. Why did something awful always happen when he had a chance to be alone with Rock?

Rock leaned forward and said quietly, "You forgot the aloe because you had the fuck of your life last night."

Charlie choked on his eggs and washed them down with juice. He averted his eyes and dabbed at his mouth, then managed to look up at Rock and nod sheepishly. "Yeah, it was pretty damn good."

Rock sat back, satisfied with his powers of deduction. "I knew it. Anyone I know?"

Charlie shrugged. "A masseuse from the ship. I met him in L.A. before we left and ran into him again on the cruise."

"Masseuse, huh?" Rock nodded. "Sounds fun. I had a masseuse once."

"I've had him four times." Charlie grinned and went back to his eggs.

Half an hour, later they stood on the dock watching a young girl bounce through the air in the parasail contraption. She sat in a flexible harness with a parachute attached as a speedboat below dragged her up into the air and carted her along the beach as she screamed and kicked her feet.

"Please tell me you're not going to scream like that when we get up there," Rock said as they both watched the girl go shrieking past the dock. She hung about one hundred feet in the air and Charlie wondered how his trail of peeling skin would look at that height. Maybe he would appear to be the witch from *The Wizard of Oz* spelling out *Surrender Dorothy*.

"Not unless the rope breaks," Charlie replied.

Rock looked at him with mild panic for a moment. He watched the girl swing through the air as the boat turned around, and said quietly, "Screaming's not so bad."

Since they had asked to ride together, they had to wait for the attendants to change out the harness. The girl who had been screaming through the entire ride laughed hysterically as she stumbled past them and approached her group of friends. She brushed by Charlie and started a small blizzard of dead skin that caused her to sputter and wave her hands.

"Ugh!" she groaned. "What is that? Is that dandruff? Eww! Gross!"

Charlie considered pushing the girl off the dock, but instead lowered his head and sighed. Rock leaned over and whispered, "If it helps any, she just threw up over the side of the dock all over her boyfriend's jet ski."

Charlie looked back and found that Rock had told the truth. The girl, apparently having had sixteen too many mimosas with breakfast, had just launched a barrage of buffet breakfast all over her boyfriend's ride back to the hotel. Charlie chuckled and turned back as the attendant approached them.

"Time for you now," the handsome young man said, and they followed him to the boat. They climbed into the many straps and watched as the man buckled them securely in place. Since Rock was taller, he stood behind Charlie and they were belted together. Rock reached out and pulled Charlie tight against him, the rounded bulge of his crotch pressing hard into the crack of Charlie's ass as he locked his hands around Charlie's stomach. The attendant buckled the last few straps, gave them a knowing grin and winked at Rock.

"Is that good?" the attendant asked.

Rock grinned back. "Better than I've imagined."

Charlie turned his head, feeling a little dizzy from his proximity to the man, but could not see Rock's face. "What are you talking about?"

"Nothing," Rock replied innocently. "Just the straps."

Before Charlie knew it, he and Rock stood at the back of the boat as it powered through the waves. The attendant said, "Ready?" and before either of them could answer, he pulled the ripcord. The chute deployed, lifting the two of them off the back of the boat and up into the air. Charlie sucked in his breath and closed his eyes as his stomach dropped. The force of the lift pressed him tight against Rock's firm, warm body, and his cock began to snake down along his thigh.

"Oh my God," Rock said with a broad smile. "Look at the color of the water."

Charlie cracked his eyes open and looked between his dangling feet. The water stretched out below, clear, blue, and beautiful. It was so clear, he could see coral reefs and sandbars beneath the surface. As the wind blew their hair back, they watched swimmers and jet skiers churn the water between their gently swaying feet.

"It's beautiful up here," Rock said with a sigh. He rubbed Charlie's stomach and leaned forward to press his lips against Charlie's ear. "Thanks for inviting me."

Charlie shivered at the touch of Rock's lips. It took every ounce of will power to keep from turning his head and kissing him. It wouldn't have been too shocking, he supposed. He had sucked Rock's dick and rimmed his ass after all. But that had always been under the guise of work. And kissing was much more intimate than a blow job or a rim job. Out here with no camera crew waiting to film a hot sex scene, it would add a different twist to their relationship. Granted, it was a twist Charlie longed for, but he couldn't fuck things up for Kinitia. Cedric despised him as it was; starting up something more intimate with Rock would surely push the director over the edge. Instead of acting on his impulse, Charlie simply smiled and nodded. "You're welcome."

Rock kept his face next to Charlie's ear a moment longer, then moved back. He pointed down at the beach and said, "Hey, there are your friends. Hi guys!"

Charlie grimaced and considered stopping him, but he could see it was already too late. Kinitia and Bernice stood shading their eyes and peering up at them through their sunglasses. Billy and Ken stood with them, but were too busy looking over the men on the beach to realize Rock had called to them. Smiling in spite of the fact he had been caught by Kinitia spending personal time with Rock, Charlie waved as well and was relieved to see Bernice start jumping up and down and waving both arms in excitement. Kinitia, however, cocked her hips and rested a hand on one as she sipped what appeared to be a bloody Mary, all the while watching them glide back and forth.

When their allotted time was up, they landed gently in the shallows of the water and disentangled themselves from the ropes. Stopping by the photo shack, they located the picture the ground crew had snapped and deemed it worthy of purchase. They each bought a 5 x 7 then headed over to the rest of the Fluffers, Inc. team.

Bernice was aflutter with excitement. "That looks like so much fun! Was it fun? Was it scary? How high were you?"

As Rock laughed and answered her questions, Charlie risked a glance at Kinitia to find her staring at him with pursed lips. He edged closer to her and said quietly, "Nothing's going on, Kinitia. We're just friends."

"You don't believe that bullshit yourself," she replied. "So don't try to convince me of it either. You may as well have been sitting on his dick right here on the beach rather than strapped into that double parachute." She folded her arms and cocked an eyebrow. "Huh."

Charlie shook his head. "We're not having sex."

"Don't you think I know that?" She removed her sunglasses to unleash the full power of her stare on him. "What you're doing is a lot more dangerous. You're getting to know him. I've told you this before, Farm Boy, and I guess I'm going to have to keep telling you over and over again because you just don't get it. This industry is built on casual sex. Sex means nothing in this business. It's a way to make a living. But when you start sharing nights on top of a mesa in the desert and mornings parasailing along a beach, that's when things get complicated. You're a threat to Cedric and his relationship with Rock, you don't have any idea how much of a threat you really are."

"I think you're overreacting."

"Am I? I hope so. Just don't get that nasty old queen riled up, Charlie. I don't want him throwing us out of our building. Got it?"

"Yes, ma'am."

"Hey, what's going on over here?" Rock asked as he and Bernice came back from watching the next parasailer. "No serious talk. This is vacation time! Let's see the city!"

They struck out along the beach and window shopped as they made their way through the crowd of tourists. Splitting off into smaller groups, Charlie and Rock found themselves wandering the street alone and stopped for iced cappuccinos. They sat beneath a shade tree to rest and sipped their drinks in companionable silence for a while until Charlie said, "Rock Harding," very slowly, drawing the name across his tongue.

Rock smirked. "You like that, huh?"

Charlie sipped and nodded. "Is it your real name?"

Narrowing his eyes, Rock said, "Are you a reporter for Gay Video World Magazine?"

"There is such a magazine?" Charlie made a note to subscribe when they returned home. "No, I was just curious."

Rock gave him an assessing look. "I made it up."

"Yeah? So what's your real name?"

"Think you can guess it?" Rock asked.

"Oh, yeah," Charlie said with a laugh. "How many men's names are there to choose from?" His laugh turned into a snort and he froze, embarrassed. Closing his eyes, he willed himself to become invisible.

"That was nice," Rock teased. "Great tonality."

"Shut up." Charlie took a breath and turned to look at Rock's face, ignoring the flakes of skin that floated off his own shoulders. "Let's see: you look like a ... Dave."

"Nope."

"John."

"Nope."

"Jake? Jeff? Steve? Tom? Allan? Kyle?"

Rock shook his head as Charlie exhausted all the male names he could come up with. Finally, Charlie slammed down his nearly empty cup, spattering them with cool liquid, and said, "Oh for God's sake, just tell me!"

Rock took a breath, wiped the cappuccino off his arm, and said quietly, "My name before I changed it was..." Charlie leaned in, holding his breath and raising his eyebrows. Rock eyed him in amusement then said, "Darrell Creeter."

Charlie blinked and sat back. "Darrell Creeter?" He

looked at him for a moment, running the name through his mind as he tried to connect the face with the name. It was no use, he couldn't do it. He would always think of him as Rock Harding.

"Hard to imagine, isn't it?" Rock said with a laugh. "You can't quite get your mind around it, can you?"

Charlie smiled and shook his head. "No, I can't. I like Rock Harding."

"Me too. And not many people know that about me, so consider yourself privileged."

"And warned not to blab?"

Rock smiled. "And warned not to blab."

They grinned at each other, then Charlie turned away and broke the spell. "I guess we should head back to the hotel... Darrell."

Rock shook his head with a smile. "Yeah, I guess so."

That evening, the cruise ship sponsored an extravagant drag show in the hotel bar. Chantilly Lace was the headliner and entertained everyone with several songs involving dancers and flashing lights. Charlie was impressed all over again with Theo's ability to move with such self-assurance in his spiked heels.

At eleven P.M. the bar closed for the night in deference to the hotel's guests, and the crowd migrated to the street looking for places to party. As he wandered through the people emptying out of the lobby, Charlie found Theo sitting on a velvet love seat, dressed in khakis and a white linen shirt, no make up, wigs or heels. As a matter of fact, the man was barefoot. Charlie watched Theo where he sat taking deep breaths with his eyes closed, obviously working to relax himself. Rod Mandrake walked by and Charlie smiled as the director stopped to stare at Theo's feet for a long, lustful moment before continuing on his way out the revolving door to the sidewalk, adjusting the placement of his cock as he moved out of sight.

Charlie sat on the love seat beside Theo. "Hi there. Coming down after your big show?"

Theo cocked an eye open and peered at Charlie. "Oh, hi Farm Boy. No, I'm trying to calm myself down. I lost one of my backup dancers after the show tonight and I don't know what to do. The bitch hooked up with some muscle bound, honest to God bullfighter and has decided to stay here in Mexico, can you believe that? Now I'm short a dancer for the show we're scheduled to perform on the ship in two days. Like bullfighters aren't a dime a dozen in L.A., I mean, really." Theo's voice, deep and masculine at first, had started to rise, and he forced himself to relax, breathing deeply. "Sorry. I'm a little worked up."

"I'm sorry to hear about your dancer. Will it affect your show a lot if one dancer isn't in it?"

Theo's eyes popped open and he looked at Charlie as if he had just asked him to have sex with a farm animal. "You haven't hung out with a lot of drag queens, have you, honey?"

Charlie smiled shyly and shook his head. "No, sir ... er, ma'am. Um, Theo. I haven't."

"Mm hm." He eyed Charlie up and down. "You're actually about his size."

"Whose size?"

"That bitch who walked out on me." Theo stood and grabbed Charlie's hand. "Come with me." He led him into the dark bar and back behind the stage that had been setup during the afternoon. Racks of long, glittering gowns and boas and boxes of treacherous looking heels took up the majority of the space behind the thick black curtain. Charlie followed Theo through the maze of clothes and accessories to a small bathroom in the back.

"Stand here." Theo stepped away and came back with a long, shimmering red dress that he held up to Charlie and eyed carefully.

"Uh, Theo? I'm not very coordinated," Charlie said. "I can't dance very well."

"Nonsense, honey," Theo said absently. "I saw you dancing in here the other night."

"I can't sing, either."

Theo looked at him and smiled a bright, friendly smile. "You are so cute." He pinched Charlie's cheek and turned away.

"Um, thanks. But I'm serious. I can't sing at all."

"Farm Boy, you're so naïve." Theo turned and approached him with a bottle of lotion. "None of us do. It's all lip synching."

"Oh?" Charlie nodded. "Okay." He eyed the bottle. "What's that for?"

"Your skin. You're shedding like some kind of nasty python and I can't have that on my stage. Take your shirt off." Theo smeared a heavy amount of the aloe vera lotion over the peeling surface of Charlie's skin. His strong fingers felt good as they passed over Charlie's body. "You've got some nice muscles here, Charlie. Keep working out, you'll be really buff soon."

Charlie sighed as Theo stepped around before him, the lotion softening his skin and the man's touch sending tingles through his system. Through the open neck of Theo's shirt, he watched the man's muscles ripple beneath Theo's dark skin and felt his cock start to harden. Out of his drag clothes, Theo was a very handsome, strong, masculine man. He stood about six foot three with a shaved head and dark, dancing eyes. His teeth were alpine snow white and flashed in the dim light of the back room as he rubbed the lotion over Charlie's bare chest. Charlie thought back to the memory of Theo lying nude beside Bernice on the sundeck and felt his cock grow another inch.

Clearing his throat, Charlie asked, "So, have you been doing this long?"

The man stopped and looked at him out of the corner of his eye. "What? Wearing dresses, makeup, and heels?"

Charlie shrugged. "Well... Yeah."

Theo raised his chin and said, "Eight years."

"Eight years?" Charlie said. "Wow. Do you have, like, a day job?"

Theo sneered. "One I don't like, but it buys me pretty things. It's boring, trust me."

"What's your last name, Theo?" Charlie asked.

"Riley. Are you done with the third degree?" Theo spread more lotion over Charlie's chest, grazing his nipples with his long, strong fingers.

"That feels good," Charlie said with a sigh.

"Just good?" Theo asked and reached down to grab Charlie's bulging crotch. "Or really good?"

Charlie grinned. "Really, really good."

Theo leaned down and kissed him softly on the lips as his fingers slid into Charlie's underwear. Theo's hand clamped around the swollen length of Charlie's prick and he grunted into the man's mouth.

Moving back, Theo looked down at Charlie as his hand remained in Charlie's pants, fondling his cock. "Would you like to have a little dance rehearsal with Chantilly, or a hot bout of sex with Theo?"

Charlie smiled. "I sort of like Theo right now."

"I thought you might say that." Theo crouched before him and slipped his shorts and underwear down to his ankles. Charlie's cock sprang free and bobbed in Theo's face. Reaching out, Theo wrapped a hand around the base, the dark skin of his fingers making a nice contrast against Charlie's pale hard-on. Theo leaned forward and opened his mouth to slowly suck down first the wide pink head, then the veined and rigid shaft.

"Oh, Theo," Charlie sighed.

Theo increased the rhythm of his sucking until his mouth slurped along Charlie's dick. He pumped the shaft with his hand, bringing Charlie up to a full, almost painful erection. As he sucked Charlie's dick, Theo reached down and freed his own hard-on from his khakis.

"Oh, God, you've gotta stop," Charlie groaned. "I don't want to come yet. I want to suck you, too."

Theo gradually slowed to a stop and stood up, smiling as he kissed Charlie on the lips and swept his tongue through his mouth. "Okay, fluffer. Let's see what you can do."

Charlie knelt in front of the man and took hold of the thick dick before him. It was about nine inches long and still growing. Charlie watched in amazement as Theo's cock struggled up to a horizontal position. It seemed to want to stand straight up along his belly, but gravity and its own monstrous size would not allow it.

"Wow," Charlie said. "That's one big fucking dick."

"Amazing what a lady can hide with some well placed tape, isn't it?" Theo smiled. "Bon appetite!"

Licking his lips, Charlie leaned in and opened wide. He took the dark, thick cock into his throat and was surprised to find himself almost nose to pubic hair with Theo's body. He had a higher gag tolerance than he had imagined. He could feel the bulging head of the man's dick deep in the back of his throat and closed his lips tight around the pulsating shaft.

Theo groaned and smiled down at him. "You got a hell of a deep throat there, fluffer."

Charlie backed off from the big prick to suck and stroke its dark, gleaming length. He reached down and stroked himself as he sucked Theo's dick.

Sliding his tongue down the twisting vein that ran along the shaft, Charlie moved lower to nuzzle Theo's low hanging, clean-shaven balls. He licked and sucked each testicle before opening wide and taking both into his mouth. With his left hand, Charlie kept up a steady rhythm along Theo's cock as he stroked himself with his right.

"Oh, that feels real good, Charlie." Theo tipped his head back as Charlie tugged and sucked at his balls. "Work up that big, hot load. Get it all stirred up in those balls."

After a few more minutes, Theo suddenly reached down and pulled Charlie to his feet then knelt before him. He wrapped a dark hand around Charlie's pale dick and began to suck him with a fast, even rhythm. Charlie groaned and put his hands on Theo's shoulders to steady himself as the man sucked and stroked his cock.

"Oh, yeah," Charlie sighed. "That feels so good. Suck my cock, that's it."

Theo ran his tongue over Charlie's balls and licked up

the taste of sweat as he coated them with a layer of saliva, continuing to stroke Charlie's cock while he licked and sucked his balls.

"Think you can handle my monster cock up that ass of yours?" Theo wondered, grinning up at Charlie from his kneeling position.

Charlie widened his eyes but said, "I can try. It's pretty damn big, though."

"I'll go easy," Theo promised and stood up. He crossed the backstage area and pulled a condom and a bottle of lube from a bag stashed near a dressing table. "I was a Girl Scout. Always be prepared."

Charlie laughed and shed his clothes as Theo stripped out of his, and then the man sat in a straight backed chair. Theo covered the long length of his cock with the condom and smeared it with lube.

"Come over here, Charlie," Theo instructed. "Turn your back to me." Theo slid two lubed fingers into Charlie's hole and worked the gel up into him. "Okay, now, nice and easy. Just lower yourself down onto me."

Charlie backed himself up and crouched down a bit as if to sit in Theo's lap. He felt the pressure of the wide head of Theo's cock as it parted his ass lips and then slid up into him. His muscles clenched and released around it, and he paused every couple of inches to give his body time to adjust. After a very slow, intense descent, Charlie found himself sitting flush on Theo's lap, fully impaled on the man's long, thick cock.

"Oh, baby," Theo breathed into his ear. "Your ass is just as amazing as your mouth."

"They're not half as amazing as that big piece of meat

you've got," Charlie said. He adjusted his position, and then rose up and sank back down, testing his body's acceptance of Theo's dick. It was so big, Charlie gasped and closed his eyes.

"Everything okay?" Theo asked.

"Just getting adjusted," Charlie said. He began to slowly bounce up and down along Theo's dick, listening to the squelch of lube as the big, black cock eased in and out of his asshole.

"That's nice, Charlie," Theo said into his ear then placed a hand on his shoulder. "Just sit right there a minute. Let me try this."

Theo held Charlie in place and thrust up into him. The big cock filled him completely and then quickly pulled out, only to hammer itself home once again seconds later. Charlie grunted as Theo pivoted his hips side to side and up and down, boring into him from different angles and to different depths.

"Oh, God," Charlie gasped. "I'm going to come. Oh, shit!" He stroked himself to climax and watched as his thick white load spurted out over the floor and dribbled onto Theo's toes.

"Oh, tighten that ass on my cock," Theo groaned. "That's it, ride that big cock. Oh yeah, I'm coming." Theo ground his hips up and pierced Charlie to the hilt as his balls emptied their load into the tip of the condom.

Theo sat back down and held Charlie in place with a hand on his belly. His fingers were spread wide as he kept Charlie secure on his lap.

"Damn, Charlie. You're more professional than half the men who get paid to fuck on camera."

"I bet you say that to all the fluffers," Charlie said, and they both chuckled.

Theo slowly pulled out and peeled off the condom as he crossed to the small bathroom and brought back some damp towels. They cleaned up and then Theo leaned down and kissed Charlie softly on the mouth.

"You're good at what you do, Charlie," he said with a grin. "You'll go far."

"You're pretty good at hiding your equipment," Charlie said and reached down to tug playfully at Theo's cock. "You obviously know the tricks of your trade, too."

The following morning, Charlie watched as Chantilly's backup group performed a complicated series of dance moves. The men, two black, one Latino, one white, and one Asian, were wearing high heels with bike shorts and tank tops and moved through the steps with poise and self confidence. Charlie watched from the front of the stage during the first run through and felt his heart sink. The song Chantilly had chosen to begin with was a fast paced, high energy disco revival remix that thumped in Charlie's chest. The dancers kicked and spun, clapped and snapped, twisted and posed with natural fluidity.

Charlie considered his own abilities at movement and rhythm and felt like a three-legged hippo in a herd of gazelle. He was going to not only embarrass himself, but also disrupt the other dancers and ruin Chantilly's number.

The song thumped away in a fade and Chantilly approached, heels clicking on the floor as he wiped the sweat from his bald head. He wore black tights and high heels and he was definitely in Chantilly mode for rehearsal. "Well? Did you get the steps down?"

Charlie glanced at the dancers gathered at the front of the stage with their hands on their double jointed hips and their pulses barely a notch above resting rate. He took Chantilly by a muscular arm and led him through the congregation of tables.

"I can't do that," Charlie said quietly. He stopped and looked up in the man's gentle brown eyes. "There's no way in hell I can learn to dance like that in two days."

Theo smiled patiently. "Charlie, baby. I've seen you move, honey. I know what your body is capable of. You can do the moves."

Charlie shook his head. "I'll fall and I'll take everyone down with me. Candles will fall over and the whole place will go up in flames. Trust me, I do this, I've done it all my life."

Theo took him by the shoulders and rubbed the tense muscles bunched beneath the skin. "Okay, Carrie? You need to calm down now. It's not the prom and no one is going to dump pig's blood over you and no one's going to get hurt, okay?"

"I can't do it," Charlie said quietly.

"Just try."

"I can't."

"Just try."

"My toe is broken," Charlie said, switching tactics. "The shoes alone will mangle my foot forever and I'll have a permanent limp."

"Just try."

"I can't."

Theo finally convinced Charlie to slip into the shoes and walk around the stage as the other members of the group sat at tables sipping bottled water and watching with bored expressions. Charlie winced a few times, almost snapped both ankles several more times, but after thirty minutes found he could walk with a sure stride from one side of the stage to the other. Theo coached him from the floor in front of the stage and had him try some kicks and other simple dance moves.

At one point, Charlie lost his balance and fell on his ass with a thud. This prompted the rest of the dance troupe to stand up and fold their arms as the Asian member of the team cleared his throat to attract Chantilly's attention.

"Uh, we didn't know this was going to be a gay version of *Dirty Dancing*," he said. "And while he's pretty, he's no Jennifer Grey. Can we be excused to do something we consider fun?"

Chantilly smiled patiently. "Harry, you may be excused. Please be back here by eight for another run through, this time with Charlie in the group."

Harry rolled his eyes and the men turned as a group to clickety-clack their way through the bar and out into the lobby. Chantilly turned back to Charlie and said, "Sorry for the interruption."

Charlie fidgeted and stumbled on the heels. "They sounded kind of mad."

Chantilly waved the remark away. "They're high maintenance. Plus I lured them on this cruise with the promise of a vacation and they have been putting in a lot of hours on this number. They deserve some time off."

Charlie nodded then followed Chantilly's instructions and began the routine again.

That evening, Charlie winced as he walked along the streets with the rest of the Fluffers, Inc. team and Theo. His calves ached from dancing in the heels and his toe had been throbbing all day. He had taken several aspirin before leaving the room, but they'd had no effect so far.

During dinner they spotted Alpha and Omega sitting at a table across the restaurant with two Mexican men. The four men spoke in low tones and every now and again glanced suspiciously around the restaurant. From where he sat, Charlie surveyed the floor around them and the seats between each of the men but could find no sign of the aluminum briefcase they had seen Omega carrying the day before.

Although he did not see the mysterious briefcase, Charlie did notice that Theo closely watched the four men. Before he could ask Theo about his interest in the Latin twins, the waiter arrived with their entrees and they all dug in. After taking a few bites, Theo excused himself and Charlie watched the man disappear down the hall to bathrooms.

"So, Charlie," Kinitia said with a grin. "I hear you've been working on a newly discovered talent."

Charlie rolled his eyes. Damn Theo! He hadn't wanted Kinitia or the others to know about the dance number, preferring to surprise them during the show. Plus he didn't want to deal with the teasing he was bound to get before he could prove to them, and himself, he could do it.

"Yeah, you could say that." Charlie raised his head and smiled bashfully. "Theo talked me into it."

"So you're a drag queen now?" Billy asked and smirked. "Are you wearing women's underwear right now?"

"Oh, Billy!" Bernice tittered. "That's not a polite question." She ate a dainty forkful of food, and then leaned over to whisper to Charlie, "Are you?"

They all laughed and Charlie shook his head. "No! I'm not wearing women's underwear. And I'm not a drag queen. I'm doing this to help out a friend."

Theo came back to the table with a box for his food. "I'm sorry, friends, but I have to rush off. One of my dancers has a little problem I need to handle." He dumped the contents of his plate into the carryout box and looked at Charlie. "Nine tomorrow morning?" Charlie nodded and watched Theo walk quickly through the restaurant.

"Huh," Ken said and turned to look at Charlie. "Wonder what that was all about?"

Charlie shrugged and continued to eat. Halfway through the meal, he realized his calves had stopped aching and his toe had ceased throbbing and he sighed. Maybe this whole Vegas showgirl act wouldn't be so bad after all.

13

BORN TO RIDE

Following a two hour practice with Chantilly and his dancers the next morning, Charlie went snorkeling one last time with Ken and Billy. He was amazed again at the incredible underwater life that surrounded him, and it was with a tiny sigh of disappointment that he boarded the ship later that afternoon behind his friends. He already missed Acapulco, and he hadn't even left yet.

The ship set sail with a bleat of its horn and a few curious Mexican citizens waved from the dock, trying to decipher the vessel's name. The passengers on board stretched out to sunbathe in deck chairs or joined in games of volleyball or shuffleboard as well as card games in the lobby. Several others gave or received blowjobs, rim jobs, hand jobs, or intercourse on deck.

Charlie and Bernice strolled the main deck sipping jumbo margaritas. Here and there they caught sight of men making out and, in one instance, a rather in depth blowjob being given off in a corner. Charlie felt himself blush as he noticed Bernice watching the oral sex act with interest.

"Wow, you gay guys really love to suck cock, don't you?" she said with a carefree smile.

Charlie laughed and shook his head. "Bernice, you have no idea."

"Yeah, I guess you're right about that." They continued their walk and paused to lean on the railing and look out over the water. The land fell away, seeming to sink into the sea.

Looking around, Bernice leaned closer to Charlie and asked quietly, "Can I tell you a secret?"

Charlie felt his gut twist nervously. With the way Bernice had been acting on this trip, God only knew what she might blurt out. "Um, okay. I guess."

Turning to place her drink on a table, Bernice carefully raised the short sleeve of her cotton blouse and exposed her left biceps. A large bandage was taped over a majority of her arm and she began to pick carefully at the adhesive.

"Oh, Bernice!" Charlie said with concern. "What happened?"

Bernice smiled at him and pulled gently at the tape. Finally nabbing a corner of the adhesive strip, she lifted the pad of gauze slowly away from her skin. Twin images of interlaced thorny vines had been tattooed around her upper arm, framing the words BORN TO RIDE which had been etched in bold letters.

Charlie's mouth dropped open and he stared in shock. Bernice smiled up at him then tipped her head to look her tattoo over.

"Do you like it?" she asked.

"Uh," was all Charlie could muster.

"I've always wanted a tattoo." She inspected the images a little longer before carefully reapplying the bandage and lowering the sleeve of her blouse. "And I just love Harley Davidsons."

"Uh."

"My ex-husband would die if he knew."

"Uh." Charlie was stunned by her revelation.

Bernice fixed him with a worried look. "Are you okay, Charlie? I didn't scare you or anything, did I?"

"Well..." Charlie broke off as Ken and Billy rounded a corner. "I like it, Bernice. I do. It's just, well, it's surprising is all. You're so sweet and Midwestern and not at all the type to get a tattoo."

Bernice giggled and picked up her drink. "I know. I am just so happy I moved to California and came to work at Fluffers, Inc. You folks have changed my life."

Charlie smiled then reached out to hug her tight, being careful of her left arm. "I'm glad you came to work with us, too. You've made me remember what the city is like to a new comer."

"Hi guys!" Billy called. "We were going up to work out, wanna come along?"

Charlie glanced down at Bernice. "I don't know, guys. Bernice and I were just chatting here and..."

"Oh, go ahead and play," Bernice said with a wave of her hand. "It's your vacation too. And thanks for making an old girl feel young again, Charlie."

Charlie smiled at her and gestured to her left arm. "I don't think you need me to feel young again, Bernice. You're doing a fine job all on your own."

He followed Billy and Ken up to the work out room

where they pulled off their shirts and grabbed towels off a counter. The room was empty, everyone else was either enjoying the sun or had moved themselves to a room for some more intimate action. They spotted one another as they bench pressed free weights, adding more and more weight until even Ken, the strongest of the three, could not lift the bar.

"Wow, did they shut off the air in here, or what?" Charlie wondered, wiping himself down and getting a fresh towel.

"I know I need to be wiped down just from watching," a voice piped up and they all turned to find their short, hunky Latin steward Jorge leaning in the doorway.

"Hi there, Jorge," Charlie said with a smile. "We haven't seen you since we docked in Acapulco."

Jorge grinned and shrugged. "You know that saying 'One in every port'? It goes for gay cruise crew members, too."

"You're looking pretty toned there, Jorge," Billy said as he walked up and felt the steward's arm. "Wow, great arms."

Jorge raised his eyebrows. "You should see the rest of me."

"If you're offering," Ken said and reached down to adjust the growing bulge in his shorts. "We're accepting."

"Come on then." Jorge led them into the locker room and stopped at a low wooden bench surrounded by lockers. He unbuttoned his shirt and let it drop to the floor then peeled the tight white undershirt over his head. He ran a large hand over his muscular chest and flexed his arms for them.

"Good Lord," Ken breathed. "How often do you work out?"

"Twice a day," Jorge replied and grinned at Charlie as he

reached down to unfasten the clasp of his shorts. "And this muscle I work out as often as possible."

His cock sprang out of his tight jockstrap and Billy immediately fell to his knees to grab it in his mouth. He sucked Jorge steadily, his hand gripping the base as his mouth worked at the head. Ken ran a hand over Jorge's impressive chest, tweaking his nipples and feeling every ripple of muscle as his free hand squeezed and massaged his own bulging crotch.

Charlie noticed the outline of Ken's erection and knelt before him. He loosened the drawstring of Ken's shorts and pulled them down to his ankles to expose the swiftly lengthening cock. Ducking his head, Charlie slurped the dick into his mouth as Ken leaned over and kissed Jorge hard.

Billy moved down to lick Jorge's hairy balls, stroking the man's saliva-slick cock with his fist. He reached out to fondle the growing bulge of Charlie's crotch with his left hand as he stroked Jorge with his right.

Ken leaned back from kissing Jorge and pulled his cock from Charlie's mouth. He stroked it a few times and slapped it across Charlie's cheek then slipped it back between Charlie's lips and thrust deep into his throat. Jorge followed Ken's example and soon both men stood side by side, fucking Charlie and Billy's faces.

"Okay," Jorge said and pulled his cock from Billy's swollen lips. "Whose cock do I get to ride first?"

"Definitely mine," Billy said and stood up. He watched as Jorge opened a locker to remove a box of condoms and a bottle of lube. Turning, Billy raised an eyebrow in Ken and Charlie's direction.

Jorge noticed the look and shrugged. "It pays to be

prepared." He slipped a condom over Billy's dick, had him lie on his back along the bench, and straddled his groin. Lowering himself onto Billy's dick, Jorge let it slide completely up into him. He groaned and grabbed his cock as he pumped up and down along the length of him. Billy reached up and grabbed Jorge's balls, pulling them taut as the steward rode his cock.

Ken straddled Billy's face and, spreading his cheeks, planted his asshole over his mouth. Billy lapped at Ken's sweaty hole as Charlie moved to the other end and knelt behind Jorge to suck Billy's balls.

After a few minutes, Jorge eased himself off Billy and had Charlie lie on the bench. The procedure was repeated, and soon Jorge was filling himself with Charlie's dick. Ken straddled Charlie's face and let his balls dangle into his mouth as he stroked himself, and Billy sucked Charlie's balls.

Jorge slowed to a stop and eased off Charlie's cock then looked at Ken with a smile. Ken lay on his back and applied a condom and lube and Jorge sat on his cock as he groaned and stroked himself. He found his rhythm and, as he bounced along the length of Ken's dick, Jorge reached back and pulled the man's legs into the air. He wrapped his strong arms around Ken's thighs and nodded to Charlie.

"Put a condom on it and fuck him," Jorge said.

"Oh yeah," Charlie replied and soon slid deep into Ken's tight, hot asshole.

"Oh, fuck!" Ken groaned. "Jesus, Charlie! Have you gotten bigger?"

"No, you've just been a top too often lately," Charlie replied, and all of them laughed.

Billy moved up to straddle Ken's face, dropping his cock

down into the man's mouth as he watched Jorge stroke himself and take Ken's cock to the hilt. Behind Jorge, Charlie held Ken's feet in the air and plunged his dick deep into Ken's ass.

"Oh, I'm coming," Jorge gasped. "Oh, your dick feels so good up in my ass. I'm going to come." He stroked himself to orgasm and blasted a load of heavy, thick semen up over Ken's chest.

"Uh, uh," Ken grunted around Billy's cock. "I'm coming." He moved his hips up off the bench and his muscles clenched around Charlie's cock as Ken blew his wad into the condom inside Jorge's ass. Jorge waited until Ken had finished then eased off him and turned to hold Ken's legs for Charlie.

Billy pulled his dick from Ken's mouth and replaced it with his balls. He jerked himself off and soon shot his spunk over Ken's belly and up onto Jorge's back. The steward turned and grinned back at Billy as the semen ran down his back.

"Nice shot," Jorge said and Billy grinned in reply.

Charlie kept up his pace and grunted as he shot his load up inside Ken.

"Great workout routine, Jorge," Ken said with a smile. "You do this every day?"

Jorge smiled. "Twice a day. Now, let's shower up, and then you may return to your vacation."

That evening, with a half moon floating over the calm, dark waters, Charlie, Ken, Kinitia, and Bernice sat in the lounge playing a game of euchre when Billy walked up to their table. He was a little out of breath and stopped to breathe deep before saying, "I need Charlie."

Charlie blinked at him. "What's wrong?"

"It's Rock again." Billy shrugged helplessly. "He can't get it up. And he's got a scene scheduled with Alpha and Omega in the wheelhouse. I've been working on him for almost an hour and it hasn't even twitched." He looked down at Ken and sniffed. "Kind of makes me feel a little useless, you know?"

Ken patted Billy's arm. "It's okay, Billy. Rock's under some stress right now. It's not you." He looked over at Kinitia who sat across from him.

Kinitia shook her head and looked at Charlie. "There's nothing we can do, Charlie. You're the only one he responds to. And if Cedric asked for you, then we have to let you go. It worries me, but it's the best thing to do."

Charlie handed his cards to Billy as he stood up. He swallowed the last of his drink and headed up to the command center of the ship. As he mounted the steel steps, Charlie thought back on the time he and Rock had spent together in Acapulco. Had it meant as much to Rock as it had to him?

He stepped out on the top deck just outside the wheelhouse and paused to look down on the ship. The moon illuminated the decks below with a soft, romantic light that etched sharp shadows from objects and people. He watched a male couple as they stopped at the railing to entwine in an embrace and could not help but sigh.

The peaceful mood of the moment was ruined as the door to the wheelhouse slammed open behind him. Charlie turned to find Cedric standing in the door, his wide hips and shoulders filling the frame. The director turned sideways and wedged himself through the doorway, tripping on the raised bottom edge and stumbling forward. Charlie had a moment of panicked flashback to the night in the bathroom of the hotel bar when he had fallen into Cedric and inadvertently kissed the man. As Cedric toppled toward him he instinctively pressed his lips together and closed his eyes. But Cedric missed Charlie by several inches, running instead into the railing to his left where he stopped himself with a heavy *woof* of expelled air.

Cedric stood up, straightened his canary yellow caftan, and lifted his chin imperiously as he finally set his eyes on Charlie. "So, fluffer extraordinaire, it seems I require your services yet again."

"Yes, so it would seem." Charlie glanced toward the open door then stepped toward the director. He was surprised when Cedric took a nervous step back. Was this powerful director afraid of him? He held up his hands palms out and leaned closer, lowering his voice to whisper, "Have you considered trying to help Rock figure out why he keeps seeing that man from his past?"

Cedric's eyes narrowed and he pressed his lips tightly together. Charlie could almost feel the anger coming off him. "Did he tell you about this man?"

Charlie fought back a nervous swallow and leaned away to put more space between them. "Not really. Just that he's been catching glimpses of someone who died several years ago. I don't know all the details." Not the entire truth, but not a lie either.

"Well, it's just from stress," Cedric said. "And I have listened to him. We're sharing a suite, you know. He is my lover."

"I know that, Cedric," Charlie replied cautiously. "I didn't mean to imply anything. I was just thinking a different approach might provide some clues as to why he's been seeing this man and help his... problem."

Cedric sighed dramatically and waved his hands in the air, the sleeves of his caftan billowing like he was practicing semaphore. "Oh for God's sake! You're a fucking fluffer, okay? Just get in there and fluff the man and get him good and hard and ready to go with those twins, and I'll handle his deep psychological issues. Is that okay, doctor Idaho farm boy?"

Charlie gave a stiff, single nod and, without another word, retreated to the safety of the wheelhouse. Inside the room, he stopped and stared at all the computerized equipment beeping quietly and glowing softly, automatically steering the ship through the waters toward their next port of call. Over by the large steering wheel, more decorative than functional he would imagine, he saw Rock sitting alone and forlorn in a padded swivel chair. He wore a jockstrap and had crossed his bare feet at the ankles as he stared blankly at a radar display before him.

Alpha, Omega, and a few crew members sat across the room watching Charlie as he assessed the situation. Turning his head, Charlie said quietly, "Can we have a few minutes alone, guys?"

The men muttered under their breath but got up and filed out the door. As Alpha passed by Charlie, he whispered, "This guy is becoming more and more worthless."

"Just give me a few minutes, okay?" Charlie closed the door on them then crossed the room to lean before Rock on the instrument console. "Still having a little trouble with the pump?"

Rock smiled without looking up. "You could say that."

Charlie stretched his neck a few times and knelt between Rock's legs. "Just relax, Darrell," he said quietly as he reached into the pouch of the jock.

Rock chuckled. "I'll never hear the end of that from you, will I?"

"Probably not." Charlie pulled his hand out and brought Rock's limp cock with it. He squeezed the base and softly stroked the dick he fantasized about so often. "Okay, we're going to get you up and ready to go, and then you're going to shoot this scene. Got it?"

Rock smiled down at him and trailed a finger along his cheek. "Got it. Thanks, Charlie."

"For what?"

Rock shrugged, still smiling. "Just for being here."

Charlie smiled back and took a breath before diving down onto the slowly enlarging cock. He took the dick to the root and let it sit in his mouth for a time, gently nursing it. Rock's legs relaxed slowly, stretching out beside Charlie's face, and then he felt the steady push of the man's cock at the back of his throat as it hardened in his mouth.

Closing his eyes, Charlie moved his mouth up and down the shaft, Rock's prick growing longer and fatter with each pass of his lips. He sucked the man to full blown erection and then backed off, wiping the back of his hand over his swollen lips. Rock opened his eyes and looked down at Charlie with a small, sexy smile.

"Done already? I was just starting to get into it."

Charlie grinned and stood up. "So was I, and that's when bad things happen. I'll go tell the others."

After Charlie opened the door, Cedric stomped past

without a word and snapped his fingers at the cameraman who had followed him through the door. Lights blazed to life, and Charlie stood off in a corner as he watched the scene unfold before him.

Alpha and Omega began to kiss and stroke Rock's body, their Latin coloring just a shade darker than Rock's tanned skin. The twins moved slowly down the length of Rock's body and Alpha sucked his dick while Omega licked his asshole.

Rock groaned and leaned forward, stretching out over Alpha to open up his ass cheeks for Omega's probing tongue. Charlie's cock twitched as he watched Omega eat Rock's hot, shaved asshole, and he shifted position as he thought back to the times he had rimmed the man himself during a few of their fluffing sessions.

Alpha and Omega stood up and pushed Rock to his knees where he sucked first one then the other. As he sucked Alpha's cock, Rock stroked Omega's, reversing the process when he shifted his oral attentions. At one point he had both heavy, thick dicks in his mouth and sucked them while he stroked himself.

Charlie licked his dry lips as Rock stood up to bend forward over the back of the chair bolted to the floor in front of the console. Alpha rolled on a condom and entered Rock from behind as Omega stood in front of Rock to pump his cock between Rock's lips. Charlie remembered the position from his time spent with the twins and fought against the urge to reach down and stroke himself. Instead, he watched with wide eyes as Alpha's cock fully penetrated Rock's hole with each thrust. He could hear the sweaty slap of skin each time Alpha's thighs connected with Rock's ass cheeks. Rock rode the big Latin cock up his ass as he sucked Omega's dick and stroked himself.

Charlie almost groaned when Alpha pulled out and stripped away the condom to jerk himself off onto Rock's back. Omega watched his brother shoot his load, and then pulled his dick from Rock's mouth and stepped up, stroking his cock furiously until he grunted and shot his cum across Rock's shoulder blades. The white puddles of semen stood out starkly against Rock's tan skin.

Rock straightened up himself, head back and eyes closed as he jerked off onto Omega's flat stomach, Alpha reaching around from behind to twist his nipples. Rock leaned his head back and kissed Alpha deeply as he caught his breath, and then Cedric yelled, "Cut!" and the hot studio lights were switched off.

Charlie noticed the temperature in the small room dropped several degrees after the lights had been shut off, and he stepped out into the cool night air with a sigh of relief. Deciding he was too worked up after watching the scene to be able to hold anything resembling an innocent conversation with Rock, he descended the steps and went to the casino to find his friends.

14

THE OVER THE TOP DRAG-A-RAMA

The morning of the show, billed with great fanfare as The Over the Top Drag-a-rama, Charlie slept in until ten. He staggered into his small bathroom and showered leisurely, being careful of his bruised and swollen toe. He was supposed to meet the others from Fluffers, Inc. for brunch around eleven, and then rehearse for two more hours with Chantilly and his group. After that, the day was his until show time that evening.

He dressed in a loose fitting button down shirt and khaki shorts. Carefully easing his injured foot into a sandal, he wished his other shoes were roomier in the toe area so he wouldn't have to leave himself open to being stepped on at breakfast. He had learned over the course of his life that if some kind of freak accident could happen, with him it more than likely would. A few minutes later he was seated at a dining table with Bernice, Ken, and Billy. Kinitia was nowhere to be seen.

"Where is she?" Charlie asked, watching with mild horror as Billy smothered his scrambled eggs in hot sauce.

Bernice shrugged. "I don't know. She didn't come back to the room last night."

The three men stopped with food halfway to their mouths to stare at Bernice.

"What did you say?" Ken asked.

"She didn't come back to the room last night." Bernice looked at them in turn, suddenly nervous. "What? What's wrong?"

Billy glanced at Ken and Charlie with a frown. "Well, correct me if I'm wrong, but this ship is pretty much stocked with gay men. Who did she spend the night with?"

"And where?" Charlie wondered. "God, I hope she's okay."

"You don't think she had too much to drink and fell overboard or anything, do you?" Ken said with low panic in his voice. "Oh my God, what if that's it?"

"Good morning people," Kinitia said as she swooped up in a swirling red caftan and sat down. She smiled broadly at each of them and picked up a menu. "Goodness, I'm starving. I could eat one of everything on the menu." She perused the menu for a moment then raised her eyes to find the four of them staring at her. "What?"

"And how was your evening?" Ken asked, his eyes twinkling with mischief.

Kinitia smiled. "Fine, thank you. And yours? Did you hook up with Marcelo like you had planned?"

"Marcelo?" Billy said and turned to look at Ken. "*I* had sex with Marcelo last night. When were you with him?"

Ken looked at Billy with amusement. "About eight."

Billy raised his eyebrows. "I was with him at ten. You mean I had sloppy seconds? No wonder his come shot was just a lot of dribble. Fuck."

Ken turned back to Kinitia, waiting until she had placed her order with the waiter to say, "And where did you spend the night?"

Kinitia glanced up as she sipped her coffee. Her eyes darted to the others at the table and returned to Ken. "I'm sorry, were you speaking to me?"

Ken laughed and sat back, folding his arms. "Yes, Princess Jones, I was."

"Oh, sorry." She dabbed her napkin to the corners of her mouth, and then looked blankly at him. "Could you repeat the question?"

"Oh for God's sake," Billy said in exasperation. "We just want to know who you could find to fuck on a ship full of cocksuckers, okay?" They all laughed as Billy blushed. He lowered his eyes and said, "Sorry, I forgot myself for a minute there, boss."

"You have heard the term bi-sexual before, have you not?" Kinitia asked, and they all nodded. "Good. And, just so you know, I had a perfectly decadent evening, and do you know what a lady says about her decadent evenings?" She leaned forward conspiratorially and looked around to make sure no one else was in earshot. They all unconsciously mimicked her, leaning in over the table. She took a breath and said quietly, "Nothing."

Charlie sat back with a smile and shook his head as he resumed eating. "Well, whoever he was, he's a lucky guy. I'm glad you got to have some fun on this trip."

Kinitia nodded to him. "Thank you, Farm Boy. And how

did your emergency fluffing session turn out? Keep him at the edge long enough without losing the pop?"

Charlie smiled. "Yes, I did. And the scene turned out great. Cedric even glanced at me as I left the room once the scene had been filmed."

"Oh, my," Bernice said with a chuckle. "Almost could be construed as a 'Thank you', huh Charlie?"

"Or a fuck off and die then rot in a vat of your own waste," Billy muttered, and they all stared at him in stunned silence. He looked up from his plate. "Sorry. Was that my out loud voice?"

When they were finished with brunch, Charlie made his way to the show room where the evening's performances were going to be held. The tables had all been arranged and he made his way through their ranks to the wide stage. He still could not believe he was going to be performing backup for a drag show in just a few hours. Wouldn't Ben Whistler back home in Idaho just fall over if he could see this?

He found Theo backstage wearing a black leotard and a massive feathered headdress with a wing span of about seven feet. He was in complete Chantilly mode, wearing bright red, three-inch heels that went with his costume, the black leotard and gigantic headdress. He smiled as he saw Charlie.

"Hello, Farm Boy. I hope you're ready to sweat your ass off."

"How many pterodactyls went bald for that hat?" Charlie asked.

Theo laughed and led him backstage to help him change. "Technically, no pterodactyls were harmed in the making of this headdress, because they did not have feathers."

Charlie shrugged as he stripped down to his underwear.

He sat down and pulled the leotard gently over his injured foot. With that done, he coaxed the heels onto his feet and sat stiff backed as Chantilly and another dancer lowered a headdress onto his head that was only slightly smaller than the one worn by Theo. Charlie felt his neck sway under the weight of the thing and looked at himself in the mirror with curious wonder. What the hell had he been thinking? He had all the grace of a drunk rhinoceros, how was he going to perform complicated dance moves wearing high heels and a twenty pound headdress?

"How's it feel?" Chantilly asked. "We just finished them this morning."

"I didn't know it was going to be this heavy," Charlie said as he tried to keep his head from swaying. "I feel like my neck is going to break."

"We had to use more foam in the back to support the feathers because they kept falling over," Chantilly explained. "Stand up and try to walk."

Charlie struggled to his feet and the heels betrayed his ankles a few times as he toppled to the left and right. Any slight tilt of his head became a frightening stumble as the headdress pulled his head and then the rest of his body to that side. He wound up on his ass several times before Chantilly removed the headdress and click-clacked off to the depths backstage to adjust the configuration.

Sitting in his chair and stretching his neck muscles, Charlie caught sight of someone standing across from him. He looked up and found Harry, the Asian backup dancer and, it would seem, the leader of the backup group, staring at him.

"Amateur," Harry said with narrowed eyes. "Now we

have to wait for you to get special treatment." He turned, the feathers of his headdress floating gently in the breeze as he walked gracefully away, his hips swinging and his headdress holding steady. Charlie marveled at the man's equilibrium and let out a sigh. Standing up, he began to practice the dance moves in his heels, wincing now and then as the pointy-toed shoes pinched his injured toe.

Hours later, having endured a long, labor intensive rehearsal that made Charlie more sympathetic toward beauty pageant contestants across the globe, he limped back to his room. He wanted nothing more than a shower and some sleep. His calves had cramped up from the heels and his toe ran a bass beat of pain through his body that could compete with any gay disco.

He luxuriated in the hard spray of water in his tiny bathroom shower and then headed up on deck. His sunburn had stopped peeling, thank God, and he was not about to make the same mistake twice. Pulling a chaise off into the shadow cast by the upper decks, Charlie stretched out in the shade and sighed as he drifted off.

Awaking slowly, he blinked and glanced around, wishing he had thought to bring his watch. He sat up and yawned, stretching as he looked around the deck. It had emptied since he had fallen asleep, and he felt a slight panic. It couldn't be time for dinner already, could it?

He got up and made his way around the deck to the bar where he would be able to see a clock. He shuffled sleepily across the deck and rubbed his tired eyes as he reached the bar and blinked to find himself standing beside two naked men. One of the men, an actor he had fluffed on Rod

Mandrake's set, sat up on the bar as another actor sucked his cock, making wet, greedy slurping sounds.

"Oh, sorry," Charlie muttered, then turned to find the young, bookish director, Simon Marshall, and his camera crew standing a few feet away. The cameraman, a burly guy named Roger, stood with his arm resting on top of the equipment, a mixture of amusement and annoyance on his face as he slowly gnawed a toothpick. Simon stood rigidly beside the camera with a stony expression on his face and his arms folded over his chest. Behind Simon and the camera crew stood a large group of people, all onlookers who had been watching the scene Charlie realized he had just interrupted. He looked at the smirking faces gathered behind the camera crew and felt his heart sink.

"We've been working on this scene for the past hour, Charlie," Simon said, his voice frighteningly quiet as he walked up to stand beside him. "And you just walked right into the middle of it like you were the only person on board this ship."

"I'm sorry, Simon," Charlie squeaked. "I fell asleep over there in the shade and just woke up and I came over here to see what time it was. I didn't know you would be filming here."

"We posted a notice."

"I didn't see it, I swear."

Simon leaned in closer and asked quietly, "Are you sure you're not some kind of double agent from a rival studio?"

Charlie let out a nervous laugh. "I'm just unlucky. Promise. I'm sorry." Simon turned and started to walk away. "Um, Simon?" The director stopped, sighed, and turned back. "Do you happen to know the time?"

Simon's lips curled into a sneer but he flicked his wrist and checked his watch. "It's five o'clock."

"Oh my God! That late? Thanks, Simon!" Charlie walked quickly, limping just a bit, back to the chaise to get his towel. He then dashed passed the bar again just as Simon called, "Action!" which was followed immediately by, "Cut! Dammit, Charlie!" Charlie called an apology over his shoulder as he walked quickly down the steps. He had to get to his room and change for dinner, after which he needed to head directly to the show room.

Turning a corner, Charlie ran full tilt into Cedric and bounced back against the wall. The director shrieked and flailed his arms as he tried to catch his balance, but it was no use. He fell on his ass with a shriek. Charlie gasped and reached down to help Cedric stagger to his feet.

As he stood up, Cedric inadvertently stomped on Charlie's injured toe with a silver platform shoe. Charlie cried out and slumped against the wall in pain, tears running down his face.

"Oh, sorry," Cedric said absently. "Excuse me, I'm trying to find someone." And he was gone.

"Oh, God," Charlie moaned, cupping a hand over his screaming toe. Turning to watch as Cedric strode away, he muttered, "Cunt," then got up and limped to his room.

Taking a handful of aspirin with dinner, Charlie was hyper alert for all possible threats to his feet. He whined to Ken about his fears until the man finally relented and let Charlie extend his leg up over the tops of his thighs, elevating his throbbing toe and keeping it from the dangers lurking beneath the table as everyone around him shifted the positions of their feet. He had a light meal, too nervous to do more than pick at his food, and left the table early. His stomach was in knots as his friends wished him luck and promised to be there for the show. What had he been thinking when he had agreed to do this?

After limping into the showroom, Charlie got dressed and, much to his surprise, thought he looked pretty convincing. He wore a painfully bright, multi-colored Spanish style dress with several layers of crinoline from the waist down and a stiff, brilliant yellow collar standing up in back. His wig, a blond flapper cut complete with curls along the sides of his face, had been stuck firmly on his head beneath the tall feathered headdress that Harry and another dancer named Kurt strapped beneath his chin. His shoes, waiting with evil intent beneath his chair, were bright red pumps with three-inch heels.

Charlie sat patiently as Harry and Kurt fussed over the headdress, their frustrated sighs and stomps of their heels making him smile. A backstage assistant crouched before him applying makeup and Charlie tried to keep his injured toe out of everyone's path. He was going to wait until the last possible moment before slipping on his shoes. Out on stage he could hear the Jewish drag queen Helen of Oy going through her routine to rousing laughter, and Charlie's stomach began to flutter with nerves. They were going on next.

Helen ended her set with a song entitled "Matzo Mia" and the crowd roared approval. She backed smiling through the curtain, then, out of sight of her adoring fans, turned and pushed past Chantilly without a word. Apparently, Helen had felt slighted at not being asked to headline the show. To her credit, Chantilly ignored Helen and stood at the front of the line of dancers, turning once to glance over each of them, Charlie bringing up the rear, and give them all an encouraging smile. The emcee called out her name and the music began as the curtains parted to what Charlie perceived as thunderous applause. He held his head high, stiffened his arms in a classic Spanish dancer pose, secured his feet painfully inside his shoes, and followed little Kurt through the curtains and into the blinding, boiling lights onstage.

"Woo hoo!" Someone shouted from the blurry faces of the audience. "Go, Charlie!"

The music picked up and they assumed their places, Chantilly at stage center and her dancers spread out behind her. Charlie felt his head teeter a bit beneath the weight of the headdress, but other than that he thought he looked pretty good. The music stopped and silence fell dramatically on the room until the audience began to applaud once again. A few seconds later, the music boomed back into life and they began their routine.

15

CHARLIE BRINGS DOWN THE HOUSE

It was all going rather well, if he did say so himself. Even his toe had stopped throbbing as his body kicked out enough adrenaline to revive a recently deceased bull elephant. Charlie did not think about anything except for the sound of the music and his next move. He was living totally in the moment, beads of sweat popping out beneath his heavy make up.

And then he took a wrong step. It was not a big mistake, nothing anyone would have readily noticed from the audience because he stood in the back of the line of dancers. But the misplaced step was enough of a mistake to put his injured toe in the direct line of Kurt's size twelve spiked heel. The man brought the back of his foot down hard on Charlie's quietly aching appendage and brought it screaming back into focus. Charlie gasped and tears flooded his eyes, blinding him as he stumbled and tipped his head back. The headdress made more than a passing acquaintance with gravity and pulled him backwards, his neck stretching as if it might tear right off his shoulders. He reached out, flailing for something to grab onto and stop his impending descent to the floor, and he caught the only thing standing between him and the back stage area: the curtain.

The crowd gasped as Chantilly struck a final pose and smiled broadly as the dancers surrounded her with their feathered headdresses. And then the music died out and the tearing, ripping sounds became clear. Charlie saw her turn with the rest of the group and watch in horror as the entire length of heavy black curtain hiding the backstage area came down in a cloud of dust and a heavy *thump*. Helen of Oy was exposed, still in full makeup and in the process of removing a painfully tight girdle. She shrieked and fled into the backstage bathroom, locking the door behind him as he cursed in Yiddish.

Charlie lay trapped beneath the heavy, dusty curtains, feet kicking weakly as he tried to breathe. He heard the click clack of heels approaching, and then multiple hands prodding and pulling the curtains apart. At last the final layer of curtain was pulled away and Charlie took a deep, grateful breath of fresh air as someone pulled him to a sitting position.

"Are you hurt?" Chantilly asked.

Charlie could see Rock directly behind her, and Ken, Billy, Kinitia, and Bernice just behind him.

"I'm okay," Charlie said, and coughed some of the dust from his lungs. "Sorry I ruined your number."

"Oh, baby, no," Chantilly said with a shake of her head, and she and Rock helped him to stand up. Charlie's legs wobbled in his heels and his headdress was, amazingly, still attached.

"Are you okay?" Rock asked, concern in his eyes. "You're not hurt are you?"

Charlie shook his head and raised a hand to steady his headdress. "Just embarrassed. I feel like an ass."

"Well, you should be used to that," Ken said, and they all managed a chuckle.

"Take those damn shoes off," Billy said. "You're going to break your leg."

"I can't," Charlie moaned. "My feet are swollen, and I need to work them off. Here, let me go over and sit down." The crowd, seeing that he was unhurt and now looking for something else to occupy their time, began to disperse as Charlie stepped carefully over the fallen curtain to sit in a chair in the middle of the backstage area. Reaching up, Charlie unfastened his headdress and sighed when Ken lifted it off his head.

"Wow, that thing weighs a ton," Ken noted as he set the headdress down.

"Tell me about it," Charlie sighed.

"Hey, isn't that Cedric? Wow, he looks pissed," Billy said and they all turned to look. Sure enough, Cedric stood at the deck railing just outside the show room door, having what appeared to be a heated discussion with someone just out of their sightline.

"Jeez, he looks angry," Charlie said. "Wonder who he's yelling at now?" He remembered that Rock was with them and felt his face flush as he turned to see if the actor had heard. Rock did not seem to be listening, however. Instead, he walked toward the door, a frown creasing his tanned good looks as he moved to see who stood on the receiving end of Cedric's wrath.

Rock stopped suddenly, his fists clenching and his eyes going wide as his jaw dropped. Charlie could not stand it any longer and struggled to his feet to wobble his way across the floor and stand behind him. Looking over Rock's shoulder, he saw Cedric lean forward and jab a plump finger into the chest of the man standing before him, his words carried away by the wind before they could reach them inside the show room. Charlie looked up along the well-built chest and gasped at the sight of Phrank's handsome, repentant, and slightly annoyed face staring down at the director.

"Holy fuck," Rock said quietly. "It's him!"

"Him? Him who?" Charlie said then stumbled forward as Rock strode toward the door. Ken, Billy and Chantilly stepped up to stand beside Charlie, and the other dancers from Chantilly's group gathered around behind them, all of them still wearing their headdresses and framing them in feathers as the four peered curiously out the door.

Then Charlie understood what Rock had meant.

Phrank was *him*, the man Rock had left for dead that morning so many years ago. Only he hadn't died, he had just been stoned out of his mind and Rock had freaked out. But why was Cedric yelling at Phrank? Had he had a bad massage experience?

Their curiosity getting the best of them, they moved forward as a unit, the backup dancers walking as quietly as possible in their heels as they approached the door in time to see Rock walk up and reach out to grab Phrank by the front of the shirt.

"You!" Rock shouted in his face. "You're supposed to be dead!"

"Oh, my God," Phrank said in surprise. "Rock! What? What do you mean?"

"I thought you had died!" Rock snapped, his cold, dark eyes boring into Phrank's face. "I've been torturing myself for all these years thinking I had something to do with your death and..." He stopped and suddenly whipped his head around, catching sight of Cedric as the director tried to sneak away. "Oh no you don't, Cedric! Get your ass back here!"

Cedric stopped and straightened his back as the dancers all said, "Ooooo," very quietly. Chantilly silenced her team with a swift glare then turned back to the scene playing out before them.

"You made me think he was dead." Rock walked up to grab Cedric by the collar and drag the whimpering man back to stand beside Phrank. "You've known all along he was alive and you let me go on believing he was dead."

"Rock," Phrank said with his palms up. "I want to go on the record right now as saying I knew nothing about my supposed death, okay? I woke up late that morning to find Cedric in my room and he told me you hated that I was doing drugs, that you hated me and wanted me out of the city and he was there to see that it happened. So I took the cash that he offered me and I went down to San Diego. I never knew you thought I was dead."

"Liar!" Cedric shouted and turned to Rock. "It was his idea from the start! He wanted to get away from you. He said you were suffocating him and he begged me to tell you he had died of an overdose. He didn't think you would let him break up with you. He thought you were obsessed with him."

"What?" Phrank leaned over to loom above Cedric. "That's a lie! Take that back."

The small group watching from the doorway turned to look as two men rounded a corner on the otherwise vacant deck. It was the Latin twins, and Omega carried the aluminum briefcase he had acquired in Acapulco. When the twins rounded the corner, they stopped in their tracks and stared at Rock, Phrank, and Cedric with anger in their eyes. At the same moment, Phrank saw the twins and froze. His face went pale, and he turned to flee. Rock saw Phrank run off and shouldered Cedric aside to pursue him. The group watching from the door leaned back as the twins ran past in pursuit of Phrank and Rock, looked at one another for a moment, then burst into motion as one and took off after them.

Phrank collided with several waiters bearing trays of drinks. He snatched a silver tray from one and flung it behind him. Rock dodged the projectile but the tray flew like a Frisbee and caught Omega in the chest. The man slipped on a puddle of pina coladas and fell on his back, the silver briefcase clanging against the deck. Alpha paused to turn back and help his brother but Omega waved him on. "Get him!"

Charlie and the rest of his group slid to a halt a few feet from Omega's head. The actor raised his eyes and peered up at them as they stared down at him, then Chantilly reached out with a red high heel to kick the briefcase out of his hand and across the deck toward the railing.

"No!" Omega cried. He crawled after the case, his eyes wild.

"Charlie!" Chantilly said. "Get the case!"

Charlie stood at the far edge of the group, only inches from the briefcase. He blinked at Chantilly, looked down at

Omega crawling speedily toward him with a crazed, angry look in his eye, then bent down and picked up the case. It was surprisingly heavy, and he tottered back on his heels against the railing. Omega's grasping fingers barely grazed the hem of his dress as the backup dancers shrieked at Charlie's close call.

"What now?" Charlie looked over at Chantilly.

"Run!" Chantilly said and waved him in the direction they had come, away from Rock, Phrank, and Alpha.

Charlie hesitated a moment, long enough to see the building fury in Omega's eyes as the man reached for him again. Then he turned and hobbled as fast as his injured foot would allow. His skirts were tight, preventing him from lifting his knees and running outright, and behind him he could hear Omega struggling to stand.

He rounded the corner of the deck and ducked into a stairway leading down into the maze of corridors below decks. Behind him, he heard Billy, Ken and the other dancers shouting and calling out instructions as they tried to block Omega's path.

After rounding a few corners, Charlie lost track of where he was within the depths of the ship. He came to a four way intersection and stopped to look behind him, letting out an involuntary squeal of panic as he saw Omega stomp around the far corner. The man shouted at him in Spanish and Charlie took off at a brisk walk, hugging the briefcase to his chest and wincing every time his injured foot touched the floor. What the hell was in the damn briefcase? And why had Chantilly told him to run with it?

Omega caught up to him in the hall near the doctor's quarters and grabbed him by the shoulder, spinning him around. As he turned, Charlie used the weight of the briefcase as a projectile to pound it into Omega's gut. The man doubled over and Charlie stepped back out of his reach. He turned to run again but the heel on his left shoe snapped off and he toppled hard against a door, hitting it with his shoulder at lock level. The door broke in and he fell in a heap of colored satin and crinkling crinoline onto the floor of Dr. Garth Tanner's quarters.

"Oh!" someone gasped.

Charlie raised his head, straightened his wig, and looked at the scene before him. Rod Mandrake stood at the side of the bed. He wore the nanny dress, hat, and clunky shoes so familiar to Charlie. In one hand, he held the doctor's hairy ankles raised high in the air, while in the opposite hand he held the wooden paddle poised for a good, hard swat at Garth's bare, reddened ass. The doctor wore his bonnet and leaned out to look around Rod at Charlie.

"Charlie?" Dr. Tanner said. "What are you doing?" His eyes lifted and he blinked in surprise. "Oh. Omega."

The large Latin man stopped in the doorway, chest heaving as he tried to catch his breath. He surveyed the men before him, and everyone was so stunned that nobody moved. Shaking his head at the scene, Omega reached down for Charlie's arm. "You just can't get enough of that, can you doc?"

Charlie lay tensed and ready, his fingers gripping the briefcase tight beneath him. When he felt Omega's fingers touch his arm, he rolled onto his back and brought his good foot up, connecting solidly with the man's groin. Omega fell with a crash and Rod and Garth both winced in sympathy. Charlie got to his knees and crawled into the hallway, then stumbled to his feet and began to run awkwardly on the three-inch difference in the height of his shoes.

As luck would have it, he nearly collided with Phrank and Rock at a three way intersection where his hallway ended. The two men tore past, spinning Charlie around until he stood dizzy and disoriented in the middle of the halls, facing back the way he had come. He blinked in surprise at the sight of Omega limping along toward him, one hand cupping his injured testicles, and then turned his head to find Alpha, continuing his pursuit of Rock and Phrank, coming at him from the left. Charlie turned and fled after Phrank and Rock, his arm growing tired from carrying the heavy briefcase.

At another hallway intersection he breezed through only to hear someone call his name. Turning, he found Bernice and Kinitia standing in the middle of the hall, drinks in their hands and concerned looks on their faces.

"What's wrong?" Kinitia asked.

"Run!" Charlie wheezed and turned to continue his flight. He heard the women fall into step behind him, each trying to save as much of her drink as possible. Behind Bernice and Kinitia came Alpha, followed closely by Omega, and behind them Charlie could hear Ken, Billy and Chantilly along with the other dancers from Chantilly's troupe.

The entire, ridiculous chase came to an end outside of Charlie's stateroom. He rounded the corner to find that Rock had tackled Phrank and was crawling up along the man's body with an angry look on his face, fists clenched and ready to fly. As Charlie came around the corner, Rock brought his fist back to deliver a blow to Phrank's face, but instead struck Charlie in the chest and knocked him off balance. Charlie fell against the door to his own stateroom, his head banging against the wood, and slid down along it to sit on the floor with his back against the door, slightly stunned. Reaching up, he turned the knob and fell flat on his back, upper half of his body inside the room as Kinitia and Bernice turned the corner and cried out.

Rock got up and stepped over Charlie where he lay in a mass of fabric then reached down to drag him all the way inside the room, a look of concern on his handsome face. He seemed to have forgotten all about Phrank as he lifted Charlie's head and said, "Oh, Charlie. I'm so sorry. Are you okay?"

Charlie nodded up at him, exhausted and sore, his hands still locked around the briefcase. Kinitia and Bernice crowded into the room, and then Alpha and Omega barreled their way in, pushing Phrank in front of them. Alpha closed the door behind him and pulled a gun from the waistband of his shorts. Everyone in the room jumped and screamed.

"Shut up!" Alpha shouted and they immediately fell silent. He turned to Charlie. "Give my brother the briefcase."

"Fine." Charlie slid the briefcase across the floor to Omega as Alpha aimed the gun at him.

"You!" Alpha gestured to Phrank who cringed and backed up against the dresser. "What are you doing here?"

"I work on the ship," Phrank said. "I'm a masseuse."

"And you owe us a lot of fuckin' money," Omega snapped as he crouched down to inspect the briefcase. "A whole lot of money."

"I know," Phrank said in a trembling voice. "I — I can pay you. I can. I just need some time to get the money together, that's all."

"That's what you said a few years ago back in Cancun,"

Alpha muttered. "And we have yet to see any of it. We want it, all of it, *now*."

Charlie saw Phrank's hand dip into the top drawer of the dresser which had come open in the commotion. His expression stilled and Charlie wondered if he had found some kind of a weapon.

"Put that thing away!" Kinitia said to Alpha with authority. She stepped forward, drink in hand and a stern look on her face. "You're going to kill someone."

"How would you like to be first?" Alpha said and turned the gun in her direction.

"No!" Charlie shouted. As he struggled to get to his feet, Phrank leaped passed Rock and himself and, with a loud, piercing cry, brought Charlie's two headed dildo down on Alpha's gun hand. Alpha cried out and dropped the weapon, which Bernice immediately bent down to retrieve. She straightened up, drink in one hand and gun in the other, then turned it on the two Latin men. Phrank stepped back against the dresser once again, the dildo bobbing and swaying in his hand like a limp, latex scepter.

Omega sneered at Bernice and folded his arms over his chest. "You have no idea how to fire a gun, you stupid woman. Give me the gun."

Bernice smiled politely at him, then lowered the barrel of the weapon and fired twice into the briefcase at Omega's feet. Everyone jumped and looked at her with renewed interest and respect.

Raising the gun to Alpha and Omega once again, Bernice said with a tight smile, "I used to go moose hunting with my husband in northern Minnesota. I bagged my limit every year."

Charlie saw Alpha and Omega both swallow nervously and the brothers slowly raised their hands over their heads.

"Now then," Bernice said conversationally after sipping her drink. "What shall we do with them?"

At that moment, the door banged open, startling them all, and they turned to see Chantilly, still in drag, crouched in the hallway holding a gleaming gun of her own. Chantilly tossed her long dreadlocks out of her face and cried out in a deep, commanding voice, "No one move! FBI!" at which point everyone began talking at once.

"FBI?" Bernice said to Kinitia, lowering her gun. "Did he say FBI?"

"I thought so," Kinitia replied and looked over at Chantilly. "You're FBI? Is this a joke?"

"FBI?" Charlie echoed and looked at Rock who, he suddenly realized, was holding his hand. "Hoover really opened the door for cross dressers, didn't he?"

Chantilly pulled off her headdress and wig before moving into the room and surveying the situation. When he saw the gun in Bernice's hand, he grinned and reached out for it, keeping his weapon trained on Alpha and Omega. "Bernice," he said with a sly smile. "Did you shoot their briefcase?"

Bernice flicked the safety on and handed over the gun handle first. "I may have accidentally fired off a couple of rounds, being a woman and unfamiliar with guns as I am." She glared at Alpha and Omega and sipped her drink.

Theo pulled a set of handcuffs from beneath his skirts and approached Alpha and Omega. He handcuffed the two men together and picked up the briefcase, placing it on the bed and opening it. Inside lay several dozen stacks of American currency and bags of white powder that Charlie assumed was cocaine. Two neat bullet holes had pierced a stack of hundred dollar bills.

"Oh, my," Bernice said at the sight of the contents of the case.

"Yeah, you got that right," Theo replied, and turned to find Alpha and Omega just slipping out the door. "Hey!"

The two men were brought up short by the dance troupe, one of whom held his own gun. Harry coaxed the men back into the room and Theo smiled and nodded. "Thanks for your help, Harry."

Harry nodded and winked at him with a grin. "No problem, partner. Glad to help."

"Oh my God," Charlie said and shook his head. "They're everywhere."

Theo grinned. "Yes we are. And not only are we G men, we're damn good dancers." He turned to glare at the two men before him. "Nice surgical job there, Jose."

Omega scowled at him but remained silent.

"Surgery?" Bernice said. "For what?"

"Cosmetic surgery. He got busted over in Cancun and he and Alpha hightailed it here to Acapulco where they stashed their cash, some drugs, and a bunch of guns. Omega had his face redesigned by a shady cosmetic surgeon to look more like Alpha then they got on a cruise ship to L.A. and started selling themselves as twin Latin brothers in gay porn. And look what's happened since: two hot Latin brothers going at each other and a whole string of men? Shit, they had it made up there. But they had to come back to Acapulco and pick up their stash." He looked at Charlie. "Which is what you saw

Omega pick up at the hotel. He got it from one of their old contacts."

"Oh, my," Bernice said and sipped her drink.

As Theo and Harry led Alpha and Omega off to the ship's hold, the dance troupe, still wearing their headdresses, wandered away murmuring excitedly among themselves. Ken and Billy pulled Kinitia and Bernice from the room to head to the bar and Rock turned to Phrank.

"You didn't know anything about what Cedric had told me?" Rock asked.

"I swear, Rock," Phrank replied. "I really liked you, you know? I thought you had great potential as an actor and as a person. And I can see I was right."

Rock lowered his head to stare at the floor for a minute then looked back at Phrank. "I really cared about you, too, Phrank. But I couldn't take the drugs and the booze and the late nights. It was catching up to me."

"I know. That's why when Cedric told me you wanted to break up and for me to leave L.A., I wasn't too surprised." Phrank shrugged. "I figured you needed to move on without me around. And he gave me enough money to get down to San Diego, so I took it. I didn't have a lot left in L.A., you know?"

Rock nodded. "I know."

"I'm sorry if I hurt you." Phrank looked to where Charlie sat on the edge of the bed in his torn dress, broken shoes, and crooked wig. "It seems, however, you may have found someone to care about a little more than you did me, huh?"

Rock turned to look at Charlie and smiled. "Yeah, I guess I have."

"Good luck, buddy." Phrank moved forward and hugged

Rock tight then leaned down and kissed Charlie on the mouth. "Good luck to both of you."

Phrank walked out the door and pulled it shut behind him, leaving them amazingly, finally alone. Rock turned and smiled down at Charlie. He sat on the bed beside him and reached out to take Charlie's face in his large, gentle hands and kissed him softly on the mouth.

Moving back, Rock smiled at the dazed expression on Charlie's face. "Hi there."

"Hi," Charlie said breathlessly.

Rock raised his eyebrows and said in a serious voice, "If I leave you alone for a little while to talk to Cedric, can I trust you not to hurt yourself somehow while you're getting cleaned up?"

Charlie smiled and nodded. "Yeah. Go on. I'll wait right here for you."

"Okay." Rock kissed him again and left the room.

Charlie sat for a moment to catch his breath and let his mind stop spinning. With a start, he realized that the morning he had answered the phone in Phrank's apartment he must have been talking to Cedric. The director had heard Phrank had returned to town and called him up to bitch him out. Charlie shook his head at the tangled relationships and stopped trying to sort them out. Instead, he stood up to head to the bathroom and promptly fell to the floor as his torn dress caught on his remaining heel.

He lay sprawled on the floor laughing with his wig hanging over his eyes until he had calmed down enough to disentangle himself, pull off the wig, and crawl toward the bathroom. On the way, he noticed the top drawer of his dresser was still open and looked around for the two headed dildo Phrank had used as a weapon. It was nowhere in sight. He wondered if the masseuse had taken it with him and reached up to close the drawer as he finished his trek to the bathroom on his hands and knees. He would have to remember to retrieve the dildo from Phrank; he and Rock may need it at some point over the remaining two days of their cruise.

He smiled at the images this thought produced and, as his cock began to harden, pulled himself up in the bathroom and looked in the mirror with a start. His makeup was a mess, having smeared and run all over his face, and his hair was a sweaty, matted tangle from being trapped under the wig.

Shaking his head, Charlie eased his feet out of the shoes with a sigh and stripped out of his costume. When he stepped beneath the spray of water he decided that a shower had never felt so good.

16

A PIECE OF THE ROCK

After his shower, Charlie tried to decide what to wear for Rock's return. Should he assume the best and wear nothing but a smile and a raging hard-on? Or should he take things a little slower and wear shorts and a T-shirt? He was muddled about why exactly Rock was coming back. The kiss had been genuine — their first! — but maybe after dealing with that old cow Cedric, he would need some space. Charlie decided to forgo thinking things to death and pulled on a pair of boxer briefs. He left it at that and sat on the bed to leaf through a magazine as he awaited Rock's return.

A few hours later, Charlie was awakened with a kiss. He had fallen asleep sprawled across his bed and, from the taste in his mouth, he had been sleeping with his mouth hanging open. Probably snoring, to boot. He ran his thick tongue over his dry lips and blinked up at Rock's handsome face.

"Hi," Charlie said in a sleepy voice, embarrassed at having fallen asleep.

"Hi. Sorry I took so long. I wanted to make sure Cedric

knew exactly how I felt." Rock leaned down and kissed Charlie softly on the lips. "Can I use your shower?"

Charlie sat up and nodded. "Yeah. Sure. Go ahead."

As Rock showered, Charlie brushed his teeth and gargled. He examined himself in the mirror and was happy to see the imprint of his hand on his chest was finally blending with the rest of his skin tone and his sunburn had pretty much stopped peeling. Once he got back to L.A., he could sunbathe on the roof in a controlled environment and even things out further. He stood and listened to the splashing sounds from within the shower and felt a warm sense of familiarity. It was almost like they were living together. The water shut off and Charlie scampered quietly out of the bathroom to lie on his side across the bed.

Rock appeared a few minutes later with wet hair and a towel wrapped around his waist. He leaned in the doorway to the bathroom and folded his big arms over his broad, hairy chest as he smiled at Charlie. Without speaking he crossed the room and leaned down to kiss him on the mouth. The kiss started out soft but quickly became more urgent, Rock's tongue sliding through Charlie's parted lips and caressing his teeth. Charlie moaned and opened his mouth wide, pressing his own tongue against Rock's as his mind spun. This was Rock Harding, the man he had been obsessed with since his first day working as a fluffer, and Rock was here in his state room with no one else around and no scene to film. It was just the two of them and this could in no way fall under the heading "work related." And they were kissing like horny teenagers in the backseat of a car.

Charlie pulled away and looked up into Rock's eyes. "Wow."

"Yeah," Rock said in a husky voice. "I've been wanting to do that for a very long time." He pulled the towel from his waist to expose the half hard length of his cock that stretched down along his thigh. "Guess I won't need someone to help me get it up before we take this any further, huh?"

Charlie grinned. "I could still use some practice."

Rock stretched out on top of him and let his mouth hover over Charlie's, sliding his tongue out and running it over Charlie's lips. Charlie grabbed Rock's tongue and drew it into his mouth as their lips pressed together. He wanted every part of the man inside him, filling him up.

Breaking the embrace, Rock ran his tongue up Charlie's jaw to his ear, licking the interior and sending tingles along Charlie's spine. Rock moved lower, kissing Charlie's neck and throat then gently biting and sucking at each nipple until they rose up into hard points. He slid his mouth to the side and raised Charlie's left arm to expose the pale, hairy shallow of his armpit. As he pulled and twisted Charlie's nipples with his strong, tan fingers, Rock kissed, licked, and sucked at the hair covering his armpit.

Charlie writhed beneath Rock's mouth, his eyes closed and his lips parted. The man's touch seemed to burn into him, every contact between their skin creating sparks. He groaned and raised his right arm as Rock slid his tongue across the width of Charlie's hairy chest to lick and suck that armpit. Charlie felt the hard shaft of Rock's dick pressed against his thigh and a damp spot where the man's pre-come oozed out into the hair on his leg.

"Oh, God," Charlie gasped. "That is so hot."

Rock slid up a little and kissed him again, his tongue tasting vaguely of Charlie's sweat as it swept through his mouth. Rock broke the embrace and slid lower, kissing the length of dark blond hair that traveled from Charlie's chest down along his stomach. Stopping to lap at Charlie's navel, Rock spread the indentation open with his hands and twisted his tongue down into it.

Charlie groaned and laid back as he ground his erection up into Rock's chest, the thin layer of his boxer briefs the only barrier between their bare skin. He sighed as Rock's tongue traveled further south, parting the dark blond hair that disappeared beneath his briefs. Rock lifted the waistband enough to allow his tongue beneath and licked back and forth across Charlie's waist. His saliva matted down the hair and left a wide, wet trail across the expanse of Charlie's stomach.

Rock released the waistband and moved down over the top of the boxer briefs, kissing and licking the firm outline of Charlie's cock. He buried his mouth in the cotton covering the soft globes of Charlie's balls and let out a warm breath. Charlie groaned and reached down to press Rock's face hard against his crotch. The man nipped and sucked at Charlie's balls through the wet fabric until he finally pulled away and moved down along Charlie's leg. Rock licked his way down to Charlie's feet and then stood up beside the bed, his hard-on jutting out from the neatly trimmed bush.

Rock held Charlie's leg up and examined his injured toe. He winced in sympathy as he carefully turned the foot and looked at it from all angles.

"This is from the morning we went parasailing?" he asked.

Charlie nodded up at him. "Yeah. And it's been stepped on a few times, too." He pouted slightly.

"Oh," Rock said softly, smiling at his expression. "Poor baby." He lightly touched his lips to the bruised and throbbing toe and Charlie cringed, waiting for pain to shoot up his leg. Nothing happened and he sighed. Then Rock opened his mouth and took the injured toe between his lips to curl his warm, wide tongue around it. The toe ached a bit, but the tongue bath more than made up for any discomfort.

"That's nice," Charlie sighed.

Rock worked each of Charlie's toes with slow, easy sucks, then finally lowered his leg and stretched out beside him. They kissed for a long time, their tongues performing a slow waltz between their mouths as their hands squeezed and groped one another.

"I've thought about this for so long," Rock said. "There's so much I want to do with you, but right now kissing you just feels so good."

"I can't believe you're here," Charlie said. "That we're here. Like this."

They kissed a little longer, then Rock eased Charlie's briefs down his legs and pulled him on top as he rolled onto his back. He wrapped his strong, hairy arms around Charlie's body and pressed his erection up against Charlie's hip.

Charlie moved down Rock's body, kissing and licking every available area of skin and reveling in the freedom of finally doing what he wanted to this man. For so long he had only been able to get him erect and then watch him walk away and have sex with someone else. Now it was his turn to experience the entire act.

Charlie ran his tongue along the smooth length of Rock's pulsing cock, and then scooped the actor's clean-shaven balls up into his mouth. He sucked the big, soft balls, reaching up with one hand to gently stroke Rock's hard-on as he used his other hand to probe the warm, moist pucker of the man's asshole. Rock groaned and raised his legs, providing Charlie clear access to his hole.

Charlie sucked Rock's balls a little longer then released them to run his tongue down the smooth skin of his taint to his anus. Sucking and slurping at the twitching muscle, Charlie used both hands to spread Rock's firm cheeks apart and dug into the opening, sucking at it and sliding his tongue inside. He spit into the hole a few times and slowly slipped his index finger deep inside. Charlie's cock thrummed with desire as he watched his finger sink into Rock's asshole.

"Oh, yeah," Rock said. He reached down to grab his legs at the back of his thighs and pulled them higher. "Get that finger up in me."

Charlie pushed his finger as deep as possible then began to twist it back and forth. He crooked his knuckle a bit and felt his fingertip graze the nub of his prostate as Rock groaned beneath him.

"Get another one up there, Charlie," Rock said. "Fill me up."

Charlie slid a second and then a third finger into Rock's hole, slowly finger fucking him. He pulled his fingers almost completely free of the hot, wet tunnel, and then drove them back in, picking up speed until he was banging at Rock with abandon.

"Yeah! Get that ass!" Rock said. "Oh, God, I want your dick up in me. Get your cock inside me."

Charlie slowed his hand and eased his fingers out of Rock's hole as his cock jumped. He had been waiting so long to fuck Rock, he almost could not believe this was happening. He crossed the room to the dresser and pulled out a string of condoms as well as a bottle of lube. Rolling a condom over his oozing cock, Charlie stroked lube over it, then slicked up Rock's asshole.

Moving to stand between Rock's, Charlie pressed the head of his dick against the glistening hole. He met Rock's gaze, then pushed steadily into him, his cock slipping inside with a quiet, slick sound. Rock groaned and grabbed fistfuls of the sheet beneath him. Raising his head, he looked at Charlie and reached up to press his big hands over Charlie's chest and twist his nipples.

"Oh, Charlie," Rock said. "You feel so good inside me."

"I can't believe I'm doing this," Charlie said and reached out to grab Rock's ankles. Lifting the man's legs higher, Charlie pulled out and then pressed back into him again. He repeated this slow process for a few moments, feeling the resistance from deep inside Rock's body. When he thought he could stand it no longer, Charlie began to really fuck him, moving his hips steadily faster. He battered Rock's ass, pounding into it with abandon, stopping now and again with his cock plugged completely into him to gyrate it in a circular motion or from side to side.

"Oh, fuck," Rock gasped. "Yeah, move that thing around in me. Oh, that's it. Get it up in me and ream that asshole."

Charlie lifted Rock's legs higher then crawled up on his knees onto the edge of the bed and leaned down over him, supporting himself with his hands on the bed. He looked down into Rock's handsome, sweaty face and started plowing deep into him, watching his expression as Rock reached down to stroke himself.

"Oh, Charlie, drive that fuckin' cock home, baby," Rock

said and opened his eyes to look up at him. "You're hitting that magic spot, Charlie. Keep it up. Oh yeah, fuck that hole. Fill it up."

Charlie leaned down and planted his open mouth over Rock's as he increased the speed of his hips even more. He could feel his own balls pulling up as the friction within Rock's ass worked along his cock. Rock tightened the muscles around him with amazing agility, clamping down on Charlie's dick as it pulled out and opening up before its fresh onslaught.

"Oh God," Rock groaned up into Charlie's mouth. "I'm coming. I'm gonna fuckin' shoot. Oh, yeah!"

Charlie felt the warm splash of Rock's semen as it splattered over the lower half of his jaw and along his chest. Rock's muscles constricted with his orgasm, engulfing Charlie's cock as he continued to pound into him. The smell of Rock's semen reached him and Charlie immediately felt his balls constrict. He grunted and rose up, grabbing Rock's ankles and tipping back his head as he plunged deep into Rock's ass and blew his load into the tip of the condom.

Charlie slowly eased his wilting cock out of Rock's body and stripped the condom from it. He flushed it away and used the towel Rock had worn out of the shower to wipe the lube from the actor's ass and to clean up himself. Falling onto the bed beside Rock, Charlie rolled into his arms and kissed him tenderly.

"That was really hot," Charlie said.

"It certainly was," Rock replied. He kissed Charlie again and the kiss quickly deepened until he reached up to hold Charlie's jaw and rolled halfway on top of him. Rock slid down along Charlie's body and took his reviving cock into his mouth, pressing his nose into the sweaty tangle of Charlie's pubic hair. Charlie groaned and lay back as Rock sucked him up into a full erection.

"How's that for turn about?" Rock said with a smirk as he came up for air. "Me fluffing you." He slowly stroked the length of Charlie's glistening cock, his strong, hair-flecked fingers wrapped around the pulsating shaft.

"I like it," Charlie replied. "But I don't think I'm quite hard enough. Keep working at it."

Rock grinned and lowered his head to continue sucking. He pressed his lips against the firm flesh and dragged them up to the tip where he opened his mouth and ran his tongue around the ridge at the base of the head. After dipping his tongue into the slit, Rock focused all his suction on the sensitive tip.

Charlie moaned and reached out to grip Rock's strong, hairy thigh as the man sucked the head of his dick. Sensations collided and exploded within him and he wanted Rock to both stop and keep on doing it forever.

Rock finally eased the power of his suction and rose up to inspect his work. The head of Charlie's cock had turned purple, as if it had a large hickey. Pre-come oozed from the slit to mingle with the remnants of Rock's saliva and he swiped his thumb through the mixture then used it to lubricate the top quarter of Charlie's shaft as he slowly stroked it. Keeping his hand moving, Rock licked and sucked Charlie's balls, taking them separately and then together into his mouth. As he stroked Charlie's dick and sucked on his balls, Rock probed Charlie's hot, tight hole with an insistent, saliva slick finger.

"Oh, man," Charlie groaned. "That feels really good. Get your finger deeper in there. Oh, yeah. Twist it, yeah, yeah!"

Rock followed Charlie's instructions and spun his fully inserted finger back and forth as far up inside him as possible. As Charlie had done to him, Rock crooked his finger at the knuckle and skimmed the soft interior, searching for and finally locating his sensitive prostate. He rubbed the mound buried beneath the muscle and Charlie gasped.

"Oh God!" He sucked in his breath and his legs flew up in the air. "Oh, God. That sent a jolt through me. What are you doing down there?" Charlie raised his head and looked down at the top half of Rock's face visible just beyond his own red, oozing cock which Rock was still stroking.

Rock smiled up at him. "I've been in this business a long time, Charlie. I've learned a few tricks."

Charlie lowered his head and rode the waves of pleasure as Rock's finger brushed his prostate again. He felt the man's finger slide free and then Rock dug his fingers in the globes of Charlie's cheeks and spread his ass apart, allowing him to clamp his mouth down over the sensitive furrow of his ass. Rock's tongue invaded his asshole, pushing into the tight confines and probing with its hot, wet tip. As Charlie moaned and shifted beneath him, Rock lapped at his hole, filling it with spit that he pushed deeper into him with his tongue.

Straightening up, Rock reached over and peeled open a condom and applied it to his thick, hard cock. He squirted lube onto it and spread it along the length, then slipped two slick fingers up inside Charlie who groaned beneath him.

"I need you inside me," Charlie said in a deep, lust filled voice. "I've wanted you in me for a long time."

"So have I." Rock adjusted his stance, aimed his cock well, and pressed steadily into the tight folds of Charlie's anus. The muscle parted before his dense, long dick and he sank balls deep into him. Charlie gasped and tightened his muscles around Rock. He never wanted to let him go. Rock held himself still, fully seated inside Charlie and his pubic hair brushing against Charlie's balls.

"Oh, God!" Charlie said. "I can't believe you're finally inside me. Oh, God, that feels so fucking good. Fuck my ass, Rock. Fuck it hard and deep."

"If you say so."

Rock took hold of Charlie's ankles and spread his legs wide. He braced himself and slowly pulled out, then drove back into Charlie again. Picking up speed, Rock banged into Charlie's hole, his abs constricting with each thrust. Charlie grunted with each thrust, and when Rock leaned over to kiss his injured toe, he nearly came.

"Oh, God," Charlie grunted. "I want to try a different position. Stop for a minute."

Rock slowly pulled out of Charlie's stretched asshole and watched him roll over and get up on his hands and knees. Rock climbed up on the bed and directed his throbbing prick into Charlie's ready and open hole, driving into him once again. He placed his palms on the pale cheeks of Charlie's ass and slapped each as he bored between them.

"Oh, fuck," Charlie said with his head resting on his hands. "That feels so good. Get that ass. Sink your big dick inside me."

Rock increased his speed, but before either of them could come, Charlie wanted to try another new position. Rock pulled out and lay on his side as Charlie did the same and scooted back into him. Charlie impaled himself on Rock's hard dick and lifted a leg to allow deeper penetration. Rock shifted a little for a better angle and reached down to support Charlie's leg as he thrust into him. Charlie groaned and turned his head for a kiss, their tongues stretching out to touch over Charlie's right shoulder.

After a few more minutes, Rock pulled out before Charlie could stop him and then flipped Charlie onto his back. He lifted the lower half of Charlie's body up into the air and stood over him. Putting one foot on either side of Charlie's hips, Rock lifted his hips higher and drove his cock straight down into him. Charlie grunted and let his mouth drop open as Rock's dick pressed firmly against his prostate.

"Oh, that's it," Charlie said, his shoulders lifting off the mattress and forcing his chin into his chest. "Oh, get that ass. Fuck that hole."

Rock pounded down into Charlie's asshole, the bed squeaking beneath his thrusts as Charlie's feet bounced in the air. Charlie was close, really close now, and soon there was no turning back. His legs stiffened and his toes curled up, even his injured one. Rock noticed and increased the speed of his pile driving fuck, watching Charlie's expression as sweat poured down his face. With a gasp, Charlie finally shot his wad. The semen splashed down over Charlie's face and into his open mouth. Rock grunted and pulled out of Charlie's hole, dropping his legs as he tore off the condom. Rock stepped up and straddled Charlie's chest as he stroked himself off over Charlie's face. The full brunt of his thick load splashed across Charlie's cheeks and jaw, mixing with Charlie's own cum. Charlie closed his eyes and rolled his head back and forth beneath the hot spray of

Rock's semen, letting to cover as much of his face as possible.

"Oh, God!" Charlie gasped when Rock had finished. "Oh, that was so fucking hot."

Rock leaned down to give Charlie a gentle, cum-smeared kiss. All he could manage was a nod of his head, he was so out of breath. He staggered to his feet and grabbed the same towel as before to clean Charlie's face, and then stretched out beside him on the bed.

Charlie pulled Rock's arm around his shoulders and snuggled up into his chest. Rock sighed and pulled him in even closer.

"That was really incredible," Charlie said. "I can't believe it happened."

"Neither can I," Rock replied. "I still remember seeing you standing on the pool deck at the set that first day. I wanted to bend you over a bar stool and just fuck the hell out of you." He leaned down and kissed him on the mouth. "But I'm glad I waited. This is much better."

They rested for a while then got up and showered together in the tiny stall. After soaping one another up and helping to rinse off, each of them emerged from the bathroom with a full erection.

"Wow, I guess we have some energy left," Rock said.

"I guess so," Charlie replied.

He stretched out across the bed and Rock laid down so they could suck each other. Charlie took Rock in his throat all the way to the root and held him there. He massaged the full length of him with his tongue and was satisfied to hear Rock give an appreciative grunt. Pulling back, he sucked harder, bringing his hand up to help pump along the shaft.

Rock began to do the same and a few minutes later, both men were breathing heavy and their balls had pulled up.

"I'm coming," Charlie gasped and Rock pulled the suddenly spurting cock from his mouth and aimed the load over his face. Charlie kept pumping his fist along Rock's dick as he watched his load spray over Rock's face, and then closed his eyes and turned his head into Rock's sudden eruption. The semen blasted over his forehead, nose, and mouth and dripped off his chin. It felt hot, sticky, and wonderful as it dribbled down his face.

"You're a messy eater," Rock said with a grin.

"You're pretty sloppy yourself," Charlie replied. He retrieved a damp towel from the bathroom and they cleaned up yet again.

After returning the towel to the bathroom, Charlie crawled into bed next to Rock and pulled a sheet up over them. He kissed Rock on the mouth and wriggled in close, almost burying his nose in Rock's armpit. With a deep, contented breath, Charlie slipped into sleep.

17

SORRY, CHARLIE

The Dominatrix reached L.A. two days later. Charlie and Rock had gone to meals and walked a few times around the decks, but other than that they stayed in Charlie's stateroom the rest of the trip. During meals, Kinitia had kept a skeptical eye on them, as if she thought things between them might be too good to be true. Charlie forced himself not to think that way, though he couldn't help it sometimes. He was deliriously happy, and Cedric was staying out of sight. Something was bound to go wrong. He just hoped Cedric wasn't going to lash out at Kinitia for losing Rock like he had, even though it had been his own damn fault.

Charlie and Rock stood side by side at the deck railing watching the people on the docks below. Their small ship pulled in between two larger, sleeker cruisers and let out a high pitched bleat from its horn to announce its arrival. A few dock workers seemed to look their way, but other than that, their arrival provoked no major activity.

"Well, here we are," Rock said with a sigh. "Home again."

"Yep," Charlie said. His stomach was in knots as he tried to think of what to say. The time they had spent together on the ship had been the ideal situation: removed from their daily lives. But now they were back to reality where Rock lived at Cedric's house and Charlie lived in a small 50 by 20 foot studio apartment. What was going to happen now? With a sigh of his own, Charlie looked up at Rock, trying to memorize the way the light touched his handsome face and the contentment he could still see in his dark eyes. "I had a really great trip."

Rock smiled, his full, soft lips parting to reveal his even white teeth. "Me too. I'm glad it's finally all worked out."

"Yeah." Charlie looked away, then glanced back as he asked, "So, what are your plans now?"

Rock took a breath and shook his head. "Head back to Cedric's house and pack my stuff. I'm going to find my own place. You know, I realized that since I've moved here to L.A. I've always had a roommate. I think I need to live on my own for awhile."

Charlie nodded. "Will you, um, still want to, you know, get together now and then? With me?" He risked a look up at him.

Rock grinned at him. "Oh, maybe now and again." He grabbed Charlie, pulled him up against his strong body, and kissed him hard. Rock's tongue swung through his mouth and Charlie felt himself swoon. After breaking the embrace, Rock leaned back and said, "Just try to keep me away."

Charlie smiled and nodded, relief flooding him. "I don't want to." Rock kissed him again and Charlie locked his hands behind his neck.

From above them, Charlie heard whoops of joy and

broke the embrace to squint up into the sun. Ken, Billy, Bernice, Kinitia, and Theo stood on the deck above them, all of them cheering him on and tossing streamers and confetti down over them, even Kinitia. Charlie smiled and waved to them then pulled Rock down for another kiss.

Charlie and Rock held hands as they walked off the ship with the group from Fluffers, Inc. At the foot of the gangway stood the captain, a man Charlie had seen just a few times during the entire cruise, and each of those times at dinner. He was a tall, handsome black man wearing his dress whites. He politely tipped his hat to each passenger that disembarked, but, when Kinitia approached, he stepped forward to grab her by the shoulders. Dipping her smoothly, the captain planted a long, passionate kiss on her mouth that caught everybody off guard.

"Oh my!" Bernice said with a hand at her throat. "Do you think she was choking?"

Billy grinned as he watched the scene before them. "She wasn't until the captain stuck his tongue down her throat. Kinitia was doing the captain! That's why she didn't come back to the room those few nights."

Ken and Charlie shook their heads and smiled. The captain finally broke the embrace and helped Kinitia to stand back on her own two feet.

"Ms. Jones," the captain said, his voice a rich, deep baritone. "It has been my intense pleasure having you aboard the Dominatrix. Please sail with us again soon."

The double entendre was clear to them all as Kinitia fanned herself and reached out to run a hand along his uniformed chest. She patted his brass buttons and gave him a stunned smile, blinking at him in a daze. "Yes, well, Captain

Addams, you can rest assured I will certainly be booking another trip with you soon."

Captain Addams smiled brightly. "I have two days in town before we ship out again."

"Then we'll have to meet and discuss the different, um, what are those called?" Kinitia snapped her fingers as she stared into Captain Addams' eyes.

"Cruise packages?" Bernice offered in a loud whisper.

"Yeah, that's it," Kinitia replied without taking her eyes off the captain. "Cruise packages." She sighed and turned to slowly walk away, her hips swaying in a seductive manner.

"Oh, my," Bernice whispered to Ken. "I do think she's rather smitten."

"Do you really?" Ken said with a grin and draped an arm around Bernice's shoulders as well as Billy's. "I would have to agree with you."

"Oh, watch the arm, dear," Bernice said with a smile. "Can't be too rough on the tattoo."

"What?" Ken and Billy both said and stopped in their tracks to inspect Bernice's arm as Charlie and Rock walked past.

Rock glanced over his shoulder to catch a glimpse of Bernice's tattoo. "Wow, Bernice got a tat?"

Charlie nodded and grinned. "Yeah. She's cutting loose these days. All those years of being a straight-laced house-wife have built up, you know?"

Before Rock could reply, a gleaming black Town Car pulled up in front of them and the back door swung open. A small man popped out and approached them with a fast stride. He wore a plaid blazer, lemon yellow polyester slacks and thick, plastic framed glasses. His thinning dark hair laid slicked back from his forehead with heavy amounts of hair oil, and a cigar stuck out of one corner of his mouth.

"Rock!" the man exclaimed. "Been trying to get in touch with you for days!"

"Who is that?" Charlie asked with a mix of amusement and unease.

"That," Rock replied, "is my agent." He clasped the small man's outstretched hand. "Barty, it's good to see you. This is Charlie Heggensford, a very good friend of mine."

Barty turned and gave Charlie the once over, slipping him a business card as he shook his hand. "Nice to meet you." He looked back at Rock. "We gotta talk! I've been working on a deal for you that'll make you weep with joy. Come here."

Rock allowed himself to be led off to the side and Charlie looked down to read the card in his hand. *Barty Bolchovski, Gay Porn Agent, You Got Eight Inches or More, I'll Get You Five Figures or More.* He turned as Ken, Billy, Kinitia, and Bernice walked up.

"Who's that?" Bernice asked.

"That," Ken said with a grin, "is Barty Bolchovski, one of the most connected and sought after agents in the world of gay porn."

"Yeah?" Billy squinted as he looked Barty over. "He looks like some kind of circus act."

"Don't let the clothes fool you," Ken said. "Barty knows how to get his clients, and himself, the best deals possible. I didn't know Barty represented Rock."

Rock approached them and Charlie cocked his head at the tense expression on his face. "What's wrong?"

"Well, Barty's kind of made an arrangement for me that I really shouldn't turn down," Rock replied.

"What kind of arrangement?"

"He's set up a tour for me. A series of guest appearances."

"Oh." Charlie felt his heart sink a little. "Here in California?"

Rock shook his head. "No."

"Oh. Well, for how long?"

Rock took a breath. "Two months."

Charlie blinked in surprise. "Two months? Wow."

"Oh, my," Bernice said. "That is a long time."

"Charlie, I'm really sorry," Rock said with honest emotion. "But if I want to keep on in this business now that I'm leaving Cedric, I need to do this."

Charlie nodded and took a breath. "Okay. It's okay, really. I know you need to do this. Are you, um, going anyplace interesting? Historical landmarks, that kind of thing?"

Rock nodded and looked away for a moment. "The appearances are all in Europe."

Charlie felt his mouth drop open. "Oh. Oh, wow."

"Oh, boy," Kinitia said quietly, then herded the others away to give them some privacy.

"I'm really sorry, Charlie," Rock said.

"You've said that."

"I know, but I can't help feeling bad about this. I mean, here we've just gotten the chance to be together, and now I have to leave. It sucks."

"When would you leave?"

"Tomorrow morning."

"Jeez. Barty doesn't waste any time, does he?" Charlie looked away and watched the other passengers streaming by, laughing and joking. "Well, I know you have to go, and

I know you don't want to, so we're both in a spot, aren't we?"

"You do believe me when I say I don't want to go but I have to, don't you?" Rock asked.

Charlie nodded and smiled up at him a little sadly. "Just be careful. And send me a postcard or something, okay?"

Rock smiled back. "Don't worry, I'll keep in touch." He bent down and kissed Charlie softly on the mouth. "I'll miss you."

"Rock," Barty hissed. "We gotta go! There's things to do before you leave tomorrow!"

Touching his hand to Charlie's cheek, Rock stepped away and slid into the back of the Town Car. Barty jumped in on the other side, leaving Charlie alone on the dock as the car turned around.

Cedric brushed passed Charlie without a glance, his carryon bag slung over his shoulder and his gauzy tangerine outfit billowing behind him. Charlie snarled quietly at Cedric's back as the Town Car completed its U-turn and headed back along the dock, passing through a large puddle of dirty water directly in front of Cedric. The water splashed up over Cedric's tangerine pantsuit, soaking him to the skin and plastering the thin material to his flabby, pale body.

"Oh, you stupid fuck!" Cedric cried after the departing Town Car. He turned at the sound of Charlie's laughter and shook a thick fingered fist in his direction then stormed off to the parking lot.

Charlie met up with Billy, Ken, Bernice and Kinitia and received condolences all around. He smiled at them with determination and said, "It's okay. He'll be back. And I'll always have my friends around me."

"That's right," Billy replied. "And you could throw yourself into your work."

Loud bursts of Spanish reached their ears and they all turned. Theo, dressed in a white cotton, short sleeved shirt and khaki pants, approached leading Omega across the dock away from the ship. Omega's hands were handcuffed behind him and he spoke angrily in Spanish. Behind them followed Harry, dressed in a similar fashion to Theo and leading Alpha. The FBI agents headed for a series of police cars waiting by the gated entrance to the parking lot. Theo looked up and smiled brightly as he caught sight of them.

"Hello, fluffers, ladies." He nodded to each in turn and winked at Charlie. "Welcome home."

"Thanks, Theo!" Bernice said. "Give us a call sometime!"

"Oh, that's a definite!" Theo laughed and pulled Omega passed their group. The man glared at them and could be heard saying to Theo, "It was a great plan! And we would have gotten away with it, too, if it weren't for those meddling fluffers!"

They all laughed and watched Theo and Harry push the two men into the back seats of separate police cars. As the cars moved off, light bars flashing, Charlie and his friends headed into the terminal to collect their luggage.

THE END

ABOUT THE AUTHOR

Hank Edwards (he/him) has been writing gay fiction for more than twenty years. He has published over forty novels and novellas and dozens of short stories. His writing crosses many sub-genres, including contemporary romance, rom-com, paranormal, suspense, mystery, wacky comedy, and erotica. He has written a number of series such as the funny and spooky Critter Catchers, Old West historical horror of Venom Valley, suspenseful FBI and civilian Up to Trouble, and the erotic and funny Fluffers, Inc. Under the pen name R. G. Thomas, he has written a young adult urban fantasy gay romance series called The Town of Superstition. He was born and still lives in a northwest suburb of the Motor City, Detroit, Michigan.

For more information:
www.hankedwardsbooks.com
hankedwardsbooks@gmail.com
www.facebook.com/groups/hankshangout

ALSO BY HANK EDWARDS

<u>Critter Catchers Series</u>

Terror by Moonlight

Chasing the Chupacabra

Swamped by Fear

The Devil of Pinesville

Screams of the Season

Horror at Hideaway Cove

Dread of Night

Critter Catchers Box Set 1

Critter Catchers Box Set 2

<u>Critter Catchers Universe Stories</u>

The Mystery of the Morelock Motel

<u>Critter Catchers: Level Up Series</u>

Grave Danger

Wet Screams

<u>Williamsville Inn Gay Romance:</u>

Snowflakes and Song Lyrics

The Cupid Crawl

Fake Date Flip-Flop

Star-Spangled Showdown

<u>Lacetown Murder Mysteries</u>

(co-written with Deanna Wadsworth)

Murder Most Lovely

Murder Most Deserving

<u>Venom Valley Series</u>

Cowboys & Vampires

Stakes & Spurs

Blood & Stone

<u>Up to Trouble Series</u>

Holed Up

Shacked Up

Roughed Up

Choked Up

<u>Fluffers, Inc. Series</u>

Fluffers, Inc.

A Carnal Cruise

Vancouver Nights

<u>Standalone Gay Romance</u>

Buried Secrets

Destiny's Bastard

Hired Muscle

Plus Ones

Repossession is 9/10ths of the Law

Wicked Reflection

Holiday Gay Romance:

A Gift for Greg (A Story Orgy Single)

Mistletoe at Midnight (A Story Orgy Single)

The Christmas Accomplice

Story Orgy Singles Gay Romance:

A Gift for Greg

By the Book

Cross Country Foreplay

Mistletoe at Midnight

The Cheapskate: Bad Boyfriends

With This Ring

The Story Orgy Singles Boxed Set

The Town of Superstition (YA urban fantasy series)
Published under pen name R. G. Thomas

The Midnight Gardener

The Well of Tears

The Battle of Iron Gulch

A Tangle of Secrets

Gay Erotic Short Story Collections:

A Very Dirty Dozen

Another Very Dirty Dozen

A Third Very Dirty Dozen

A Fourth Very Dirty Dozen

<u>Salacious Singles Gay Erotic Short Stories</u>:

Bear Market

Convoy

Double Down

Exchange Rate

Finding North

Hotel Dick

Kindred Spirits

Sacked

Stroking Midnight

Vanity Loves Company

Wet Lands